THE PERIL TREK
A Western Trio

MAX BRAND

Five Star
Unity, Maine

Five Star First Edition Western Series.

Published in 2000 in conjunction with Golden West Literary Agency
"The Man Who Followed" by George Owen Baxter first
appeared in Street & Smith's *Western Story Magazine* (12/10/21).
Copyright © 1921 by Street & Smith Publications, Inc. Copyright ©
renewed 1949 by Dorothy Faust. Copyright © 2000 by Jane Faust
Easton and Adriana Faust Bianchi for restored material.
Acknowledgment is made to Condé Nast Publications, Inc., for their
co-operation.

"The Boy Who Found Christmas" by George Owen Baxter first
appeared in Street & Smith's *Western Story Magazine* (12/22/23).
Copyright © 1923 by Street & Smith Publications, Inc. Copyright ©
renewed 1951 by Dorothy Faust. Copyright © 2000 by Jane Faust
Easton and Adriana Faust Bianchi for restored material.
Acknowledgment is made to Condé Nast Publications, Inc., for their
co-operation.

"The Peril Trek" first appeared under the title "Reata's Peril
Trek" by George Owen Baxter in Street & Smith's *Western Story
Magazine* (3/17/34). Copyright © 1934 by Street & Smith
Publications, Inc. Copyright © renewed 1961 by Jane Faust Easton,
John Faust, and Judith Faust. Copyright © 2000 by Jane Faust
Easton and Adriana Faust Bianchi for restored material.
Acknowledgment is made to Condé Nast Publications, Inc., for their
co-operation.

The name Max Brand™ is a registered trademark with the
United States Patent and Trademark Office and cannot be used for
any purpose without express written permission.

Set in 11 pt. Plantin.

Printed in the United States on permanent paper.

Library of Congress Cataloging-in-Publication Data
Brand, Max, 1892–1944.
    The peril trek : a Western trio / by Max Brand.
      p. cm.
    ISBN 0-7862-2112-7 (hc : alk. paper)
    1. Western stories. I. Title.
  PS3511.A87 A6 2000c
  813′.52—dc21   00-037175

TABLE OF CONTENTS

The Man Who Followed

"The Man Who Followed" was published in the issue of Street & Smith's *Western Story Magazine* dated December 10, 1921, appearing under the George Owen Baxter byline. At the time Frederick Faust had been contributing to *Western Story Magazine* for a little over a year. The relationship would prove to endure for nearly two decades, Faust contributing literally hundreds of stories and serials to this, one of the best of the pulp magazines. This story involves one of Faust's common themes: Blarney Joe Peters and Harry Quale, two giants of men as well as bitter enemies, forge a temporary alliance to help the heroine, Mariam Claude, in a time of need. This is the first appearance of "The Man Who Followed" since its original publication.

I

"The Horse Thief"

They rode in silent fury, which is the most consuming kind. They rode with their eyes fastened hungrily far down the valley, and, from time to time, each man of the five patted with affection the butt of his Winchester beneath his thigh or the dangling holster of his revolver. For they were on a man trail—the trail of one who had stolen a horse.

And to their savagery of purpose was now added a grim touch of hopelessness. He had doubled on them, running like a hare from hounds, and with astonishing boldness the rascal had slipped past them and cut straight back down the valley. He gained more than distance. By the time the little posse had sprinted its ponies here and there in a great effort to find the trail again, they were sadly wearied, and when, by a steady pressure of hard riding, they came in sight of the scurrying fugitive, they found that they could never catch the prey they sighted. For he was riding the gallant roan well within its strength, and now, although he turned and looked back at them occasionally, he refused to accelerate his pace and thereby wear out his mount.

In vain they yelled. In vain they tried pot shots from the distance. He kept steadily on, scorning to exhaust the horse needlessly. Another mile and these Y Bar J boys would fall away, and he would canter off into safety. It had been a very cunning maneuver, that doubling back. For the new direction carried the fugitive straight toward the Y Bar J Ranch, the last place in the world toward which one would expect him to head.

But it was just such cunning, after all, as one might expect from such a customer. They had all seen him when he applied to the boss for work in their outfit. He was a fellow of thirty-five, perhaps, hard as leather, with a sneering, thin mouth and shifty eyes. So when the alarm was spread that Molly Purchass had lost her roan under suspicious circumstances, and when it was further found that the hard-looking stranger was still in the neighborhood just before the roan disappeared, the Y Bar J boys made up their own minds on the subject. The suspicion was easily confirmed. When the five, scouting about, came in full view of the stranger, he had put off at high speed. And half the day he had kept them in play. Now, at last, he was about to shake them off as soon as he cared to call on the honest roan. But, in the meantime, he preferred dallying close, mocking them by his slow gait, as it were, and making them spur the hearts out of their mustangs.

When he reached the long gully with flat sandy bottom and precipitous sides in which water flowed in times of heavy rain, and which was known as Johnson's Creek, it seemed that the thief made up his mind that he had played the game long enough. So he turned in the saddle, waved them a careless farewell, and then called on the roan for greater speed. And what an answer the roan gave! In half a mile the posse lost two hundred yards, and finally Kirk, the recognized leader for age and wisdom, drew back his pony to a slow lope.

"No use, boys," he said, as the others turned toward him. "We can't get the coyote. He's gone!"

He was interrupted before he could speak again by a shrill yell of triumph from another of his riders. And following the gesture of him who had shouted, Kirk and the rest saw a man on a black horse ride out on the edge of the ravine and sit the saddle looking down on them and on the fleeing roan.

"It's Blarney Joe Peters and Colonel, sure enough," cried Kirk. "Let's get to the top of that hill and watch the fun! It's Blarney Joe! Could he've come luckier?"

Kirk led the way to the top of a small eminence that was, however, high enough to overlook clearly the valley floor, and there he and his men drew up their horses which stood swaying and heaving in their exhaustion, their heads pendant. It was strange to see the absolute and joyful confidence with which the five strong riders, the five fighting men, resigned the work that had proved too much for them into the unassisted hands of a single cowpuncher.

However, this was plainly their intention. Neither did they seem to admit the slightest possibility of failure on the part of him they termed Blarney Joe and his beautiful black horse.

"The skunk sees Blarney," said Kirk, who was watching through his glasses. "He's throwing the spurs and the leather into the roan. The fool must think he can outrun Colonel. But the black'll just play with him . . . just plumb play with him!"

"Blarney'll have to ride along the top of the cliff," remarked one of the men, "until he comes to the crossing."

"The devil he will!" shouted Kirk. "There he goes! Look at that! That's riding for you!"

It seemed that Blarney Joe, while he sat motionless in the saddle on the height, had been overlooking the situation and planning his blow. But when he struck, it was almost literally like the sudden stooping of the hawk from the central sky. Straight down the precipitous slope of the ravine he rushed in a cloud of dust and flying pebbles that partially obscured him.

And in another moment he was a flying streak that gained upon the fugitive hand over hand.

"The skunk is pulling his gun," exclaimed Kirk, swaying with excitement in his saddle. "But now . . . *whang!* It's all over. The fool ought to've known better than to pull a gun on Blarney!"

As he spoke, the rider of the roan suddenly pitched from his saddle and, striking the earth, rolled over and over before he lay still. But he was motionless before the heavily echoing report came speaking up on the ravine and reached the ears of the watchers.

They spurred ahead at the same time to come up to the scene of the fall. They arrived to find Blarney Joe in the act of lifting the thief to a sitting posture, and they heard him inquiring gently: "How you coming? Any busted bones? Anything but scratches?"

At that the captured man lifted a face that was much

bruised, for the sharp gravel in which he rolled had incised a thousand small cuts, and his clothes were torn to shreds. Yet in spite of the agony that must have been burning him he uttered not a sound in reply, but scowled in sullen hate into the eyes of Blarney Joe.

The latter, having stepped back to observe the condition of his captive more carefully, now seemed to be satisfied that the fellow was in no immediate danger of death, and, accordingly, with a shrug of his broad shoulders, he produced the inevitable tobacco and brown papers and rolled and lighted a cigarette. He was in every respect a fine specimen of young manhood, strongly but not cumbersomely built, deep-chested, and with one of those strong necks that are apt to give a certain nobility to the carriage of a man's head. There was that nobility about Blarney Joe. In fact, viewed from the rear, his was a proud and almost awe-inspiring figure, but, when one saw his face, the awe departed. He had very keen, very smiling, blue eyes. His mouth was too large, to be sure, but a smile of inward good humor was continually playing about it. His nose, if not absolutely a pug, was assuredly far from the Grecian ideal. In a word, it was a boyish, mischievous face, with point given to the scope of mischief by the size of the shoulders and the steadiness of the eyes when occasion demanded. His companions looked upon him affectionately and respectfully, and it was with many a "Good old fellow!" and "That was sure riding!" that they gathered about and slapped him on the back.

One of them went on to repasture the roan, which was soon done, since the Purchase girl had raised the horse as a pet. Being a pet, the sin of stealing the roan was doubly great.

"I guess," said Kirk, "that there ain't any use in wasting sympathy on this gent's bruises. We've got him with the goods, and they's only one thing to do with him. We've got

11

the time, we've got the rope, and yonder's a tree all handy for him! Get up, you skunk, and come along!"

So saying, he prodded the victim cruelly with a spur and brought him to his feet with a bound and a yell. His gun was now taken from him. A search revealed a knife of murderous possibilities. His arms were pinioned behind his back. While this was going on, the captor stood by, still smoking, but growing more and more solemn of face, until, when the thief was started toward the designated tree, Blarney Joe stepped forth and halted the procession.

"I just been thinking," he declared, "that, if our friend here who gets all mixed up about the brands on hosses is hung, it's me that'll be doing the hanging."

"Because you caught him? Well, and it's a good job. We'll all be behind you if any trouble comes out of it."

This speech brought a smile to the brown face of Blarney Joe.

"I ain't never been particular about dodging trouble," he said. "But getting a gent hung is something new to me. And I don't take to it. Not a devil of a bit! It's like hitting a gent when he's down. Only worse!"

"Now," urged Kirk, "don't be a fool. Why, look at this one in the eyes. If he ain't cut out to do murder, I'm a coyote. Don't believe he's ever done a lick of honest work in his life. Hanging's a favor for a gent like him. It keeps him out of a pile of trouble."

Blarney Joe finished his cigarette with one enormous inhalation and snapped the fuming butt away. "You see, partner," he said in his smoothest tone—and how oily smooth was the tone of Blarney Joe when he chose to use it—"you see, you're one of these terrible, man-killing kind of fighting gents. And that's what makes you so hard on the rest of the folks you meet up with. But a gent like me, that's all mellow and easy with people . . . well, partner, I just can't see this poor skunk hung. And I ain't going to, neither. I guess that'll have to be final!"

There was, in this speech, a prodigious sarcasm that a casual listener might not have detected, but which was so apparent to the other bystanders that they looked from Kirk to Blarney Joe in alarm. One might have said that there was expectation of damage in the measuring glances that they cast at Kirk, but their leader did not move to pick up the soft-worded challenge of the younger man. Instead, he stepped back suddenly, and laughed.

"I know you, you devil," he said cheerfully. "And if you've plumb set your mind on turning him over to the sheriff, instead of using him for stretching a rope, why, you're the doctor."

"Thanks," said Blarney Joe in the same softly ingratiating voice. "Now, I sure take that kind of you, boys!"

With this, as though the rest of the captors had agreed to the deed of mercy, he turned and sprang onto the back of the black horse. The stallion, Colonel, bursting with eagerness to be off and with excess of strength and spirit, reared, whirled on his rear legs, and was off. Straight at the sheer side of the ravine rode Blarney Joe. At least, it seemed a straight wall from a distance, although it was at this point much lower than it was farther down the gulch. And the terrific impetus of the black shot him up the slope to the very top. There, all forward motion lost, he reeled, staggered, seemed about to topple but, regaining his footing at the last instant, struggled on to the level above.

The laughter of Blarney rang back to them as he cantered across the plain beyond. There was an exclamation of relief and wonder from his friends. Then they turned to the captive.

That worthy was eyeing them with furtive, darting glances, swift as snake tongue motions. "Now what?" he said uneasily. "Now what, partners?"

The whining voice made Kirk sneer. "You think we'll string you up now that his back is turned on us? No, son, we know him too well for that, and you can thank your lucky stars that Blarney Joe felt generous today!"

At this information the horse thief gasped. "That? Him? Is he Blarney Joe?"

And the little group enjoyed his amazement with chuckles. "That's him. But how'd he knock you out of the saddle?"

"His slug hit my gat," said the thief, "and knocked it out of my hand when I was just about to pot him. And the gun flew back and nicked me alongside the head. That's all I know."

There was a great lump on his forehead as proof.

After that he refused to talk. Not a word did he utter until they had ridden him into the town, handed him to the sheriff, and then escorted him to the door of the jail. Here, in hand-cuffs, he turned on them with a departing snarl.

"To the devil with you all, you sneaks," he said viciously. "And about this Blarney Joe you think such a pile of a man . . . I'm going to let Harry Quale know about him. Then Harry'll come along and tame him the same's you'd tame a two-year-old. You can lay to that!"

II

"Challenged"

"Who's Harry Quale?" was a question often asked around the Y Bar J outfit during the days that immediately followed. Not until they went to the sheriff did they receive the answer.

"Harry Quale ain't been hung yet," he said, "and that's

the most that can be said for him. You don't know him. But you'll know him soon. He's up north. Away up north around Montana way. And around there they swear he's the hardest gent in a fight that ever pulled a gun out of leather, the best hand at busting a hoss, and riding the best hoss in the mountains . . . Pat, they call the big gray he owns. Matter of fact, they claim everything for him that you folks down this way claim for Blarney Joe. Except that Blarney is plumb good-natured. He fights for the love of fighting. But Harry Quale fights for the love of killing. And there's a difference. He's cleaned up every badman in them parts. They don't need no fighting sheriff while Harry Quale is around. Minute he hears about a hard one coming anywheres within five hundred miles, Harry's mouth sure begins to water. He climbs on Pat and goes till he finds the gent, and then he lays around till he gets into a mix-up. And the end of the mix-up is always the same. Yep, Harry Quale is quite a man. They'd don't come no meaner, some says."

"What sort of a looking man is he?" they asked.

"Never seen him," said the sheriff. "But I been told he's a big, dark, good-looking gent."

"Well," said the men of Y Bar J, when they had heard all of this report, "if he wants to keep his good looks, he'd better keep clear of Blarney Joe, because, when Blarney gets through with him, he sure won't be no lady's favorite!"

So they rode back to the ranch house in great excitement. Indeed, during the next few days there was little talked about save the probable qualities of Harry Quale, and what would happen to the master of Pat if he should ever meet with Blarney Joe. They discussed his death over and over. They devised ways and means of his ending. They painted pictures of Blarney Joe destroying this enemy with gun, or knife, or smashing fists, or the mere bone-breaking grip of hands. For

15

Blarney Joe was one of those naturally powerful men whose strength can hardly be measured. It is an elastic quantity. It rises to the occasion, and that is all.

It may be seen that Blarney Joe was in a measure the recipient of such admiration as often comes the way of a champion pugilist, except that there was a greater seriousness in the regard that he was favored. For in the mountain desert, skill with weapons becomes a factor notable in public life. And, feeling that they had a world's champion in their midst, the men of the Y Bar J outfit were tremendously proud of their possession.

But beyond his fighting qualities there were lovable characteristics in Blarney Joe Peters, and he was loved for them. Those who knew him could never entirely forget that the gentleness of voice that never left him was sometimes used to mask deadly threats as well as to tell pleasant tales.

At any rate there was prodigious excitement in the ranch outfit when, on a day, a letter arrived for Blarney Joe bearing the postmark of an unknown Montana town. That day Blarney was riding on a distant part of the range, but when he returned, late at night, he found that no one in the bunkhouse was, as yet, asleep. All were propped up on their bunks, reading magazines or telling stories—half a dozen or more stalwarts of all ages, for all ages are active in the West. When he entered, nothing save yawns and careless side glances greeted him, so he knew instantly that something important was in the wind, and, when he found on his bunk the letter, he looked sharply about the room. It was to find every eye turned elsewhere. But the moment he had opened the envelope and shaken out the paper within, he was vaguely aware that every glance had focused on him again.

He pored over the letter for a long time, and then he said: "Boys, this is a world beater. Want to hear it?"

There was a single shout of assent, and he read aloud:

"Dear Mister Blarney Joe Peters: I have just had a letter from a gent who used to be a friend of mine. His name is Skinny Watkins."

"That's the hoss thief, ain't it?" queried one of the 'punchers.

"That's him! Go on, Blarney."

"Leastwise, Skinny claims to have been a friend of mine. And he sure has done a friendly turn for me. He says you been talking pretty large and liberal about me around those parts. He says you been saying that, if it wasn't for the distance between you and me, you'd ride up north and show me up proper."

Blarney lowered the letter.

"It's sure a good thing I didn't let Skinny be hung," he said. "I'd hate to be the cause of a grand liar like him passing out of the world."

He went on with the reading.

"Me being one of the most peaceablest gents in the world I was considerable surprised to hear all this sort of talk. But I been thinking it over, and it seems to be a shame that a gent with all your ambition shouldn't have a chance to blow off steam. I got a couple of things to hold me up for a while. But when I get through with 'em, I'll climb on my horse and come down to see you-all. Then we can stage a little party. Harry Quale.

"And that ain't all. Here's a postscript saying that he's

17

enclosing his picture so's I'll know him when I lay eyes on him. That'll give me a good break. And he wants to have my picture back." He tossed the singular letter to one side and studied the photograph. It showed a long, darkly handsome face, stern-set lips, aquiline nose, jutting chin, high cheek bones—a cruel and purposeful face. And then he passed the photograph to his companions.

There was a chorus of opinions, phrased in different words, but all to the same point.

"If he wants to commit suicide, why don't he just use his own gun?"

"Always knew that those cold Montana winters froze the sense plumb out of a man."

"I hope he brings the price of a coffin with him."

But finally they asked in a chorus: "What are you going to do, Blarney?"

"Ain't you got a map of the mountains, Charlie?" Blarney said, addressing one of the seasoned cowboys.

"Sure," said Charlie, and straightway produced from his pack a large map that he unfolded. It covered the mountains from the Canadian boundary to the Río Grande, with two yards of thin linen paper showing, almost literally, the smallest town, the most obscure road.

"Now," said Blarney Joe, "let's find this town he mails the letter from. Where's Coachville?"

Only after a long search it was located in the heart of the mountains. After which Blarney took a piece of string, measured the distance to the proximity of the Y Bar J Ranch, cut this distance exactly in two, and replaced the string on the map. The end now reached, of course, to the spot midway between Coachville and the ranch, and it was found to fall exactly on the Craven River, between the two towns of Jasper and Trail's End.

The others watched him in bright-eyed silence.

"What you going to do, Blarney? What's the map for?"

But he refused to answer, and they saw him go back to his own bunk, draw forth writing materials, and poise a pencil in his big hand. Kirk offered his pen and ink for the composition of such a document as the one that Blarney must have in mind. It seemed almost sacrilege that the reply to such a challenge as that of Harry Quale should be inscribed in so perishable a medium as pencil. But Blarney waved the suggestion away.

"A pen ain't much good to me," he said. "Every man to his own tools. I'd rather ride ten bronchos and bust 'em than write one letter, but I'm going to send this Quale person as good as he sent me. Trouble with a pen is that I get to using it like a pick. It keeps sticking into the paper and littering everything up with spots. Besides, before I get through, I'm ink up to my neck. Lemme have a pencil and *peace*. That's all I ask for writing a letter."

He proceeded with his composition, drawing the letters carefully, so that they looked very much like the painful work of a child of five or six. It read:

Dear Mr. Quale: I am glad that I did not let the boys hang your friend Skinny. Because if they had, I maybe would never have got your letter. Nobody knows you around these parts except the sheriff, and he says that the best game you play is a gun play, and that there ain't nobody as popular as you with the undertakers up Montana way. Seeing that you do a rush business up there, I sure would hate to take you away from your happy hunting grounds. But it appears to me that, if you're willing to come all the way to the Y Bar J Ranch to have a chat with

me, I ought to do something to match you.

What I suggest is that you and me meet up on the Craven River, north side of the bank, between Jasper and Trail's End. I been looking at the map and it seems to me I could get up there in about five days, pretty comfortable. I'll wait five days for this to get to you. Then I'll start out, and I aim to be looking forward to meeting you eleven days from now, wet or dry, rain or shine.

Hope that you ain't late.

Joe Peters

P.S. Them that call me Blarney are my friends. J.P.

Having finished this exquisite composition, Blarney Peters heaved a prodigious sigh of relief, stamped and sealed his envelope, and rose to stretch his muscles.

"It ain't the way writing cramps my muscles that bothers me," he remarked to the hushed circle of friends watching his every move. "It's the way it plumb cramps your brain."

"What's it going to be?" asked Kirk. "Rifles, gats, or knife work, partner?"

"I dunno," said the big man, stretching again. "I just been asked to a dance, and it ain't up to me to tell 'em what sort of music ought to be played. I hope the floor's smooth, that's all!"

III

"On the Road to Craven River"

The floor for the dance, however, as Blarney Joe Peters referred to his meeting with Harry Quale, was far from smooth. The Craven River he found to be a swift stream that had cleft a rough-sided valley through the heart of the Craven Mountains, a lofty range whose summits shot up well above timberline. And, indeed, the valley itself, between the little villages of Jasper and Trail's End, was so lofty, so barren of soil and rich in rocks, that almost the only trees that could find footing there were the lodge pole pines, those hardy pioneers that prepare the way for the upward march of nobler forest trees. Over the southern and lower crests the pines rolled and washed in dense thickets across Craven Valley, and then straggled up the chilly northern slopes, diminishing in numbers and in size to the verge of timberline.

To Blarney, accustomed to kindlier skies and gentler topography, this region was a dismal and terrific landscape. He turned west out of Jasper, having crossed the river at that village, and rode through the snows that lay fetlock deep, crunching under the hoofs of Colonel. The black stallion, unused to such footing, was continually lowering his nose to sniff at the frosty going. Or he would throw his head high and whinny a soft question to the master. These questions Blarney was never too preoccupied to answer with a pat of his hand or a reassuring word. For to him Colonel was something more than a horse. His very life had more than once depended on Colonel's sureness of foot, inexhaustible speed, and doughty courage, so that the black stallion had to Blarney a peculiar relationship of servant and friend.

Receiving that assurance from the mind of man that all was well, Colonel went on again and presently broke into his long-striding gallop and gaily went up the valley, scattering a cloud of the dry, friable snow dust behind him. It had been storming for the last week. The lowlands had not yet received the full violence of the storm, but the summits were still veiled or blotted out, sure proof that winds were sweeping the dangerous lands above timberline, and that the snow was falling in gusts and volleys. Indeed, timberline itself, with its advanced guard of tiny, stunted trees and shrubs, was quite overwhelmed with the piles of snow, and far down on that steep northern slope the snow was heaped so thick that here and there, as he rode west, Blarney Joe saw a dozen little land-slides begin, each to have its motion quenched, before long, in a thicket of trees. But if once a free stretch opened for the avalanche, how terrific would be its sweep down to the Craven River!

Indeed, there was so much to be seen on those mile-long northern slopes that Blarney rode with his head constantly turned in that direction. Also, Blarney paid much attention to keeping his circulation going. Harry Quale, used to these northern storms and northern cold spells, would have a tremendous advantage unless Blarney kept the muscles of his hands and forearms active. So, as he rode, he massaged his arms and kept his fingers in play, and more than once he tried his revolver in the holster and brought it smoothly and swiftly forth.

But, after all, he was not depressed. The iron-gray sky overhead, the distant murmurs, from time to time, of the storm that was howling on the far-off summits to the north, could not dampen his spirits. For he was riding to enter his greatest adventure. Of that he was sure. That strong and solemn face of Harry Quale fitted with such a country as this. And although Craven River was as far south of Quale's haunts as it was north of Blarney's, it seemed to belong to the man of the north. The snowstorm would make it like home to him. And with the advantage of familiar weather, with eyes unharmed, no doubt, by the glare of the snow that had been bothering Blarney for the last day and a half of riding, Quale should give the man of the south land a terrible battle for supremacy. Blarney knew it, and he rejoiced in that foreknowledge. Not that he was sure of winning. But he possessed that instinct of the true sportsman that makes him rejoice in a contest whose end cannot be guessed and who despises a struggle whose termination can be accurately forecast.

He had come like Alexander, out of a world where he was the acknowledged master, the acknowledged hero. In those parts where he was known, half a dozen strong and courageous men would have given way to him the moment he raised his voice. And a single man, no matter how expert a fighter, would as soon have planted a gun at his own forehead and pull the trigger as face Blarney in a fighting mood. This position had not been won by a single exertion, or a single feat. It had been the result of a calm confidence that began even in his boyhood when he discovered that nature had endowed him with a certain quality of muscle, a quickness of eye, and a reserve of nerve power that enabled him to overwhelm men far more mature and far bigger in bulk. That consciousness of superiority was nursed by time. And, taking pride in himself, he had used the utmost pains to develop the natural talents.

In a country where every man is apt to spend hours and hours each day acquiring skill in the use of guns, it requires a basis of unusual natural adroitness and adaptability as well as infinitely prolonged training for one man to make himself stand out above his fellows. Blarney Joe had given himself that training. He had practiced in secret for countless hours. He had spent thousands of minutes merely practicing the draw, until he could simply *think* the gun into his hand. He had learned from the first all the intricacies of shooting from the hip, with its implied necessities of a smooth draw rather than a convulsive jerk, so that the revolver will slide out into position for shooting and not require an instant for steadying before the shot. He learned all these things until he could do them without thinking. He taught himself to whirl and aim at an imaginary enemy who had come up behind. He armed himself with readiness to meet any sort of foe under any sort of conditions. From a Mexican who, in the largeness of his generosity, he had saved from starving one winter of little work, Blarney had learned the art of knife play. This in itself was a most mysterious and complicated art. It required a different set of muscles to get out a knife and throw it with a flip of the fingers, but with such terrific power that it would drive halfway to the hilt in a tree trunk. But, bringing his natural adroitness to bear, and reducing gun play before, Blarney was eventually able to surpass the skill of his teacher. Not that he used his knife in such a manner. But all that pain of profound study was to equip him for eventualities. There might come a time when, disarmed of his gun, he would need the throw of that weapon to win him a chance for life.

Nor were gun and knife play all. Being supreme in these fields of endeavor, he found that the world expected other things of him. Men would meet him, from time to time, who, shunning battle to the death with such a master, were nevertheless anxious to match him with the skill of their fists. Then there were others who would not use the fists, but contented themselves with a desire to grapple with him and wrestle with him to a state of helplessness.

It should not be assumed that Blarney Joe went through all these contests unbeaten. More than once, before he attained maturity, he recalled fierce struggles in which he had been overwhelmed. He remembered one occasion, in particular, when a professional pugilist of some note had been specially imported by a malicious foe. That had been a fearful battle. He had run against a solid wall of fists. He had been battered and torn and smashed beyond recognition. But when, at last, he wakened out of a pit of darkness, he found his conqueror holding his head in his lap. That same warrior of the roped arena had stayed with him for weeks and given him priceless days of instruction until, in the end, he groaned because Blarney would not take to the ring for a profession. There was another occasion when a wrestler, a little lithe man, had made a fool of Blarney—and then had taught him the mastery of that art of arts—catch-as-catch-can wrestling.

So, gradually, the education of Blarney grew, and the sphere of his culture was increased until, to the men of the Y Bar J Ranch and other outfits through a great section of the cattle ranges, there was a belief in the prowess of Blarney as in a superhuman individual.

But now Blarney Joe Peters was advancing outside of the kingdom where he was known, and where the mere mention of his name was half of a victory. He had come to a strange land, and he was to meet the king of another district, perhaps a man who had grown into significance even as he had grown. Perhaps a man even larger, stronger, swifter of hand, surer of eye.

So Blarney Joe Peters kept his hands from the nipping chill of the air and rode west up the Craven Valley, constantly on the lookout for the enemy, the big-shouldered, dark-faced, handsome man. A man on a big gray horse, he would be, a gray horse that would, perhaps, blend with the background of the snows. While he, on Colonel, would stand boldly out, in plain sight of men miles away. Would this Harry Quale take advantage of the fact? Would he use it to stalk from behind, instead of striking like a man from the front?

That thought had been growing large in the mind of Blarney Joe Peters, when, in a lull of the howling wind that was now cutting down from the mountains, he heard the crunching of the hoofs of a galloping horse behind him and whirled in the saddle to see a mighty man riding on a mighty gray horse.

IV

"Champions Meet"

It did not need the color of that beautiful, dark-gray horse to identify the man. It did not even need the dark and handsome face. The lofty carriage of Harry Quale's head, the broad shoulders, and an inexplicably proud and haughty air about the man identified him. He bore himself like a king. Indeed, he was a king. And, by his manner alone, Blarney Joe Peters could have picked the fellow from a crowd.

For a tingling instant Blarney was on the verge of going for his gun. But Harry Quale showed no signs of hurry to commence the battle. One hand gripped the reins. The other rested jauntily on his hip. He rode close to Blarney. Very close—insultingly close, in fact, and, sitting his saddle, he looked down on the man of the south land.

He looked down! For an instant Blarney would not admit

the fact. Colonel stood a full sixteen hands and three inches; and he himself, standing six feet two in his bare feet, out-topped by far any man he had ever met on horseback on his home ranges. But here in the north they seemed to breed a different bone, a heavier flesh. Pat must have stood an inch over seventeen hands—a giant of a beast, but compactly built beyond credence. At a glance Blarney Joe knew that a master of Pat was both a bigger and a stronger man than himself. There must be an extra inch of height. There must be an extra twelve or fifteen pounds of weight, and all that iron-hard muscle, perfectly trained. Yes, he was a bigger and stronger man. All that huge body must be perfectly controlled by the mind behind those keen eyes.

The heart of Blarney Joe sank. His throat became dry. With a terrific effort he fought away the chilly waves of fear that were assailing him. For the first time in his life, indeed, he was really afraid. Was this man his master? Ah, he had never before even admitted that question. But now he was thinking hard and fast. And he knew that, if they were to close in battle at that moment, the larger man would have the advantage. For he was not only larger in body, he was stronger, also, in the spirit and the mind. He was more domi-nant. He was fiercer and more kingly. He was less liable to imaginary fears.

Now he was smiling contemptuously down at Blarney Joe Peters. And Blarney, in spite of himself, could not meet the eye of his enemy full. His own glance wandered a little to the side and far away, and, distinctly outlined against the white-ness of the snow, he saw a girl riding.

Would she come close enough to hear the explosion of the guns? Would she see his body fall from the saddle? When fierce Harry Quale rode off, sliding his gun back into the hol-ster, would she spur wildly down the slope and spring from the saddle and take his limp, dead head in her lap? Suddenly he found himself wondering what manner of woman she might be. And why had he known at once, from that distance, that she was young and good to look on? Then he forced his glance back and centered it on the eye of Harry Quale.

"Blarney," said the man of the north country, "I been cussing my luck for having to ride so far south as all this, but since I followed up the valley and seen the way your hoss ran, I've made up my mind that it's a pretty good thing. Pat is a better hoss than your black, but the black will carry me, and I've always wanted to have two hosses. And that's something I've never had."

He spoke slowly, in a deep, rough bass. Blarney's own tones, so smoothly pleasant, were almost feminine in contrast. At the moment he hated that gentle voice. He wished for a large and gruff voice to mate that of Quale. But he welcomed the spark of anger that burned up in him suddenly. It thawed the fear in his soul.

Who was it first said that one may often curse a man with impunity, but never his dog? The imputation cast on his horse enraged Blarney like a blow in the face. He saw the picture of Colonel's matchless beauty, matchless strength under the saddle of Harry Quale, and suddenly he was ready to fight.

"It's sure easy to see," he said, "that Pat would make a better hoss than Colonel if it come to pulling a plow. And I figure that's what I'll use him for. Speaking of long trips, it sure does rile me to have to come this far to get a plow hoss. But now that I'm here, let's get through the business!"

But if he expected to enrage the other, he was mistaken. The larger man merely tilted his great head back and laughed. How huge that laughter made him seem!

The wind fell away suddenly. The world seemed hushed

to listen to the voices of the champions.

"I like to hear a gent talk up big," said Harry Quale, when his laughter had so far diminished that he could speak. "But I'd like to know what sort of gents they have in the south that you could've got your rep for being a man-eater? Up where I come from, they use the likes of you for the chores. Skinny sure has a sense of humor, or he'd never have wrote to me what he did."

"Skinny, and the other hoss thiefs that you call men up in your part of the country," said Blarney Joe Peters, smiling, in turn, "had a lot of time to use his imagination. He was resting quiet inside a jail. Come down that way and we'll give you the same sort of a rest."

The big man closed his teeth with a snap. "I got a long way to go back," he said. "How you want to run this little job through?"

"Dunno," said Blarney. "But on foot or on hossback I'm ready for you, Quale. Knife, or rifle, or Colt, fists, or wrestling, or rough-and-tumble, I'll meet you the way you say. It don't make no difference to me."

He filled to the lips with joy to see Harry Quale blink at that assurance. Far away, the girl still drifted across the background of pure snow, having left the pines and entered an open stretch of the mountainside.

"Suppose," said Harry Quale, "we throw a coin. Fists and things like that are right enough in their place. But I ain't got the time to waste playing. Rifle or revolver, son, is what I'd choose. We'll throw a coin. Heads it's revolvers. Tails it's rifles. That go with you?"

"Anything goes. Throw the coin."

Harry Quale removed the glove from his right hand. A huge hand it was, the fingers square-tipped and with a suggestion of power that astonished Blarney. Quale drew forth a fifty-cent piece, snapped it into the air, and, when it landed with a spat in his open palm, he showed it to Blarney. It was revolvers—heads. And in spite of himself Blarney could not help an exclamation of pleasure.

Suddenly he was laughing into the sneering face of the man of the north.

"Luck's ag'in' you, Harry," he assured Quale. "That flip of the coin means that you're going to be buzzard food . . . if you got buzzards up this way!" He added: "D'you shoot straight enough with a gat for me to risk staying on Colonel? Or should I get off and have it out on foot?"

The sarcasm made the man from the north flush a terrible and dark red. Plainly in spite of his great pride, or perhaps because of it, his temper was no very steady thing. Having unbalanced it, Blarney could not but feel that perhaps the battle was already more than half won.

"Keep on your hoss, and get back a ways," said Quale sternly.

They reined their horses apart. There was now perhaps twenty yards between them.

"Ready?" Quale asked.

"Go for your gun, son!"

"Me make the first move? I ain't never done that," answered Blarney. "But before we start, I forgot to ask who you want me to write to and tell how you had an accident while you were cleaning a gun. Who'll I let know?"

The big man was grinding his teeth in fury. "Nobody, because they ain't nobody will need to know what ain't going to happen. Are you ready, Peters?"

"More'n ready. Plumb tired waiting."

Now he saw, as they both sat their horses in silence, that the right hand of Harry Quale was trembling. At first he thought, naturally enough, that it must be the nervousness of fear. But then he knew, almost at once, that it must be only the nervousness of a man whose whole nerve force was being centered in the movements of that single hand. In spite of the bulk of the hand, the bulk of the arm, the draw of Harry Quale would probably be as lightning fast as the stroke of a cat's paw.

Speed on the draw would decide, beyond doubt. For this fellow must have practiced even as he had practiced. In fact, here was a man of his own breed, unconquered, unconquerable! Which of them, then, would possess the luck, or the skill, to whip out his gun a fraction of a second quicker than the other? Or would both the guns dart into the air at the same instant, at the same instant explode, and both the riders fall lifeless to the earth? There had been such occurrences in the memory of Blarney Joe Peters.

A rumbling sound from the north broke in on him, a dull and sullen roar traveling across the windless air of the valley, while behind and beyond there was the faintly ominous moaning of the storm that was thundering above timberline so many miles away.

Then a sudden uneasiness appeared to Blarney.

"Sounds like a landslide coming our way!" Quale said, turned, and then pointed with an exclamation.

Blarney followed the direction of the other's hand, and he saw, far up on the slope, a thin wisp of shining snow dust whipping up into the air, and in front of it was a lunging white monster that ricocheted down the mountain with gathering speed, twisting and turning with unseen contour of the ground; and Blarney knew at once that he was viewing the beginning of a great snow slide such as he had often heard of, but never seen.

A moment later he glanced down and saw another thing that was of greater importance. The girl on the horse, riding

31

far down the mountain slope, was straight in the path of the descending ruin, and the slide was coming down with terrific momentum.

V

"In the Path of an Avalanche"

"Save her!" burst out Blarney, instinctively turning to one who must know more about such affairs than he of the south land. "For heaven's sake, Quale, save her. I'll tend to you later, but now, save her!"

"You fool," groaned Quale, his flush of anger quite gone and deathly white coming in its place, "nothing but God can save her now. She's plumb in the way."

"She don't know it's coming," Blarney said. And with one voice they shrieked their warning.

Doubtless she was too far away to hear. But perhaps at that moment she detected the sound of the slide for the first time and distinguished the difference between this roar and that of the storm for which she must first have taken it. At any rate, they saw her horse dart out with sudden speed.

"She's saved!" Blarney cried, laughing suddenly in the pure joy of relief.

"No," answered Harry Quale. "Look!"

The slide had started in a deep, steep hollow where the wind had gathered the snow and packed it hard and deep. Almost from the first, therefore, the slide was a bulky movement, and, when it tore out of the hollow and reached the open slope, it shot away at dizzy speed. It had grounded down to the bottom of the thick snow. It had caught up mud, sand, gravel, small rocks, boulders, which served now as teeth to cut all obstacles out of its path. Its front grew loftier and loftier until it towered high. Behind it there was the diminishing triangle, ending in the sharply upshooting column of snow dust, and behind this trailing wisp there appeared a raw black scar—token that the slide was gashing the soil from the mountainside.

It careened now like an express train that, in its tremendous speed, rocks along the rails like a ship staggering through heavy seas. Even so the front of the slide rocked and veered. And, watching the passage of the great white death of the mountains, Blarney saw a sudden attestation of its power. A stanch little grove of pines squarely blocked its path, and it was the sight of these that made Blarney cry out that the girl was saved. For certainly the stanch trunks would block the surge of the snow. Little he knew the power lunging with that mass!

To his horror and astonishment he saw the slide cleave through those strong trees as though they were standing straws of brittle wheat, going down before the scythe. The trunks were tossed up like reeds, whirling high above the onrushing mass, and then dropping again into its midst.

The girl was spurring directly below. Yet she rode fast, and certainly she would get past the danger. No, for above her, as though guided by demoniac intelligence, the slide swerved, following a contour of the slope, and reached out a mighty white arm to the left—then the whole mass of the slide thundered off to overwhelm her.

Harry Quale covered his face with his hands, moaning like a frightened child. But Blarney Peters was too horrified to move his eyes. Then his yell of agony made his companion jerk up his hand to watch in turn.

There was still a ghost of a chance, when the snow slide

veered malevolently to the left, that the girl might outride the danger and get past its reaching arm. But now the horse she was riding, panic-stricken by the uproar above, terrified by that wild clamor which drowned the reassuring voice of its rider, whirled, thrust out its head, and jerked the reins through the hands of the girl, and now, blind with fear, was rushing straight down the slope toward the river.

Only the sight of the water could check that headlong flight, but the horse would never reach the bank of the river. It might as well have fled straight down the tracks to escape from a speeding train. Behind the fugitives the snow slide rushed on its way, now cramming the valley with a tumultuous shouting and, as it struck small rises of the ground, leaping and tossing aloft gigantic white arms as though it exulted in the prey of beast and man it was about to devour.

The girl had not surrendered to the panic of the horse. They saw her head go back as she strained and struggled with the reins to check the flight and swing the animal aside where safety might be reached in half a dozen leaps. But her task was hopeless. It would have needed the gigantic power of Blarney or Harry Quale to achieve that feat of strength.

Blarney Joe started forward, giving Colonel the word, and with a yell that was drowned at once by the roaring of the avalanche he rushed straight toward the girl.

A great shadowy form rushed forward at his side. He turned and saw big Harry Quale driving Pat forward on the same errand of mercy and fear, his teeth set, his eyes glaring with a desperate resolve. And the heart of Blarney went out to the fierce rider beside him. For here was ample proof that there was something beside the soul of a bully in the man from the north. Another thing would be proved by this ride. And that was the comparative speed of the horses. With a gesture he called upon his rival to watch. Then he threw himself forward, bringing the burden of his weight more across the withers and forepart of the horse.

Colonel responded with a mighty burst of running. The huge gray beside him answered the challenge, flinging him forward with tremendous bounds. Colonel could hear the shouting of his master close beside his ear and above the growing thunder of the snow slide, and that voice was more than a spur to urge him on. He went like the wind, settling low as his stride increased, and stretched out straight with the labor. The gray went back slowly and surely. Moreover, while Colonel heard and saw nothing saving the will of the master, the big gray could not help swerving a little south instead of running, apparently, into the very jaws of the roaring death above them.

Back went the gray and drifted out of sight, while Blarney bent to the work ahead. He was darting close to the fugitive. He could see the fear-maddened eyes of the horse. He could see the white and desperate face of the girl with her hair flying behind her in a shining golden stream. Now, as if in mockery, there was a sudden rent blown in the clouds, and through the gap brilliant sunshine poured against the face of the snow slide and set it flashing. That front of the slide was like a confusion of a thousand horses galloping in headlong charge through dense fog. The snow pushed forward jutting arms. It leaped and surged. It roared and growled with eagerness and anger. It sent long echoes thundering up the valley and down, and mourning from the distant southern hills. Right under that overhanging wall of fear Blarney rushed with the black stallion. He ranged beside the girl. He reached and gripped the rein of the wild horse she rode. At his first terrific tug the leather parted. And with it all hope was gone.

No, for the beast staggered at that check, and while it

reeled, straining to regain speed and dart away, Blarney Joe swung close to the girl, swept her out of the saddle with a mighty effort, and then spurred on across the face of the slide.

But it was close, now, terribly close. In the interval of pause, when he swung south beside the fugitive horse and the girl, the slide had borne down on them with appalling speed. It seemed to Blarney, glancing toward it, that the mass of snow reared so high that half of the sky was blocked. And the snow-laden ground before it quivered with the approach.

A length before them and turned in the saddle and shouting back as though his presence might give the gallant black more strength for the final and vital burst of running was Harry Quale on the gray. He had refused to rein back out of the danger when he saw that he could be of no assistance, but with a fine and generous courage he had stayed close to share the disaster, if disaster came. But Blarney Joe Peters gave the big man only a glance. He had swayed forward again, touching Colonel with his heels as the black shot away with gathering speed again. Swaying the girl like a child over one arm, Blarney distributed his weight and hers again in such a fashion as to burden least the sprinting horse. For now, half the distance of a leap might mean life and death.

Over them the thundering wall of snow lurched downward. The shriek of the girl at his ear was like the thin murmur of a distant wind in the prodigious uproar. And Blarney felt her weight grow limp. So much the better. She would not impede him with hysterical struggles, and, throwing himself forward, he yelled again and again in the ear of the black.

Nobly Colonel answered. His was no common broncho blood, but the strain of fine Thoroughbreds, crossed and re-crossed with the ranch breed until only the toughness and durability of the Western horse was left in the blood of the black. He gave all his muscle, and he gave his heart and spirit, also. There was a great crashing behind, about, underfoot, it seemed. Some force from behind seemed to pick the black up and hurl him forward. Suddenly Blarney was aware that he had been carried past the avalanche, and that now the snowy surface, at a diminished height and a dizzy pace, was sliding harmlessly past him.

He brought back Colonel to a walk, and then stopped him. Already the slide was an incredible distance down the slope of the hill. In a moment it struck the bank of the river, leaped out into thin air, and smashed across to the farther bank of the stream, filling all the gorge between with a ruin of churning snow, stripped tree trunks, mud, and rocks. Against that barrier the Craven River boiled and fumed. But the noise of its complaining was nothing. After the turmoil of sound that had filled the valley a moment before, what remained to the ringing ears of Blarney Joe was dead silence. And when the man from the north came close and spoke, it seemed to him that Quale must be shouting at the top of his lungs.

"Good boy!" the dark man was saying. "The finest thing I ever seen done!" His hand fell with a kindly pressure upon the shoulder of Blarney.

VI

"Rustlers"

Weakness came over Blarney now. With the great strain of danger past he felt a mist floating before his eyes. Quale had thrown himself to the ground, and into his hands Blarney now yielded his burden.

As he dismounted, he had heard his companion say: "A beauty, by the Lord, eh? Just a faint, Blarney. She'll be around in half a minute."

Blarney, still half stunned, looked vaguely down upon the broad shoulders of the man he had come to battle with and who had now joined him suddenly in a work of mercy. Then he saw the face of the girl, and his brain cleared. At the same instant her eyes opened and looked up at him, blue and clear. In recognition she smiled faintly.

After that, the sense of the danger she had passed through came to her. She struggled to her feet, stared down at the mass of wreckage now jamming the Craven, and said faintly: "And Jeff? Poor old Jeff?"

"Was that the name of the hoss?" asked Harry Quale gently.

"Poor Jeff. Yes."

"He's gone where all hosses go sooner or later," said Quale. "But he near polished you off before he went. Would've done it if it hadn't been for my friend, Blarney Peters, here."

There was something so ridiculous in being introduced by Harry Quale as a friend that the man from the south land laughed faintly.

"We're not going to waste time talking about that," Blarney protested.

She had a queer, indirect way of thanking him. "But I saw you both come at the same moment. And I thought you were both mad. Because I knew that I couldn't get away, and the moment you came inside the path of the slide I was sure that you were goners, too. Then you came close enough for me to see your faces, and I was sure you were insane."

"I was plumb scared," confessed Blarney, in that smooth, pleasant voice of his.

"And me, too," added Quale. "But . . . we didn't start together. It was Peters that got the idea first, and that's why he got to you first."

Blarney shook his head.

"He's making excuses for his hoss, lady," he said, smiling. "He started the same jump with me. But . . . you see that hoss of his? . . . well, you never seen my hoss with such a bunch of weight in the shoulders that could really do much running. No, sir, it ain't in 'em . . . real speed. When I put Colonel to it, he just walked away from the gray." He turned to Quale, still chuckling. "Pat may be a pretty good hoss for looks," he said, "but, if I was you and wanted to show him off, I wouldn't get him out of a walk!"

The face of Quale had been blackening gradually during the speech.

"Pat slipped," he insisted. "Otherwise, I'd've walked right past you."

But Blarney Joe turned an insulting shoulder on his companion and faced the girl. The little byplay between the two huge men had caused her to look from one face to the other with keen, prying glances. She saw enough to determine that they were not ordinary men, even if their incredibly daring ride of the moment before had not convinced her. With the danger hardly a minute past, and her own heart still hammering, her body cold with dread, they had already forgotten it, in seeming, and were now badgering each other about the comparative merits of their horses.

"Maybe," said Blarney Joe, "you'll take my hoss, lady, to finish your ride?"

This brought a scornful laugh from Harry Quale.

"You better break him first! Look at him, dancing there like a fool! Why, I wouldn't be seen around with a hoss that I hadn't taught better manners to!"

The remark called forth a murderous glance from Blarney Peters. "Colonel," he called, "come here!"

The black approached slowly, thrusting forth an inquisitive nose. But at sight of the stranger and as he drew nearer to them, he crouched with every step and trembled as though in fear and distaste. Plainly he was a one-man horse.

"Comes up more like a mountain lion than a hoss," commented Quale. "I'd about as soon trust a girl to a lion as to a hoss like that."

The girl saw her rescuer grind his teeth.

"Pat him on the nose," said Blarney Joe. "He's like a man. He don't make up to strangers. But he's plumb easy to get along with once you've been introduced all proper. Sure, he's quiet as a lamb! Look at him now? Easy, Colonel, you black fool!"

The last stern cry was brought forth by a sudden snort and stamp of Colonel, who had laid back his ears and bared his teeth like a dog about to snap at the hand of a man. He quivered at the sound of the master's command and allowed one ear to prick forward, which gave a most whimsical expression to his head. The girl had stepped back, but now, with a brave smile at Blarney, she came forward again, and this time succeeded in laying her hand between the gleaming eyes of the stallion.

"Like patting a chunk of dynamite, ain't it?" commented Harry Quale reassuringly. "Look at Pat, now, steady as a lamb!"

The girl, to be sure, had stepped back somewhat hastily from the head of the black, and Pat of his own accord approached her and started sniffing at her head as though in search of sugar. Her eyes brightened at this exhibition of kindliness.

"You must treat him like a pet," she said to the dark man.

Indeed, this gentleness was far from what one might have expected in the horse of Quale. Blarney himself wondered at it.

"Sure," said the big man, "he was raised up in the house, you might say. Pretty near talks to me, old Pat does! He's the hoss for you, lady, if you want to get home."

The girl looked from his eager face to the ominous expression of Blarney, as he had been called. What children they were! What could she make of them? Great-hearted, generous, and brave to the point of the most headlong recklessness they unquestionably were. But they were dangerous men, as well. Of that there could be no doubt, and, during her life, she had had rare opportunities of learning to know the danger in a man by his ways and his face. How should she judge between the two? They were full of contradictions. Harry Quale was unquestionably a handsome man, far handsomer than Blarney. But the voice of Quale was huge and rough as his own body, and the voice of Blarney was soft as running water. But had not that very deceiving quality of his voice, perhaps, won him the nickname of Blarney? And was not the heart of the other far kinder? As for gratitude, she owed more to Blarney, but then he had simply been the one who reached her first. The dark man had attempted just as bravely—and only failed because he was forestalled.

All these comparisons she made in the space of a single breath. She must do something and say something quickly, for the atmosphere between the two men was becoming loaded with thunder, with all probabilities of a quarrel. She was replacing the hat which had blown off and been retained only by a chin band.

"You have done so much for me!" she cried suddenly. "You've both risked your lives with such a wonderful readiness and generosity for a girl you never saw before, that I'm going to tax your kindness still further. Indeed, I almost think God has sent you to me."

There was something so thrilling and grave in this declaration that both the big fellows were suddenly abashed.

"My father is William Claude . . . of course, you know him?"

"Lady," said Harry Quale, "this gent comes out of the south. I come from up Montana way. So I guess neither of us never come within a hundred miles of this neck of the woods before."

The girl explained swiftly: "He's the sheriff of the county. And I . . . they told me this morning . . . that while he. . . ."

"Steady up, Miss Claude," said Blarney Joe kindly, as she grew entangled in the headlong explanation. "Take your time and tell me what I can do. Your father's in trouble, eh?"

"He's gone to stay a few days with his oldest friend, Mister Sanson, over the mountains. At least, we've always looked on Mister Sanson as our best friend. After he left . . . a man came to the house and told me a strange story. Where he learned what he called facts, I don't know. But he is a man my mother and I nursed last winter. From his voice and his manner . . . well, I could swear that he was telling the truth!

"What he told me, in a word, was that Mister Sanson has asked Dad to his house to throw him into the hands of the cattle thieves. You see, for three years a gang of men has been running cattle off the ranges, and my father has never been able to locate them. Only recently he ran across some clues that gave him an idea that he could locate the guilty man before long. Now, the man who came to me this morning says that Mister Sanson himself is the leader of the gang, that he has always planned the work, and that he has kept his thieves supplied with money and with hiding places. I can't believe it. And yet I know that lately Mister Sanson has seemed very prosperous. He has bought a great many fine horses. He has improved the old Sanson house. He has built new barns. Yet his ranch apparently is paying less than ever before, when he was running more deeply into debt every season.

"And the message I had this morning is to the effect that my father has been invited to the Sanson house because Sanson knows that Dad is on the right trail at last and he fears that he will be exposed. Dad is to be turned over to the gang. And . . . oh, don't you see? It's murder, black, black murder that stares Dad in the face! There was no help I could get. We live alone. There were no men on the place. I haven't the time to get to Trail's End or Jasper for help, because I have to reach Sanson's place across the mountains before dark. And now . . . isn't it the work of Providence that has brought you two across my trail? You've offered me a horse. Oh, I want more than that! I want you to ride to the Sanson place and give my father a warning, and . . . once you're there . . . I know you'll fight to help him as you'd fight to help your own fathers!"

"I ain't got a father," said Blarney solemnly, "but I'll ride as hard and fight as hard for him as though I had. Just tell me where to go!"

"And you?" inquired the girl, looking at Quale.

"Me?" said Quale. "For every lick Blarney hits, I'll hit two! You can lay to that!"

She paid no attention to the challenge, or to the ugly interchange of glances. She had stooped and was charting the way with her finger in the snow.

"There's only one way and that's down yonder, around the side of the Craven Mountains, and then around to the north until you come to Sanson's place. You don't have to go all the way around the mountains. There are a lot of blind cañons that run into the mountains. One cañon, though, cuts straight through, and that will save ten miles and give you a chance to get there in time."

"How do we find that cañon?"

She paused, clenching her hands in a desperate effort to remember.

"Why not strike straight across the mountains?" asked Blarney. "That'd cut off more'n half the distance, according to the plan you've drawn."

"Yes, yes, but look!"

She pointed to the veil of storm wrapped around the summits of the Craven Mountains.

"Nobody in the world could get across there," she said. "No horse could live through it. There's nothing but that cut through the cañon . . . and I can't remember the description of it!"

"Could you lead me to it?" asked Blarney eagerly. "Could you take Harry's hoss and lead me to that cañon?"

"Ah, yes. I could find it blindfolded!"

"Then . . . we're off! One man'll be enough to carry the message to Sanson's place, and, if it comes to a scrap, I'll do what I can!"

"God bless you!" returned the girl.

"Wait a minute," said Harry Quale's rough voice. "How come you got the call over me? How come you're to go and not me? Are you better with a gun, or quicker on the draw? How come, Blarney?"

"Are you going to hold us up now?" exclaimed Blarney hotly. "Ain't you already proved that she couldn't trust herself on my hoss, but that your hoss would carry her like a lamb?"

"I take that back," said Quale through his teeth. "Your hoss seems quiet enough. Besides, my gray's kind of tricky, now and then, and bullheaded, and. . . ."

"Are you going to let her have your hoss, or not?" thundered Blarney Peters.

Then all the good humor that the girl had marked in his face before was gone. With the hard ring in his voice there was a companion glint in his eye. In the face of Quale, also, she saw the stubborn anger rise. They were both furious, both trembling with passion. In another moment they might clash together.

She threw herself between them. "Don't you see," she pleaded, "that everything is lost if you fight about it? Time is what we have to save, and we're losing priceless time! If either of you will go . . . if I have to go along to show the way, and there doesn't seem another possibility, won't you throw a coin to see which one is to stay behind?"

Blarney took off his sombrero and bowed to her.

"I might have knowed," he said, "that you'd find some way around Quale's selfishness! Here's the coin."

She stepped back. What manner of man was this who called it selfish in another who proposed riding on what might prove a wild-goose chase or else a desperate adventure against heavy odds? And what manner of men were they both to fight for the grim honor?

The coin spun into the air.

"Call!" cried Blarney.

"Tails!" shouted the tense Harry Quale.

The coin came down; Harry leaned forward.

"Tails it is!" he shouted. "I go. You stay here!"

VII

"Blarney Follows"

The head of the man of the south land fell as though he had received a stunning blow. As one dazed he helped the girl into the saddle on the black. Then he stepped to the head of the stallion.

"Colonel," he said, "take her safe there and bring her safe back. And keep your feet and act like a gentleman to a lady. Miss Claude, good luck to you!"

"I shall see you again to give back your horse safe and sound," she said. "And I hope I can say that I've found all well. And . . . Mister Peters, no matter what comes, you've saved my life, and your horse may be the means of saving my father!"

He waved his hat, forcing a smile to his lips, and the two started off at a hard gallop, with Quale turning in his saddle and waving a mocking farewell.

Swiftly they streaked across the snow, against which Colonel stood out in every small detail like a glorious picture. He ran like a blowing bubble for lightness. Compared with his stride, the gray seemed, indeed, a plow horse. And so they swept up a rise, over it, and dipped out of sight.

Blarney Peters, in a passion of anguish and disappointment, dashed his hat into the snow. In truth, he was very much like a spoiled and sullen child when he was thwarted.

"It's the snow," he said, picking up the hat again and knocking the snow off it. "Down in the south country we don't have the stuff. Otherwise, I'd be over them mountains

46

like they was nothing and. . . ." He paused, his hat in his hand, and stared yearningly toward those huge, solemn peaks, with the shifting fog of storm about them. Suppose he were to try them, in spite of the iced paths, the crevices, the dangerous slides and drops such as the girl had mentioned? No, it would be insanity. The girl, desperately rushed though she was, had not even thought of taking that chance. And suppose night were to overtake one in that wilderness of wind and snow? It would mean death by freezing if one stayed still, and death by a fall over some cliff if one moved forward.

Yet, slowly and steadily, as though drawn forward by his wishes, he found himself striding toward those summits.

Once he made that discovery, the die was cast. He had never yet drawn back from a venture to which he set his hand, and this should not be an exception to the rule. He settled into a steady pace and swiftly he went up the slope. With each upward stride it seemed to Blarney that the air grew colder, and in half a mile he reached the region of the upper storm. Faintly at first the wind fanned his face, and then with increasing violence, until, a scant half hour of journeying from the start, a veritable hurricane was raging about him.

He had to lean far to one side against it, staggering in his step when there was a slight let-up in the force of the gale. Suppose, along some precarious trail, such a gust should strike him? It would dash him from his foothold and down to horrible death in the ravine below! Still he kept on.

There was worse before him. A solid fog of driving snow was not far ahead, and yet he kept steadily on. In time he entered it. In fifty paces the gloom of late twilight was around him. Cross the summits in the night of that storm? He was forced to a halt by the madness of the thought. But the moment he had paused, his heart rose up in revolt. Setting his teeth, he leaned again to the side sweep of the wind and strode on.

He could hardly see his hand before his face now. The whipping snow stung his face in closely packed volleys. It made the wind a thick, palpable thing. It scourged and pounded him. Always there was the yelling of the gale, sometimes overhead, sometimes before him or behind, sometimes shrieking like a demon at his very ear.

Then he reached the shelter of the lodge pole pines again. Shelter? They were an open sieve through which the currents of the fierce wind poured. They were worse than nothing, for they had served to collect huge drifts of snow, and through these, buried to his very head, he beat and floundered his way, half choked, perspiration streaming from him in spite of the cold.

Now the trees were diminishing rapidly. Now they were hardly waist-high, and finally he came to a dense hedge, bent back from the summits, hardly knee-high. This, he knew, was the timberline, and where the hardy trees could not advance, what utter folly it was for him to set foot!

Yet he went on. He knew, now, that he could never cross the summits in the storm. The girl was right. In this dense fog of snow he would certainly blunder to death. Still he kept on. A nightmare impulse drove him along when reason urged him back.

Meantime, his footing was easier. The wind had blown the snow from the slope to a great degree. It was hardly more than ankle-deep, and the ascent rose smooth and steady. Then the wind leaped at him suddenly from a new corner of the compass. Straight out of the north it screamed against him, down the mountainside, belching the snow at him in stifling clouds. All sense of direction was now gone. He was simply keeping uphill. And then, after long labor, with all his leg muscles cramped and exhausted, he found a diminution in the force of the wind and a corresponding increase in the light that streamed through the driving snow and surrounded him with an atmosphere of brilliant and pure white.

Here the ground began to pitch down. He paused, feeling that he must have reached the summit. Below him must be the tortuous and dangerous way. While he paused, the storm broke and fell away as though recoiling. In the space of ten minutes the snow ceased blowing; the air grew clear. Looking up, Blarney saw gigantic rents torn in the cloud canopy. The clouds rushed hither and thither down the curve of the sky as though borne by half a dozen different air currents. Suddenly the whole sky was clear, except that to the northwest there was a dense wall of lavender mist slowly climbing up the sky. Otherwise, all was clear, and the snow world below him dazzled his eyes.

Blarney could see the difficulties of his path now, and he shuddered at the thought of attempting the crossing in the dark of the storm. Yet, it was almost like a reward for boldness, this clearing of the sky. The summits were crossed and chopped with a thick interlacing of ravines, as though an immense hatchet had been used to chop the ground and hew it here and there without rhythm or reason. Even with the sun to light him the way would be difficult.

He commenced the descent toward the opposite timberline, a dark streak far down the slope. Another enemy came to torment, a mysterious and subtle foe. His hair began to prickle. There were faint but harsh murmurs beside his ear, and strange sensations began to crawl over his skin. A native of these parts of the higher mountains might have told him that these symptoms were precursors to an electrical storm, which was annoying but not necessarily dangerous except to one with weak heart action. But to the man out of the south land it was a strange and terrible thing. He felt his muscles tingling and growing cramped as though muscle-bound. Presently, darting near the ground, there passed wave after wave of luminosity. Sometimes many colored balls of light glimmered an instant before him and then flashed out.

It was a dazed and bewildered Blarney Joe Peters who strode on, surrounded, he felt, by supernatural visions. Indeed, the mental confusion was so great that he sometimes wondered if he were not going mad. Meantime, the waves of electricity passed with greater frequency and greater speed, with a louder and more crackling noise. When they passed, there was a distinct twitching at every hair on his head, and his eyes burned painfully. Meantime, strangely tormented as he was, it was not long before he was in the thick of the intricacies of the climbing. He chose the straightest cut for the northern timberline and its comparative safety. But to make that cut he had to climb down the wall of a ravine, a precipitous drop where hands were of more use, clinging in small crevices, than his feet, shod in the most hopeless gear for mountain work—thin-soled riding boots.

Yet the descent was not so difficult as the climb on the other side. At the bottom of the gorge he broke through a mass of snow, crunched through a thin shield of ice, and was drenched to the waist in freezing water. Wet and chilled and discouraged he fought his way up from this bog, still with those prickling, maddening waves of electricity sweeping about him.

The opposite wall of the ravine was fierce labor. Once, halfway to the top, both feet shot from their hold on an ice-coated ledge, and he swung over five hundred feet of nothingness by the tips of his fingers, with a gust of wind whizzing down the ravine to tug him away from his precarious support. He swung in, found a new footing, clung there until the thundering of his heart had ceased, and then began his climb again.

He reached the top, weak and shaken. But the most difficult part of his task was done. Scarcely a mile of steep slope and he would be again at the safety of timberline. So over that white, gleaming descent he strode swiftly. For it was time for speed. The sun was dropping rapidly toward the western horizon, and the distance must still be considerable to the house of Sanson even if he could find it at all in the wilderness of foothills below the mountains.

There was a sudden acceleration of his gait. The very ground was moving beneath him with increasing speed to help him along. He thought for an instant, with a leap of the heart, that he had lost his reason in that strange climb. But now, standing still, he found that he was, indeed, moving forward with greater and greater speed. The snow beneath him moved. The snow to the side remained stationary. And suddenly he knew that his walking had jarred the snow into the beginning of a slide. It was already rustling down the slope as fast as a man could run. All of this within the space of half a dozen seconds!

He ran to the edge of the slipping snow and sprang toward the firm white surface at its edge. Alas, his weight knocked a whole ledge loose and the velocity of the whole mass, joined to the original slide, was redoubled. He half rolled, half scrambled to the side again, marked a place where a rock jutted above the surrounding snow, and leaped for it.

The result was a dazing blow, but his perilous descent was stopped.

He stood up and watched the progress of the slide. He had seen one in the full course of destructive action. He saw another now in its moment of birth. Viewed from the little distance it was a thing of beautiful motion, a white serpent of

51

unspeakable grace sliding down the hills, giving like water to every change in the contour of the ground. But now it cut deeper, sweeping up all the snow and leaving a black trail behind. It scoured rocks and brush from its path. It increased in momentum with astounding rapidity, and, finally, a thundering mass, it reached timberline, vaulted aloft so that Blarney could see the trees beneath it, and fell again in indescribable uproar.

Blarney rubbed his knuckles across his forehead. Three times that day he had rubbed elbows with death. Now he stepped forth into the well-known path of the slide and started forward and downward more swiftly than ever. There was still an hour before sunset, but how great was the distance before him?

Just before he reached timberline, he paused on an eminence. Below, with trees crowding about it and only the red of the roof showing—a faint spot of red on a distant hill—he saw the house of Sanson. But as to the miles that lay between, Blarney could make no estimate. He merely bowed his head and bent to the work before him.

VIII

"Sanson Interferes"

Meantime, Miriam Claude and her huge companion, Harry Quale, had reached the entrance to the ravine which, cutting through the tumbled heart of the Craven Peaks, saved them a full ten or twelve miles. Down this they turned the horses, the black Colonel still struggling with ceaseless energy to keep his head in the lead until the girl's strong arms, used as she was to a life in the saddle, ached from the constant pull.

That long detour along the sides of the Craven Mountains to the ravine, however, had cost them a great deal of time, and now it was hardly more than a half hour before sunset when they swung out over the last rise of the ravine floor and came in view of the northern foothills, the same instant when Blarney Joe Peters, perhaps, reached the trees of timberline farther to the west. The girl now freshened the pace until the gray was snorting in the effort to keep up, for he was carrying a tremendous burden compared to the light weight which now sat the saddle of Colonel.

Over the hills they rushed, bearing straight on without regard to the cattle paths and the horse-worn trails that they began to come upon, faint indentations in the overlying snow. As they galloped, the girl and her companion formed their plan.

"What excuse shall we give?" she said. "How shall we explain the fact that you are with me?"

"Tell him the truth about what you've heard in a dozen words," said Harry Quale, "and then we'll get him out."

"You don't know my father," said the girl, smiling ruefully. "He'll probably scoff at my warning and say it's all stuff and nonsense. Besides, we may have no good opportunity to warn him. When we arrive, if Sanson really has planned to attack Dad during the night, he may guess why we have come and he may simply make his attack earlier than he had planned. We may cause the very trap we're afraid of to snap together."

"Why, then," said Quale, "it ain't hard to say something else. I'm out of the mountains. I been working a claim right below timberline, me and a partner named Bud Denver. Along come a gang of rough ones the other day and killed Bud while I was off hunting meat. I come back to find Bud dead, the gold we'd washed all cleaned out, and nothing but a bunch of signs leading west. Suppose I come in with a yarn like that. I'd come down out of the mountains to find the sheriff. I went to his house. He wasn't there. You offered to show me to Sanson's house. Ain't that clear as day?"

"Yes, yes! And Dad . . . because that's his nature . . . will be in the saddle inside half a minute. When we have him out by himself, we can tell him the truth and make him believe it!"

Quale nodded.

They had fallen back to a canter during the time they were framing this simple but effective plan, but now they increased the gallop once more to a headlong pace. For the time of night was coming, and although they might reach the house of Sanson before full dark, who could tell what might take place in the lonely farmhouse as soon as the sun was down? If there was murder in the air, the very first hint of coming night might bring it forth.

As the girl had prophesied, they reached the last stage of the journey just in the twilight and pushed their sweating horses up the grade. The big ranch house and its depending shacks and cattle sheds and barns were sprawled across the top of a broad knoll—a dozen acres were littered with the remnants of what had once been the core of a great estate.

"Mister Rodney Sanson," said the girl, as they drew near to the big house, "is a man who makes a pretense at bluff honesty. If what I've been told today is true, then his frankness is a monstrous hypocrisy, but with it he has deceived everyone in the mountains for years. His honesty, in fact, is so thoroughly believed in that he is called in as a referee when there are disputes here and there which men don't want to bring into the law courts. You'll have to watch him closely. If you're not careful, he'll twist you around his finger, and inside a minute or two you'll be laughing at me and my story of danger. You'll be listening to nobody but Mister Sanson. Will you be careful, Mister Quale?"

Quale merely laughed, and there was such a fierce assurance in that sound that the girl smiled with pleasure, although the smile was almost instantly replaced with a shiver of apprehension. She might be taking this brave and generous fellow to his death. Because no matter what odds he found against him, he certainly would fight her quarrel to the bitter end.

"We're rushing," said Quale, as they swung from their saddles before the house. "The gray will stand. Just throw his reins. Here we are."

Quale helped her down from the saddle. Stepping into his hand was like stepping into the strength of a rock. Then she was scurrying to keep up with his immense strides. Down to the right of the house, their steps rattling on the long verandah, they passed into view of the dining room windows. And then the low hum of voices, the rattle of dishes, came out to them. Even in the distance they could sense the large number of men in the room. The girl held up her hand in dismay.

"He's got a whole table full of men," she said gloomily. "Listen!"

The table stretched across the width of the three windows. The shade of each window was drawn, and across each shade appeared the black, misshapen silhouettes of the diners. As the girl had said, the whole length of a very long table must be occupied.

"It's almost proof," she said. "It's almost proof in itself! What does a plain rancher want with as many men as that?"

"Then your father will know that something is wrong?" said Quale hopefully. "He'll be watching for a break so he can get away?"

"He'll see nothing," answered the girl sadly. "He trusts Mister Sanson as he'd trust me. But . . . have you got the courage to go in, Mister Quale?"

"Ordinarily," chuckled the big man, "the sight of a dinner table don't set me all quaking. I'll chance this one."

With that he approached the door, threw it wide without a preliminary knock, and entered. Miriam Claude, coming close behind him, found her utmost fears realized.

There was Sanson at the head of the table. At his right hand was her father. And down the rest of the length of the table were stretched a motley collection of cowpunchers. Men of every complexion, and of almost every age, were numbered in the dozen hardy fellows who occupied chairs. As they entered, there was a general turning of heads and an expression of alarm at sight of the huge figure of Harry Quale.

How truly gigantic he was she appreciated now as never before. His shadow was a secure mask to cover her presence.

"Where's Sheriff Claude?" he asked.

"Here, friend," said her father, rising. "What's up?"

"Trouble, bad trouble, and lots of it! Murder, that's what the trouble is, and I want action. And action quick!"

Sheriff Claude instinctively reached for his gun at that word murder, and so, Miriam noticed, did all the others at the board, with a certain lowering of the brows that chilled her blood. Unless all her experience with men was at fault, they were fellows capable of violent action and plenty of it. She slipped around her companion and ran toward her father, waving a hasty greeting to Sanson.

The latter sat with his head drawn down, peering up through the shadow of his brows with keen old eyes. If ever she had seen suspicion in a human face, it was now in the face of the old rancher. Plainly he would probe to the bottom of this alarm. Perhaps he would give the signal now and turn his bloodhounds loose against the sheriff even in the presence of the two newcomers. But such action was hardly in keeping with his character. He would be more apt to try some sort of trickery. What that might be remained to be seen.

"You here, Miriam?" said her father, frowning. "How come all this?"

"He came down out of the hills and straight to our house," said the girl, steadily enough, "and he said that he was out hunting, and, when he came back to the mine he and his partner were working on the side of Grizzly Peak, his partner was dead . . . shot from behind . . . their gold they'd been washing was stolen . . . and there were hoof marks of half a dozen horses which had been ridden up to their claim and away again."

Such was the story that she and Quale had hastily agreed upon. Here the old rancher spoke to the man at his left, who nodded and instantly left the room, fixing a steady glance of curiosity upon big Harry Quale as he left. What did that maneuver mean?

Her father was coming around the table. He was, as she had hoped, instantly on fire, and not at all disposed to ask dubious questions.

"Where's my hat, Rod?" he shouted, addressing Sanson. "Where's that hat? Never can keep it around. Partner"—this to Quale—"how far'd you trail the gang?"

"Not more'n half a mile. No use in one man trailing six, is there?"

"You showed sense there. But you got their direction?"

"They hit northwest."

"Did, eh? Well, we'll make that the hottest trail they ever followed. What did I say, Sanson? Didn't I say that news would get around about that bunch of cattle-rustling skunks that's working through the Cravens? Now everybody in the range thinks that this county is going to be a happy hunting ground!"

He snatched the hat that someone had brought to him and turned toward the door.

"We'll be going in about ten minutes," he assured Quale. "Get a bite of food, stranger, before we start. Miriam, you stay here at Rod's place overnight and ride back in the morning and. . . ."

The voice of Sanson broke in for the first time. At the sound of it the girl's heart sank.

"Just a minute, Bill."

"Not half a minute, Rod. I'm plumb rushed."

"Sixty seconds," insisted Sanson. "I want to ask the big fellow a couple of questions."

"All right," fumed Miriam's father, "but we're losing a lot of valuable time."

"Maybe we are," said Sanson, "and maybe we'll save a lot of valuable skin by wasting a little valuable time."

He came slowly around the table until he was confronting her champion, big Harry Quale. The latter glanced askance at her as though to implore aid in the test of words that was apparently coming. She could only bid him, with a gesture, to be resolute. He fixed his naturally stern and forbidding glance on old Sanson.

The latter now stood squarely before Quale, with his legs a little apart and his hands clasped behind his back. What did he intend to do? She could only guess that in some way he was going to attempt to throw suspicion on Quale's honesty.

The very first question dispelled all doubts.

"How long," he said, "have you been working that claim?"

Miriam dropped her head. He was going to riddle Quale with cross-examination. The big man would not have an inch of ground to stand on in another five minutes.

IX

"Under Arrest"

"How long have I been working it?" repeated Quale. "Oh, just a few weeks." He was admirably careless.

"I was up along Grizzly a few days back," said the rancher. "Kind of funny I didn't see you gents working."

"Not a bit funny," broke in Miriam, trembling for the exposure. "He says his claim is on the creek, and I suppose you might ride within only a few yards and not see it on account of the shrubbery."

"On the creek, eh?" said the rancher, and, turning on her although he continued to smile in the most friendly fashion, she thought that his eyes contracted and gave forth a bright gleam of suspicion. "But you see," he continued, "I rode right along the side of the mountain. It sure is queer that I didn't see your claim, partner. Didn't catch your name?"

"Quale," said the other, controlling himself with an effort that was visible to the girl. "That ain't strange, though. We're working in a little cut . . . back from the east bank of the creek . . . and, unless you heard us working, you mightn't know we're there if we stayed a thousand years!"

"Hmm!" murmured the rancher. "Maybe this gent is all right, Sheriff, but I'd sure talk to him a while if I was you. You know that you're pretty close on the heels of the rustlers, and who knows? Maybe they've sent out this gent to get you and trap you. They try to make it seem a fair play by working through Miriam, there. But if I was you, I'd ask him a little bit more about his claim, and how he's been working it. I seen that the creek on Grizzly, the other day, was clear as crystal. No sign of anybody using water to wash dirt with . . . no sign of any cut back from the bank, so far as I could make out!"

"Look here!" interrupted Quale, "you mean to let on that maybe I'm a crook, or something like that?"

"You can't bluster with me, young man!" cried Rodney Sanson with anger. "I ain't going to back down just because you talk loud. I dunno you. You say your name is Quale. Maybe it is. Maybe it isn't. But I don't know any gent named Quale, and I won't go your bail. But I do know my old friend the sheriff, and I ain't going to see him drawed out on what may be a wild-goose chase after nothing particular."

The sheriff patted the shoulder of his friend with a reassuring hand. "Don't be too hard on the young gent, Rod," he said. "I can take care of myself, big as he is. He don't look like no mama's boy, but I can handle him. I've handled bigger and worser than him."

"You have, Bill," said Sanson heartily, "and it ain't one man that I'm afraid of, for your sake. But I say that, if you want to ride out with this gent that runs a gold mine nobody ever heard of on Grizzly, why, some of my boys are going to ride out along with you! I'm firm on that! But ask him a few questions, Sheriff!"

In vain Miriam strove to catch the eye of her father. The fiery old man had whirled on big Harry Quale and was looking him keenly in the eye. And Quale, embarrassed by this unexpected examination, and furious at the baiting to which Sanson had subjected him, was crimson with rage that might very well appear to be guilty mortification.

"Partner," said the sheriff, "I sure want to do you justice and help you to find the gents that've killed your partner, as you say he's killed. But they's something in what Sanson says. I want you to answer me a couple of questions. Where . . . ?"

Suddenly the rage of Quale, which had been rising steadily during the past few minutes, broke all bonds of restraint and good judgment.

"I'll answer nothing," he said fiercely. "I been told that the gents around these parts were a bunch of thick-heads, and now I believe it! I ain't going to ask no more help from the law. I'll be my own law. And to the devil with the lot of you!"

So saying, he turned on his heel.

"Let him go," suggested Sanson eagerly. And his eagerness seemed to the girl to betray the fact that he had penetrated the entire secret of her coming with Quale.

"What? Let him go?" roared her father, his gray beard shaking with excitement. "I'm cursed if I will! You, there, Quale, stand where you are!"

The big man turned again on his heel. His face was now convulsed with passion, and his eyes glinted wildly from face to face about the long board. He was truly at the fighting temperature. In another instant the fire might break out. Just at that moment the door behind him opened, and the man who had been sent out by the rancher returned silently, as though to report. He closed the door noiselessly behind him, and the raised finger of Sanson warned him to remain where he was.

"I'll tell you the facts," Harry Quale was thundering, "and you can swallow 'em whole or let 'em go by. I don't care. This friend of yours . . . this Sanson . . . he's the gent that's running the rustlers around these parts."

He was interrupted by the sudden uproar of laughter from the sheriff.

"Let him talk," said Sanson, his eye fixed with a side-glance upon his henchman who stood passively by the door. "Let him talk. Maybe he'll say something worth while!"

"What? Let him slander you, Rod? I guess you and me ain't been pals all these twenty years for nothing. You a rustler? If I wasn't so damned mad, I'd have to laugh at the fool for having the nerve to stand there and look me in the eye and tell me such fool things as that!"

It seemed to the girl that Sanson settled back a little in his chair, to which he had returned, and it seemed to her, also, that each of the men about the long table, who had leaned forward a little at the accusation that Quale delivered, now also relaxed. She was close to the huge, trembling bulk of Quale, and she found occasion, during the muttering of angry voices that closed in around the end of the sheriff's speech, to whisper to her champion: "Whatever happens, don't try to resist. There's a man behind you with a gun. You can't fight back! Don't try!"

Quale rolled on her a glance that she would never forget. It was like the look of a baited bull, feeling that he can crush any one of his baiters to powder with his overwhelming power, but unable to reach them on account of the surrounding barriers. She pitied him with all her heart. She had brought him into a situation where only adroitness with words could be of use to him. And such adroitness he did not possess. He had the strength and the fighting skill to handle three men with bare hands, or even with weapons, perhaps. But against a dozen he was helpless. Perhaps she was sacrificing him in vain. But, at least, if she could prevail upon him not to lift his hand or move to draw his gun in resistance, she would postpone the time of his fall. Although the veins stood out on his forehead in his agony of rage, there was struggling, mute acceptance of the truth of what she had said in his eyes.

Here the door from the kitchen flew open. The Chinese cook ran in and leaned at the ear of his master. Sanson listened and then raised his hand and nodded, as though bidding the cook wait. At this the latter returned hastily to the kitchen.

Now the sheriff was running on hotly: "Are you scheming out another fool lie, Quale, or whatever your name is? I tell you this, you ain't going to leave my hands till I've found out more about you, and why you want me to ride out with you tonight. You look bad to me. You look plumb crooked, and I'm going to get the facts about you if they's any facts in reaching distance."

"You're going to arrest me because I come down here to warn you?" said Quale slowly.

"It sounds like you got enough sense to understand something. That's exactly what's going to happen to you, son. D'you give yourself up peaceable?"

The struggle went on for another long moment in Quale. His head bowed with the intensity of that inward strife, and, when he lifted his face again, it was seamed and wrinkled in a thousand small furrows with the pain of restraint.

"All right," he gasped out. "You got the numbers ag'in' me, Sheriff. But if you ever live to see tomorrow, or the day after, I'll make you sweat for being a fool!"

"Well," said the sheriff, eyeing him sternly, "how you could ever have come to such a crazy idea as to think that I'd believe the best friend I got in the world . . . old Rod Sanson, here . . . runs the same gang of cattle-rustling skunks I'm hunting down is more'n I can see. But whatever kind of a bluff you're running, son, it's sure called."

He turned to the rancher, smiling coldly and quietly. "Got a place where I can keep this gent, Rod? I'd like to have him put safe out of the way till we've finished dinner. Then I'm going to see what I can get out of him. He's sure a queer one."

"I got a safe room down in the cellar," answered the rancher. "Jack, will you and Pete take the big gent down there? Get his gun first, and then take him down. And if he tries to get away, shoot him like a dog!"

"That's right," said the sheriff. "He's under arrest, and if he tries to get away, drop him!"

Harry Quale gave up his weapon without a murmur, while rolling his eyes slowly and fiercely around the room, as though he were printing a picture of every face on his mind. Then he strode out, followed by two cowpunchers who prodded him along with their revolver muzzles.

No sooner had he seen this accomplished than Sanson, first seating Miriam at the table, excused himself and hurried out to the kitchen. There he saw a man well-nigh as big as the giant who had just been escorted to the cellar. He was wet to the waist. His clothes were covered with rents. He seemed to have been torn and battered by all the force of the storm of that day. It was Blarney Joe Peters.

X

"In the Room with Quale"

He grew excited the moment he saw the rancher.

"You're Sanson?" he asked eagerly.

"What you want with me?"

"Come over here a minute. I want to talk to you!"

There was such a guilty secretiveness about his manner that the rancher immediately obeyed, although always keeping a sharp lookout on the new visitor.

"Are they here yet?" asked Blarney.

"Who?"

"The girl and the big fellow. The sheriff's daughter and Quale?"

"Hmm. Yes."

"The devil!" exclaimed Blarney in vexation. "Then I've had my trouble for nothing. But, no, if they's told the sheriff, you wouldn't be here without irons on."

"What?" the rancher muttered. "Talk soft, you fool. What are you driving at?"

"The girl knows it all," said Blarney, frowning. "And she and Quale come on to tell the sheriff. They know that you've set a trap to bag the old goat."

Suddenly the face of Sanson became a curious study of mingled emotions. Curiosity, denial, fear, anger, suspicion were all finding a place in his mind.

"That's queer talk," Sanson said.

"You know it's straight talk," said Blarney. "Listen, while I tell you just who I am and why I'm here. I'm Blarney Joe Peters. Go south to the Y Bar J outfit and they'll tell you who I am. Anyway, I got track of a gent up Montana way named Quale. Him and me agreed to meet and have it out in the Craven Valley just on general principles. We met and were about to tangle when we seen a slide start and come close to blotting out a girl riding along the slope. We managed to grab the girl off her hoss, which was running wild, and we got her out of the path of the slide just in time. She fainted, being pretty nigh scared to death, and, when she come to, she told us what she was bound for . . . her father was the sheriff of the county . . . he was hunting some rustlers . . . had got an invite to spend a few days with you . . . had gone to your ranch . . . then along come a gent and tells his daughter it's a plant . . . that you're backing the rustlers yourself and keeping 'em safe and covering their tracks, and that because the sheriff is close on your heels, you've planned to have him bumped off to get rid of him and keep yourself from being discovered. She tells us this. She wants us to start on and try to rescue the old man. But I won't listen to it. You can guess why. I've done a bit of rustling myself, now and then, just to keep a hand in. Meantime Quale has been blinking at the girl's pretty face. All at once he pulls a gat and covers me, ties my hands behind my back, puts the girl on my hoss . . . you go outside and you'll find a big black . . . and rides off with her. But when she was talking, she'd told the way to your house. I was plumb wild. I worked the rope off, found my gun, and started across the mountains in the storm."

The rancher gasped, glanced over the ragged clothes, and then stared at the big man with a new respect and belief.

"But this is a mighty queer yarn," he said noncommittally. "What d'you expect to get by telling me all this stuff about snow slides, and murder planned, and what not?"

"I don't give a curse what you believe," said Blarney Joe Peters with heat. "All I want is Quale. Lemme at him. Give him a gun and me a gun and turn us loose. Or turn us loose without guns. I don't care as long as I get a chance at him!"

Sanson looked down to the floor, rubbing his chin thoughtfully with his knuckles.

"Then suppose," he said, "that I believed you and that I took you down into the cellar and put you into a room with Quale. . . ."

Blarney swallowed with apparent joy.

"Just do that!" he said fiercely. "Just do that, partner, and I'm your man. I'll bust the skunk in two!"

"He's tolerable big," said the rancher cautiously. "You sure got ambition. Would you give me your gun before you went into that room with him?"

Instant was the answer of Blarney: "Take my knife, too. I don't want nothing but bare hands and light to see his throat."

A sudden conviction lighted the face of Sanson.

"Then give me your gun and knife and follow me!" he said

tersely, and he led the way through the kitchen and down the stairs into the moist darkness of the cellar, vaguely illumined by a lantern that hung from the beams overhead. Voices and a rectangle of light came from about the edges of a door to the right.

"Now," he said suddenly, "you're the father and the king of liars! I'm going to show you it don't pay to lie to me."

But Blarney merely shook his head at the leveled revolver.

"Don't be a fool, Sanson," he said. "You know, I'm talking straight. Lemme in there at Quale . . . I hear his voice . . . and I'll show you that I mean what I say!"

Slowly Sanson lowered the revolver.

"It sounds like a fairy story. Matter of fact, they's too much in it to be imagined. Blarney, I believe you, and . . . I'm going to turn you loose on Quale. Come here."

He led the way to the door, knocked on it, and, when it was opened, he introduced Blarney to a comfortably large room, lined on every side with heavy logs. What it could have been used for was a mystery. It was as secure, as soundproof, as a dungeon. The two men, both with drawn guns, were still guarding Quale, who sat sullenly in a corner. At sight of Blarney he gasped and started.

"You!" he gasped out. "You here?"

"I'm here, you hound," said Blarney through his teeth. "And what's more, I've blown your whole game, Quale. I'm here, and I'm here to finish you the way I please."

An expression of bewilderment swept over the handsome features of the man from the north land. He leaped to his feet with a snarl of inexpressible fury and sprang at Blarney Joe.

"Don't shoot!" cried Sanson to his men.

Their guns hung poised in mid-air and between them. Careless of his danger Quale leaped at his old enemy. His hands were extended with gripping fingers. He had only one thought, and that was to sink his fingers into the throat of Peters. Far different was the action of Blarney. Poised on tiptoe, for an instant he measured his man, then stepped with incredible swiftness a half pace forward with his left foot, flung his whole weight forward, and with his whole power drove his right fist into the face of Quale. It landed flush on the point of the latter's chin. Quale went back as though a wave of the ocean had tossed him. He staggered. His hands went down to his sides. His face took on a stupid expression of unconcern. And into that dazed face, brutally, Peters struck again. This time it was his left, hooked with perfect science and terrific force. The sound of the blow on the loose chin was like the fall of the cleaver thudding into the soft wood of the chopping block. Quale whirled and pitched onto his face, an inert mass.

"Now," said Blarney through his teeth to the other three, "get out of the room. I got something to do. I want to be alone. Get out!"

In face of his snarling and bestial ferocity he saw the others, hard men though they were, shrink and change color, while at the same time their lips lifted in a sneer of disgust. Sanson touched his arm.

"Thought you were faking," he said. "But I guess your whole yarn is right. But not that way, Peters. Here. Slip these irons over his wrists. That'll keep him. Here's the key for 'em. If you want to finish him . . . well, you can do that later. I don't want too much noise right now."

With a grin of understanding Blarney took the handcuffs, fixed them over the wrists of the unconscious man, and then stepped back and looked down at the inert body, moistening his lips with an air of peculiarly animal-like satisfaction. Sanson examined him with a mixture of horror and interest.

"Blarney," he said, "if I let you finish Quale, would you

want a good job with me . . . along the line of some of the work you used to do?"

"You give Quale to me," said the man of the south land, "and you can make your own bargain. I won't fight about the terms."

The rancher nodded, his expression a strange mixture of disgust and satisfaction.

"I guess you boys won't be needed down here," he said to the others. "Here's the key to the door, Blarney, and your revolver. But mind you, don't do nothing to him tonight. I want quiet. You can guess why." He waved farewell for the moment and stepped out, closing the door after him.

"Ever see anything like that?" he said to his men. "Ever see a devil like that before?"

"Like a wildcat," said one of the cowpunchers. "Don't he carry a punch in them arms of his?"

"He'll be a good man for us," said Sanson. "The kind we need when we get in a pinch. Now step along. We don't need to worry about Quale, I guess. If he don't get his throat torn out, he's lucky. Now we got to get up and handle the old man. Won't do to leave him alone with the girl. Once we have him in bed . . . well, he'll never wake up . . . the old fox."

The moment the door had closed behind the three men, the manner of big Blarney Joe underwent a strange change. He stood a moment listening to the noises of the retreating trio. Then he turned the key in the lock, strode to the fallen giant, turned him on his back, and examined him closely. There were two slight bruises on his jaw. Otherwise, having shielded his face with his arms when he fell, he was not injured.

Then Blarney sat down to wait.

XI

"The Fight in the Ranch House"

There was no long pause. Harry Quale recovered rapidly from his daze the moment he was turned on his back and his breathing thus made easier, for presently he opened his eyes, glared about him in bewilderment, and, when he saw the face of Blarney above him, intelligence suddenly dawned in his eyes, and fury with it. One furious growl, one profound groan of despair escaped from his lips when he found that his arms were pinioned behind him. Then the rapid voice of Blarney broke in upon him.

"Will you listen to me for half a minute, partner?"

"You dog!" panted Quale. "You sneaking, treacherous dog!"

"Cuss me out. I know I've treated you rough. I'm going to tell you why I done it. And, when I get through, I'm going to take off the irons and stand up and let you wallop me a couple of times just the way I done to you."

"Wallop you? I'll wring your neck," said Quale snarlingly.

"Maybe. But just hear me talk. I came here after you folks by cutting across the mountains . . . the storm let up just in time to keep me from getting a broken neck down one of the ravines. I sneaked onto the porch. I saw what was going on in the room. I knew you were a goner. I couldn't break in with a gent there watching the door. So I came around to the kitchen, got hold of Sanson, and pretended that I was on his side. I told him enough truth to make him pretty sure. But he's suspicious as a fox. For all I know he may have sneaked

70

back to listen at this door, and that's why I have to whisper now. When he took me down here, I had to prove that the reason I wanted to see you was because I wanted to kill you. I proved it in the only way I knew, and I sure didn't take any pleasure in doing it, partner."

Quale ground his teeth.

"I'm going to give you your chance at me back again," Blarney promised him. "Meanwhile, we got to work together, and I ain't going to take these irons off till you swear that you'll wait till we've got the sheriff and the girl through this mess before you start in trying to smash me to bits. Will you promise?"

"What can we do?" said the other growlingly. "We two ag'in' a houseful?"

"But we two," said Blarney, "working together, can sure try a strong hand ag'in' them all. Will you give me your word?"

"Take it, then," said Quale. "Sooner or later, though, I'm going to kill you, Blarney."

"You black hound," answered Blarney, with equal rage. "When you kill me, they won't be nothing but white blackbirds around these parts. I like you the same way you like me, and no better. You can lay to that."

"I hear you," said the other. "But what you want to do now?"

"Turn you loose. The girl is in there pretending that she don't suspect nothing wrong but that you've plumb deceived her with your story. Sanson knows the truth. I had to tell him that much. He'll try to get her out of the way and up to her room. Then he'll get her father out, have the dirty work over with, and try to lay the blame on someone else . . . you or me, most likely. We got to get doing before the dinner is over. Will you help?"

71

"You do as much as me," said Quale, "and you'll be a better man than you ever proved yourself before."

"That's good," said Blarney, still whispering. "I've got your word?"

"Yes."

With that Blarney unlocked the handcuffs, and Quale leaped to his feet. For a moment he stood swaying, fighting against a desire to leap at the throat of his former tormentor. Still he controlled himself.

Blarney nodded. "You'll have your chance later on," he promised. And he unlocked the door.

The two friendly enemies stood in the cellar, looking about them.

"Now," said big Harry Quale, "what's the problem? What's the way the two of us are going to have a chance ag'in' more'n a dozen, because you got to figure the old sheriff joinin' in the fight ag'in' us!"

"You take this revolver and then you go out through the cellar window," ordered Blarney in a whisper. "If you find both the hosses where you left 'em, all right. If you don't, go to the barn and get 'em and saddle 'em. Then bring out two more . . . the best ones you can pick out of the lot, mind you."

"I hear you," replied Quale, taking the revolver. "Then what?"

"Sneak 'em back to the front of the house and leave 'em standing there under the trees, all together. Then come back to the door of the dining room where it leads out onto the verandah and whistle."

"Well?"

"And then," said Blarney Joe Peters, "you're apt to hear a lot of noise. You can start in praying for me. If I come out through the door, you can help me with what I'll have with me. If I don't come out after about two seconds after the noise starts, you go and jump onto Pat and start off . . . and take Colonel along with you, because I'd sure hate to have him rode by skunks like these." He added: "You understand?"

But still Quale hesitated. "Whatever's about to happen," he said slowly, "seems to me that you're taking most of the risk."

"I got to. I'm the one that's in the place to take the risk."

"Which sounds," said Quale, "like you wanted to hog the glory."

"If you got a plan handy," said Blarney Joe, "I'm free to say that I'd like to hear you talk. Otherwise, shut up and help me. But of all the most out-suspicioning gents I ever see, you're the worst, Harry Quale."

Quale cursed softly, but with profound feeling.

"I'm going to do what you tell me to do," he said. "But no matter what happens to the fool sheriff and his girl, I'll sure be mad if one of those gents in there gets you and I didn't have a chance to make my play. If it wasn't for the girl, I'd let the sheriff hang and finish you now, while I got you here."

"But being that the girl's in it," said Blarney calmly, "you're going to play square and fair and give her a fighting chance to get away. Eh?"

Quale nodded, glared sourly at his companion, and then turned and strode off toward the window. Blarney watched him disappear into the outer night and then turned—to face Sanson himself!

The little withered rancher had approached with the softness of a bodiless spirit, and his lean face was wrinkled and devilish with suspicion. In his hand a heavy Colt was balanced ready for a snap shot at an instant's notice, and because Blarney had given the gun that he had had to Quale, he knew instantly there was nothing he could do.

73

"How come," said the rancher snarlingly, "that you're out here, and not in there with that gent you said you wanted to get at so bad?"

The calmness of Barney for one instant was utterly shattered. But he managed through a desperate effort to maintain a smile. There was desperation in the face of the other. Plainly Sanson was pushed so far back against the wall that he did not care what he did. One murder must be done in his house that night. Why not more than one? Aye, as many as necessary, for his game was nearly up!

All of this Blarney saw in the vicious, contorted face of Sanson. Through years Sanson had played his part as an honest citizen. Now, whether it was financial difficulties or some other reason that had started him on a career of crime, the real evil in his nature was being developed with astonishing rapidity. He affected Blarney as the nearness of a monstrous rat might have done, or some poisonous viper.

"I'll tell you what, partner," said Blarney, and his voice was steady, "you're terribly handy with that gun. I give you a promise tonight. Well, when I seen him lying there . . . and nobody around . . . and when I thought about the dirty trick the skunk had played on me today . . . well, it was like putting a drink before a dry man. I just nacherally couldn't resist, Sanson. I just reached down and gave him a grip around the throat. You know? Just digging my thumbs into the hollow of his throat. It didn't need much more'n a squeeze. He stopped breathing for good."

The little man gasped. His eyes widened as though he had seen a ghost, then contracted suddenly as before a great light. "You done that?" he muttered. "You done that before he come back to life?"

"Why not? Didn't he take a drop on me when I wasn't looking? Didn't he do me dirt so's he could run off with the girl? Answer me that, Sanson. He looked bigger'n ever . . . but he'll never speak out loud again. Never."

The little man drew a great breath. "What . . . what a devil you are!" he gasped out.

"Maybe you're a saint, eh?" returned Blarney sneeringly.

"Never mind. I can use you . . . maybe I can use you tonight."

"The sheriff?" asked Blarney. "Sure."

"And there's somebody else. We can't have any witnesses. We can't have people around who know too much, eh?" He thrust his head forward. His grin was diabolical. "No matter what happens here tonight, we could take the bodies out and drop 'em over a cliff into the snow. Wouldn't be found for months . . . not till spring. And who'd turn to the sheriff's old friend, Sanson, and ask questions?"

Then a curious horror swept over Blarney, although he only half guessed all the unspeakable atrocity of the double crime the rancher intended.

"Who's the second?" He forced himself to add calmly: "The girl?"

"Her . . . yes," panted the rancher. "She . . . she knows too much. Blarney, if you get rid of her . . . I couldn't trust any of my other boys to get rid of a woman . . . I'd make you rich . . . rich! You hear? She can do me as much damage as any man . . . she. . . ."

When he had slipped the heavy revolver back into the holster and stepped close, explaining, the great hand of Blarney shot out and caught that detestable, withered throat. The temptation to kill was great. Only the weakness of Sanson and his age saved him then. Instead, while the eyes bulged out from their sockets, Blarney made a gag of his bandana, thrust it into the mouth of the victim, carried him to the cell that had been occupied by Quale and, having taken Sanson's revolver, snapped over his wrists the handcuffs with the arms behind the captive's back. He slammed the door, locked it, and hurried up from the cellar to the floor above. He did not expect to use the revolver in carrying out his plan for the rescue of the sheriff and the girl, but it was as well, he thought, to have a gun when he could get one.

The Chinese cook gave one glance at his face, and found in it something so terrible that he shrank suddenly back against the wall. Blarney sent him scurrying out the back door with a single glance, and then he forced his features to a smile, and, in this fashion, he entered the dining room jauntily enough.

At a glance he took in what was going on. The sheriff was talking gaily. His daughter, at the other end of the table, was listening, white of face, but forcing herself to appear attentive. The cattle rustlers eyed the speaker with ferocious sullenness. Things had gone so far, now, with the capture of Quale and his attempted exposé of the gang that they were no longer even pretending. They were inviting the catastrophe with their manner. But the sheriff, blind in his fancied security in the house of his old friend, and apparently immune to the warnings which his daughter had time and again attempted to convey to him, talked on contentedly, laughing at his own stale jests until the entrance of the ragged figure of Blarney made him lift his eyes in surprise. The others turned.

"Go ahead, gents," he said, "don't let me bother you none. Just seen Mister Sanson, and he says he'll be in here in a minute or two."

He was sauntering across the room toward the sheriff, when he heard from the door of the room a sharp whistle. His heart stood still. It was the signal of Quale who must have moved with astonishing speed to execute his half of the plan. And Blarney had been too long delayed with Sanson in the cellar. The signal came too soon, and now it brought every man from his chair to his feet.

"Wait a minute, gents," said Blarney, stepping to the table beside the sheriff. "I got to explain what Mister Sanson has just told about that whistle." He dropped his great hands on the edge of the table and tested its weight, glancing down at the two lamps that illumined the double row of grim faces.

"The fact is," said Blarney, "that Sanson sends word by me that he is unable to be with you now!"

As he shouted the last word, he heaved upward with all his might. The table swung up, the lamps rocked over. In spite of his speed of hand there was time for two guns to be drawn, two shots to be fired, but a hasty aim saved his life. The table crashed over. There was a jangle of knives and forks and smashing crockery. The lamps, crashing into a thousand fragments, spilled their flaming oil across the floor, and the room, from a steady and sufficient light, was suddenly plunged into a twilight of reeling shadows. Instantly all was confusion. There was shouting of wild voices, the explosion of guns, and yonder three men, their clothes having been splashed by the oil and ignited, were rolling on the floor to extinguish the fire.

Before the remaining men could rush Blarney, and while the first instant of confusion reigned, he seized the sheriff beside him, swept him up like a child, crushed him to his broad breast so that his arms would be powerless, and darted for the door.

Could he reach it in safety? Would the girl see what was being done and follow? There was a confusion of yelling behind him. Half a dozen guns exploded, and the bullets *whizzed* perilously close to his head. But the only light to guide that shooting was the ragged play of fire on the floor. Through the doorway he sprang with the struggling sheriff, and behind him—he gave a shout of triumph—raced the girl!

She had seen and followed his move with the speed of thought.

Behind them came the pursuers, yelling their rage and astonishment. But they met a strange and unexpected reception. While Barney Joe Peters plunged away toward the horses, carrying the shouting sheriff, and the girl ran beside him, Harry Quale, covering the retreat, emptied the revolver shot after shot through the doorway. They were unaimed shots, but the cries of anger and fear showed the men inside were scattering to corners of the room to return the volley.

Quale had no intention of remaining to receive that fire. No sooner did he see the three in place on the horses—for ten words of frantic entreaty from his daughter had pacified the sheriff and made him swing onto his saddle—than Quale turned and raced like a deer for Pat.

As he gained stirrup and saddle, the rout issued from the door of the house, and a volley rattled behind them. But they were instantly lost in the darkness of the trees in the first rush of the frightened horses. Down the hill the four raced, and then on and on across the gleaming snow, faintly white beneath them in the darkness.

Epilogue

The weary riding of that night was never forgotten by the sheriff and his two newfound, gigantic assistants. First they brought the girl to the town of Jasper, and, leaving her there, they returned with a posse of twenty men, gathered at midnight, armed to the teeth and ready to meet desperate resistance. But they returned to find the house falling to pieces in the flames of the fire that had started in the dining room when Blarney Joe Peters overturned the lamps. Even through that sea of flames Barney dared to penetrate to the cellar for fear that the unfortunate rancher had been left there when his gang fled from the place. But the door of the room was open and no one was there. Sanson had fled, and, indeed, he disappeared as completely as though the fire had burned him to ashes and the wind blown the ashes away. But the cattle rustling ended in the sheriff's county.

It was noon, the next day, before the excursions through the neighboring hills to find the trail of the fugitives were given up. A new snowfall had covered all signs effectively. So the weary men of the posse threw themselves down about a hasty campfire and made coffee.

Then it was, when he had drained his first cup, that Quale, who had been sitting for a long time with his eyes fixed thoughtfully on distant spaces, turned suddenly to Blarney Joe Peters.

"Blarney," he said softly, "what you thinking about?"

"Honest Injun?"

"Yep. Tell me straight."

"Why, I was thinking that it would sure be purgatory when you and me had to stand up and fight it out. Partly because I dunno whether or not I'd win, and partly because . . . well, we been through quite a pile together lately."

The other nodded, still thoughtful. "Sometime," he said gravely, "I figure you and me are going to have it out proper. But you sure done a pretty decent turn by the girl and the sheriff, Blarney Peters. Take it all in all, you're so much man that I sure would hate to mix up with you right now. Still, I never been much on partners, Blarney."

"Nor me."

"Because I never met my match before. But now I've met him . . . and what say, Blarney?"

A great hand extended to meet his. The two sets of fingers closed with force that would have crushed the bones of a normal man to shapelessness.

"If we stick together," said Blarney joyously, "nothing can beat us."

"And nothing can separate us but the devil," said Quale.

"Or a woman," said Blarney.

"Aye," returned Quale, sighing, "or a woman."

He looked again into space.

The Boy Who Found Christmas

"The Boy Who Found Christmas" was published under Faust's John Frederick pseudonym in the December 22, 1923 issue of Street & Smith's *Western Story Magazine*. In fact, in 1923 Faust's output was seen almost exclusively in the pages of *Western Story Magazine*, where between January and December sixteen short novels and seven serials were published. In contrast to Faust's often larger than life heroes who tower over all the other characters, his hero in this touching story is a puny twelve-year-old named Lew Maloney. Don't let his size fool you, he's as skilled in the art of survival as any other Brand hero. But he possesses something far greater of which even he is unaware until he learns about a holiday named Christmas. This is the first time, since its original publication, "The Boy Who Found Christmas" has appeared in book form.

I

"The Land of No Work"

When I asked the judge about writing this, he said: "The way to begin, Lew, is to start out like this . . . 'I, the Kid, alias the

Oklahoma Kid, alias Oklahoma, alias Lew, being twelve years of age and in my right mind, do affirm that. . . .' "

"Judge," I said, "hand it to me straight, will you?"

The judge scratched his chin and said: "Tell them the whole truth and nothing but the truth." Then he winked. So I'm doing just what he said: telling the whole truth and nothing but the truth—with a wink.

I was born on Black Friday. The same day, my mother died and my dad lost his job. Them two things took the heart of him. She was a black-haired Riley, and he was a red-headed Maloney, and, when she died, everything went wrong for Dad. He never did no good for himself nor nobody else after that. The only way I remember him was when I was four or five years old. He used to put me on the bar and drink to me and tell me I was to grow up past six feet with a punch in both fists. The booze got him.

After he died, I went to live with Aunt Maria in a terrible clean house. Aunt Maria was a queer sort. She'd had a great sorrow in her past, someone told me, and was kind of sour on life in consequence. She was a good soul in a hard, severe way, but nothing religious about her, though. On the contrary, she hated church and ministers and all that like poison, wouldn't let 'em have anything to do with her, and was always reading books written to prove that they were all wrong in their beliefs.

This aunt of mine had four sons of her own, and what with me doing odd jobs around the place, fighting her boys, and getting lickings from her, times was hard. Her place was a ways out of the town and it was too far away for us—me and her sons, that is—to go to the district school even if she'd wanted us to, which she probably didn't. In the mornings, she'd put in an hour teaching us kids to read and write and figure, and that was all the schooling we got or were likely to get. It was all work and no play with Aunt Maria. She worked herself and made us boys work seven days a week, fifty-two weeks of the year. She never took a holiday herself and never gave us one. She was a hard taskmistress.

Then Missouri Slim blew in one day and seen me chopping kindling in the woodshed. I took to Slim right away. I'd seen plenty of rough and tough ones in my time, but Missouri was different. He was long and skinny. He had a big, thin nose and a little mouth and chin like a rat's, and a pair of small, pale blue eyes that never stopped moving. He was wearing seven days' whiskers, and he didn't look like soap bothered him none.

His clothes was parts of three different suits, and none of the three could ever have fitted. His coat sort of flapped around him with bulges in the pockets, and his trousers bagged at the knees and the seat, which showed that he done most of his hard work sitting and thinking. He looked like today was good enough for him and like he didn't give a hoot what come tomorrow. I figured he was right. He didn't talk much, neither, and, after Aunt Maria, that was sort of restful.

He says: "How old are you, young feller?"

"Seven," I says.

He watched me chop wood for a while. Then he pulled an old violin out of an old battered case and tuned her up. When he begun to play, smiling and with his eyes shut, I started seeing dreams. He finished and packed up his violin.

"Where you going?" I asks.

"Where nobody works," says he.

I asks him if that was heaven, and he allows that maybe it was. He says his first stopping place was down in the hollow just outside of town, near the railroad bridge, and that, if I wanted to see him and talk about the land where nobody worked, I could come down the next morning. He says he

83

couldn't do no talking while I was chopping that kindling. He says it made him sort of sick inside to do any work or to see anybody else work.

"Look at that cow over in the field," says Slim. "Is she happy?"

"Sure," says I. "She's chewin' her cud."

"Has she done any work?"

"Nope."

"Look at them two dogs," says Slim. "Are they happy playin' tag?"

"I hope to tell!" says I.

"Do they do any work?" says Slim.

"Nope," says I.

"Nobody but fools work," says Slim.

I watched him out of sight. When I come to, Aunt Maria had me by the hair of the head.

"Not finished yet!" she says. "You lazy, good-for-nothing! Like father, like son!"

"My dad," says I, "was the strongest man in the county and the best fighter, and he never said quits!"

"It's a lie," says Aunt Maria. "He was a loafer, and he let a whisky bottle beat him and kill him!"

When it came to a pinch, I had a way of doing my arguing with my hands—until Slim taught me better. Now I grabbed a chunk of wood and shied it at Aunt Maria and hit her funny bone. It made her yell, but she was a Maloney, too. She caught me by one foot just as I was shinnying over the fence. When she got through with me, I couldn't stir without raising an ache. Besides, she sent me to bed without supper. I lay in bed, twisting around, trying to find a comfortable way of lying, but I couldn't invent none. Then I thought of Slim.

I went to the window and looked out. There was an old climbing vine that twisted across the front of my window. I smelled the flowers; I looked beyond and smelled the pine trees in the wind. Before I knew it, I was on the ground. I stood there a while, sort of scared at what I'd done and wondering if I could climb back the same way that I'd climbed down. I heard Billy and Joe snickering and laughing in the front attic room; I knew they was talking about me and my licking. I heard Aunt Maria rattling in the kitchen and finishing up her work. I smelled a couple of apple pies that was standing in the kitchen window, and they made me sort of homesick, but I told myself that I'd started along so far, that I'd better get the worst of it over before I come back to take my licking and go to bed again. I looked around me.

Take it by and large, the dark is pretty creepy inside of a house, but I seen that on the outside it was tolerable friendly. I could hear the frogs croaking out on the flat; I could hear crickets singing up and down the scale; the smell of pine trees was sweeter and stronger than it ever could be by day; and the sky was full of star dust and of stars.

There was nothing to fear as far as I could see or hear, except the black windows of Aunt Maria's house with a glimmer of light in 'em like the light in a cat's eye, and the noise of Aunt Maria in her kitchen. So I seen that there was nothing to worry about and lit out for the hollow beside the railroad bridge.

I come down through the trees and out into a little clearing, with the creek cutting through the middle, and firelight dancing across the riffles or skidding across the pool. There was four men sitting around the fire, drinking coffee out of old tomato tins, and in a sooty old wash boiler near the fire I could smell all that was left of a fine chicken stew. Maybe the Plymouth Rock rooster Aunt Maria had missed that day was in that stew. I hoped so. Three of the men had strange faces. The other was Slim. I come out and spoke up behind the place where he was sitting, sipping his coffee.

"Slim, will you let me eat while I listen to you talk about the land where nobody don't work?"

He didn't even look around. "It's the kid," says he, "the one I was telling you about. Are you hungry?" says he to me.

But I was already diving into the mulligan. I ate hearty. *Now,* says I to myself, when I couldn't hold no more, *no matter how hard Aunt Maria licks me, this has been worth it!* Then I looked up and seen they were all sitting around and watching me with their eyes bright, looking every one like the grocery man when he's adding up a bill.

"You've ate," says Slim in a way I didn't like at all. "Now what you got to pay for what you ate?"

I blinked at him and seen he meant it. "What's it worth?" asks I.

He looks at the others. "Forty cents," he says. "There was one chicken alone in that stew that would've cost anybody but me a whole dollar and a half. That ain't saying nothing of the two fryers that was alongside of him, and the onions and the beans and the potatoes and the tomatoes, and the work of bringing in the chuck, the cleaning of the pans, the building of the fire and the watching it, the picking of the chickens along with the cleaning and the cooking of 'em, the peeling of the potatoes and the slicing of 'em, and a lot of little odds and ends that's throwed in for nothing. Forty cents is dirt cheap. It's lower'n cost, and what I got to have is cash!"

"I got no money," says I.

"Then you can pay with work."

"I thought that there was no work in your land," says I.

"Work or get money by your wits," says Slim. "It's all just the same."

"I got to work, then?" says I, backing off a little, for I could tell dead easy now that there was real trouble ahead of me, and a lot worse trouble than any I'd ever gotten into with Aunt Maria. "I'll do my work running," I says, and turns and run with all my might.

I'd taken three steps when a stone as big as a man's hand hit me and knocked me on my face, but still I could understand 'em talking.

"You've killed the kid, Slim," says one of 'em.

"Then he's died knowing that I'm his master," says Slim. "But he ain't dead. He's too chuck full of hellfire to die like this. No rock will end him . . . it will take steel or lead to do his business. Mind me, pals!"

I got my wind back and tried to duck away again. Another rock hit me and dropped me. I come to with water in my face and sat up, asking where I was.

"With your boss," says Slim, leaning over, "and here's my signature."

He showed me his bony fist doubled up hard.

"Leave go of that idea," one of the others says. "How d'you figure in on him more than any of the rest of us?"

"By reason of this," says Slim, and eases a long knife out of his clothes. "Does it talk to you?"

After that, they scattered and there was no more argument. After that, too, I belonged to Slim. I tried for six months to get away from him, but I never could work it. He kept an eye on me all day, and every night he tied my wrist to his wrist with a piece of baling wire. By the time that half year was up, I wouldn't have left him if I could. I'd got used to him and his ways, and I liked the life.

Besides, he learned me a lot. He learned me to sing a lot of songs by heart, playing the tunes to me on his violin. He showed me how to dance the buck and wing, or straight clog dancing. He showed me how to handle a knife so as to take care of myself if anybody else tried to get me. He taught me how to throw it like a stone and sink the point into a tree twenty yards away.

Once I says: "Slim, how come that you work so hard teaching me things?"

He says: "I work for you now . . . you work for me later on."

And I did. After that first six months, when he found out that he could trust me away from him because I was sure to come back, Slim never raised his hand. I used to knock at doors and ask for hand-outs. Mostly the womenfolk used to fetch me inside and set me down at a table and give me three times as much as I could put inside me, so I'd take it to Slim in my pockets.

Sometimes they got real interested and tried to adopt me. They'd wash me clean, dress me clean and new, give me a name like Cecil, or Charles, or Robert, or some other sort of fancy name like that, that a dog wouldn't have taken and kept. They'd put me to sleep in a fine bed covered with cool sheets. They'd come in and kiss me good night and cry over me; but in the middle of the night I'd come awake when a railroad train whistled for the stop, or because I felt the weight of the ceiling above my face, or because I choked with the smell of cooking and other folks that hangs around inside of any home.

Slim used to say that nothing this side of a good, first-class murder and then a ghost could clean a house of that smell of being lived in. I asked the judge about it. He said that Slim was just smart enough to be mean, that the first half of most of the things he said was right, and the second half was sure to be wrong. This shows how close the judge could figure things. I never knew him to go wrong.

Me, speaking personal, I never could make up my mind, but when I woke up like that in the middle of the night, the first thing I used to think about was the open sky. The second was a picture of Slim over a fire, cooking, and the smell of the mulligan. So I'd slide out of bed, dress up in my new clothes, and duck through the window.

Right here I've got to say that roast chicken, or 'possum and sweet potatoes, or roast young pig, is no better than chewing dead leaves compared to a real mulligan, the kind that Missouri Slim used to cook. He could make a stew out of a tomato skin and an old bone, if he had to, or else he could put in everything you brought.

Once I got into a grocery store on a Saturday night. I brought out one can of almost everything, hot peppers, a chunk of ham, and everything else I could find. It didn't faze Slim. He started the fire, opened the cans, and began putting 'em in and stirring the stuff with a stick. Once in a while he'd taste the goozlum on the end of the stick and then dump in something new. When he got all through, I was almost afraid to taste that mess, but, when I did, it beat anything I ever tasted before and anything I'll ever taste since. It was good.

"What d'you put in to make it so dog-gone good, Slim?" I asks him once.

"Good thoughts, kid," says Slim.

That was his way of talking.

Battering doors for hand-outs was the smallest part of my work. Mostly I kept cash rolling in to Slim. When we hit a good town we hadn't worked before, we'd lay up till evening with Slim playing his fiddle or sleeping, and me hunting around the town, seeing without being seen. I used to ask him how he could sleep so much.

"I'm like a camel, Lew," he used to say. "A camel puts fat on the hump in case it runs out of fodder. I put sleep in my pocket in case I hit hard going."

In the dark of the evening, we'd stroll into that town and

Slim would play his fiddle while I danced and passed the hat, or else he'd come in, hobbling on a cane and acting sick, and I'd walk along and sing, with my cap in my hand and everything from nickels to silver dollars dropping into it.

"Keep looking up at the stars, kid," Slim used to say to me, "like you expected to go to heaven along with the next note you sing. The way to make 'em reach deep into their pockets is to put tears in their eyes."

Well, we made enough money to get rich, but Slim used to lose it playing poker, about as fast as it come in. Speaking personal, I liked it best when we wasn't too flush. When the coin was in, we'd lie up and take it easy, maybe a week at a time; when the coin was out, we'd be moving and seeing the sights. We went from New York to Frisco and from Montreal to El Paso during the five years I was with Slim. Then Slim began to drink pretty hard, and, when he started hitting up the moonshine, I knew it was time for me to shake loose. I begun to wait for my time.

That same winter a shack pulled us out from under a car where we was riding the rods. He basted Slim in the face with his lantern and kicked me off the grade. When the train rolled along, Slim used up the last of his cuss words, and then started groaning and holding his nose, where the rim of the lantern had landed.

"What d'you make of a man like that shack?" he says. "One that hits a man when he ain't expecting it? Ain't it low, Lew? That shack is so low he could crawl right under the belly of a snake!"

I didn't hear him. It was a mighty cold night. We'd been near to freezing on the rods, and now we seen the mountains walking up into the sky all around us and the wind come scooping down with the feel of the snow in its fingertips. A wolf began to yell on the inside edge of the skyline, and my stomach shriveled up as small as a dime.

"It don't make no difference to you," Slim says to me. "Poor old Slim that taught you all you know and worked for you and slaved for you! Now he's down and sick and weak and getting old, and you laugh when you see him hurt!"

That was the way Slim used to carry on. I knew he'd made a good thing out of me, but sometimes I couldn't keep the tears out of my eyes when he told me how I'd abused him. Well, after a while, he got out his flask of homemade whisky, so strong it would peel the varnish off of a table. He poured some of that down his throat, and then we started out to find a shelter against the wind. We had luck right away.

When we curved around the side of the hill, we could see the lights of a town in the hollow underneath, and, when we aimed straight for it, we ran plumb into a jungle as neat and as comfortable as any you ever seen, with a fine lay of boilers and tins handy, plenty of dead wood, trees so thick that they was like the roof of a house, and three hobos lying around a dead fire, sleeping warm and snoring—which showed that they'd been living fat.

II

"The Question"

It was coming to the gray of the morning. The sky was beginning to show through the trees, and the mountains was turning black in the middle of the night, when we heard a rooster crowing on the inside rim of the skyline, and then other roosters answering the way they do.

"Do something for your country," says Slim. "Here I am,

a poor, weak, old man"—he wasn't a year more than forty—
"and you stand around and wait for me to starve. Ain't you
got no shame in you, Lew?"

I left the jungle after I'd boiled a cup of coffee and ate a
chunk of stale punk. Then I cut across to the town. I come out
of the woods in the rose of the morning, and there was a neat
little town with a white roof of snow on every house.

A mighty comfortable-looking town, I thought it was, as
pretty as I ever seen. It sat down in the arms of the mountains
with evergreen forests walking up away from it and a creek
talking and shining through the middle of it. I seen a boy
about my own age delivering milk, driving his wagon down
the street, jumping off every minute to leave a bottle, coming
back slapping his hands together to keep 'em warm. But there
he was all wrapped up so thick with clothes that he could
hardly move, and here I was with not even an overcoat.

You see, when you're laid out on the rods and let a winter
wind comb through you for three or four hours at a stretch,
there ain't anything else in the world that can really make you
feel cold. I felt all snug and comfortable when I looked down
at the town. I listened to the bells on the milk wagon go out,
then I started for breakfast. The hobos I seen in the jungle
had a lot of punk and other fixings; all we needed was meat,
and there was meat asking to be taken.

I slid into a chicken yard and watched 'em prance around.
I'll tell you how to catch chickens. Just go and sit down in
their yard and wait. A chicken is the most fool of anything in
the world. Pretty soon they come to have a look at you and a
peck at you. Then nab one in each hand. You can always tell
the fat ones. They're the busiest. The reason they're fat is
because they work harder for bugs and worms and seeds, and
the harder they work, the fatter they get.

If you're in doubt, don't feel the breast of a chicken to see if it's fat because the last place where they put on fat is the back. When a chicken is nice and round and soft in the back, you know that you got a good bird; if she's full of bones and ridges under the wings, you know you got little to chew. I grabbed a couple of beauties and went back into the trees, where I wrung their necks and then snagged 'em on a branch.

While I waited there, I heard a door open and a screen slam. Then I seen a woman come out on the back porch and call across to the next house: "Hello, Missus Treat! Oh, hello!"

Mrs. Treat shoved up a window and tried to lean out, but she was too fat to get her shoulders through. "Are you up so early, Fannie?" says she.

Evidently Fannie was.

"Was there ever a time," says Fannie, "when I wasn't up as early as you? Besides, this is the day before Christmas, and I guess womenfolk can't afford to sleep on such days."

"Not on days of festivity and merrymaking like Christmas," says Mrs. Treat. "We got to work while the men-folks sit by and fill up fat."

"We got happy lives," says Fannie. "We watch the sick, we hear the babies, we take care of the houses, and, when the big softies are blue, we got to smile and cheer 'em up. I can stand everything but the having to smile!"

She looked like smiling was a real trial, too. But Mrs. Treat, she just kept smiling and chuckling and bubbling all the time.

"Men are silly dears," she says. "You take everything hard, Fannie!"

I picked up the chickens and went off toward the jungle, because I knew that when a pair of womenfolk begin to get sorry for each other, they talk foolish for a long time. In the jungle, I found everybody up and awake. The three 'bos was still yawning and rubbing the sleep out of their faces while they fed up the fire, but Slim was real neat. He's gone to the creek and washed. His hands was reasonable white up to the wrists, and the front of his face was clean, but his neck and ears was never bothered by being wet except it rained on 'em.

As for baths, Missouri Slim never troubled much about 'em. He used to say that they was bad, because they took all the protection away from the skin. "Look at a dog or a horse," Slim would say. "Ain't they got something on over the skin? Same way with a man. He needs protection." There was no use arguing with Slim about a thing like that. He'd made up his mind for good and ever. Baths were not for him.

The hobos took the chickens and began to work on 'em, while Slim sat by and told 'em what to do. He'd brought in the meat supply, through me, and so he didn't have to work with his hands. They started a mulligan, while I rustled more wood, but when the stew was simmering, I asked my question, because it had been riding me for a long while back, ever since hearing the two women talking.

I says to Missouri Slim: "What's Christmas, Slim?"

Slim stopped stirring the mulligan, took another drink of his moonshine, and then corked the bottle, and put it up—all before he started answering me. Then he called to the other hobos.

"Look here," says Slim. "Here's ignorance, for you. Here's what the kids are growin' up to these days. Smart lookin', but they don't know nothing. No eddication. No refinement. No manners, by gosh! Here's a sample of 'em. Would you guess it? He wants to know what Christmas is!"

They all sat around and laughed at me. I could have knifed 'em all and enjoyed it, but I rolled me another cigarette and cussed 'em good and hearty. There is ways and ways of swearing. I knew a 'bo that had been a longshoreman. He could talk a bit. I knew another that used to be a muleskinner, and he could talk a lot more. But for taking a gent's hide off with cuss words, there was never anybody like Missouri Slim, because he sat back and thought things over and picked out words that meant something. With a knife or with his tongue he was a champeen, but he wasn't much good in any other kind of a fight. I'd laid by and studied the way he done it, and after a while, practicing to myself, I learned how to out-cuss even Missouri Slim himself. I'd got so's I could make the toughest 'bo that ever done a stretch foam and tear and rage when I cussed him. I've had a 'bo sit under a tree for thirty-six hours waiting to get me. Well, I talked right back to these three until I had 'em ready to fight. They stopped laughin' and showed their yellow teeth.

"Christmas," Missouri Slim says finally "is the day when folks get things without having to pay for 'em."

"Why," says I, "every day must be Christmas for you, then."

Missouri shied a rock at my head. He could throw a stone like a snake strikes—that quick. But I'd learned to dodge even quicker. The stone sailed by.

"What *is* Christmas?" I asks them all.

"Go and find out!" all four tells me.

They wouldn't say any more. Through breakfast, Slim kept saying how hard he took it that, after all the hard work he'd put in teaching me, I didn't even know what Christmas was. He said that I was a trial and a shame to him.

I didn't listen. I just ate my share of the chuck, smoked my cigarette, and then curled up near the fire to have a snooze. The last thing I heard was Slim telling the other 'bos to keep shut of me while I was sleeping, because if I was waked up quick, I got my knife out before my eyes was open. Slim had taught me that, if he hadn't taught me about Christmas.

When I slept, I had a dream that I had a fine black horse brought to me, all saddled and bridled, and that when I whistled, he came up and nuzzled my hand. I'd always wanted a horse. I used to beg Slim to get me one, but he used to point to the steel rails of the track and say: "There's our horse, kid, and it'll step faster than any four-legged horse in the world!" This dream made me so happy that I called out: "What's the name of this horse?" And a voice sang out in the air over me: "Christmas!"

I woke up. The four tramps was sitting around, grinning at me. So I knew that I'd shouted that last word out loud. I told Slim I was going for a walk and started off through the woods, but what I was really doing was hunting for Christmas. It made me feel like a fool to be laughed at by four 'bos. Aunt Maria had never taken a holiday or given me one or had any festivity at this time of the year, and with Dad and then with Missouri Slim, every day was a holiday. That was how I happened to miss knowing. I went back to the edge of the town and laid low.

Pretty soon a couple of boys came out into the back yard of a big house. I climbed up and sat on the edge of the fence.

"Hello," says one of them, "what are you doing up there?"

"Sitting on the fence," says I.

They frowned and looked at each other. They were a shade older than me, and heavier. I could see them sizing me up.

"That's *our* fence," says the biggest of the two. "You got no right to it."

"I'm just borrowing it," I tells 'em.

They begun to sidle up to me, talking all the time. I acted like I didn't notice.

"What you looking for?" they asks me.

"Christmas," I says.

They stopped and begun to laugh.

"What's funny about Christmas?" I asks 'em.

"D'you believe in Santa Claus?" says one of 'em.

I'd never heard that name before. I hedged. "Partly I do and partly I don't," I says.

They laughed again. "He doesn't know much, Tommy," says one of the two, "Where'd you come from, boy?"

"Yonder," says I, and waves to the sky.

"Who's your father?"

"The sheriff," says I.

"That's a lie," says Tommy. "Pete Saunders's dad is the sheriff. Who *are* you?"

Asking wasn't good enough. Tommy made a dive and caught my feet. As he pulled one down, the other one grabbed me around the neck.

"We've got him!" they yells, and they begun to pommel me.

It was all a cinch. When I laid hold on 'em, my fingers sunk 'way into them, they was so soft. I hit Tommy in the stomach, and he rolled on the ground, gasping. I got a half-nelson, that the Denver yegg, Tom Larkin, showed me how to use, and rolled Charlie on his back. Then I tapped him on the nose until he hollered quits. When I got up, Tommy was coming again, like a bull. I hit him on the jaw so hard it made my shoulder ache, and he dropped on his face and lay without a wiggle. It was good fun. I wiped that blood from Charlie's nose on my pants. When I looked up, a fine-looking man was standing in the yard with his hands on his hips, looking me over.

"Cheese it," I says to myself. "Here's where I get the boss licking of my life!"

III

"I Meet the Judge"

"Uncle John, Uncle John!" yells Tommy. "Help! Help!"

I looked at the fence. It was higher from the inside than from the outside, and I saw that there wasn't a chance for me to go over it. Then I looked at the man. He was about thirty-five, but he had no more stomach than a greyhound, and by his way of standing I knew that he could run like one. So I made up my mind that I wouldn't try to run away. A boy is a fool to run if he can help it. When you're caught after running, you get three licks for every one you would have got before. I leaned against a tree and rolled a cigarette and waited to take what was coming.

The big man didn't seem in a hurry. He give me a look, and then he gave Tom and Charlie a look apiece. He didn't seem no ways satisfied.

"There's two of you, and there's one of him," says he. "Am I right?"

"He . . . he . . . ," Charlie begun.

"Be quiet," says the big man in a way that made 'em both stand stiff and still. He goes on: "Did I see you two fighting that one boy . . . two on one?"

They didn't have nothin' to say. Me, I blinked at him and couldn't savvy what he was driving at.

" 'S'all right," says I. "They didn't do me no harm . . . just scratched me up a bit."

"Listen to me, boys," says the uncle, "if this were not the day before Christmas, I'd make you remember this as long as

98

you live. And if I ever again hear of you combining against another boy of your own age and size . . . by jingo . . . ," he busts out, "I do believe that both of you are bigger than this little chap!"

It made me mad. I never gave promise of growing up to and past the six feet that Dad promised me when I was a little kid, but it always rubbed me the wrong way to have folks point it out. I stood up as big as I could stand.

"I ain't so small, mister," says I. "And them two . . . huh, they ain't nothing. If they was twice as big, I could eat 'em!"

I'd got the cigarette going pretty good, and then I steps up and blows it in their faces, but even that didn't make 'em fight. They'd had plenty.

"I think I understand," says the big man to himself more than to the rest of us. "I think I understand."

He hitches up his shoulders and drops his hands on his hips.

I thinks to myself: *If he don't pack a wallop in each mitt, may I never grow up to be blowed in the glass. Hope he don't take his exercise on me today.*

He hooked his thumb over his shoulder. "Go inside, boys," he says.

They went hopping; pretty soon they come to the back windows and must've frosted their noses looking out to watch me get my hiding. But the big guy didn't seem in no special hurry.

"Is that tobacco?" he says to me.

I told him it was and waited for him to start a lecture, like the rest. It's a queer thing that folks that's growed up can't leave a boy alone. They got to give advice. But the big guy was different.

"Lend me the makings, will you?" he asks me.

I handed them over. He rolled the pill with one hand; it was mighty slick work. I asked him how long it had taken him to learn, and he said that he got the trick of it when he was punching cows on the range. He didn't look like a 'puncher. He stood too light on his feet, and he wasn't brown enough, and he didn't have the wrinkles around the corners of his eyes. I told him that I was surprised.

"What would *you* make of me?" he says.

"Why, a banker." Then I had another idea, because of the way he looked straight into me and made me blink. "Or a sheriff," I says.

At that he started a little and let the match go out between his fingers without lighting his cigarette. "Why is that?"

"Because you look at a feller like he had a gun hid in his pocket," I tells him.

He managed to light his cigarette this time, and he grinned at me through the smoke. "You made a close guess, son," he says. "But I'm not the sheriff . . . I'm only the judge."

"Oh!" I says, and took another look at the size of that fence. It was bigger than ever!

He was a judge, and, of course, they're even worse than sheriffs. I started backing away.

"How long have you been smoking?" he asks me.

"Four or five years," I says. "Is that wrong?"

"Wrong?" he says, and cocks his head to one side like he was considering it. "Certainly not. If you wish to smoke, why shouldn't you? It's a comfort, isn't it, after a hard day's work?"

"It sure is," says I, and took a long breath, seeing that he wasn't one of them lecturers. For a square guy, the judge was a bird. He had the world stopped.

"I suppose that you're traveling through?" says the judge.

"Yep."

"With your dad?"

"Nope."

"Older brother?"

"I play my own hand," says I.

He took another breath of smoke and blew it out in rings. "Been playing your own hand for long?"

"About five years."

He whistled.

"What's wrong," says I.

"A touch of rheumatism," says he. "I got an old bullet lying up in me, and once in a while it gives me a reminder that it's there."

"A bullet?" I says.

"Yep."

"Somebody plugged you once?"

"A pair of crooks started out to get me," says the judge.

"A pair of 'em? What kind?"

"Yeggs," he says. "I gave one of their pals a long sentence. A fiver, if you know what that means."

"Listen, was I born yesterday? Sure, I know that lingo. I used to pal around with Sammy Mobile. Well, you're lucky if you got out with only one chunk of lead in you if there was *two* yeggs after you. Did they corner you?" I stopped, anxious for him.

"They got me from behind," says the judge.

"Behind! Shot you down and then flagged it?"

"No, they ran to finish me."

"Jiminy!" says I, beginning to think that he was maybe just a ghost. "What happened then?"

"I finished them, instead."

"While you was lyin' on the ground?"

"I got the drop on 'em. The ground steadied my arm."

"Oh," says I, running out of any words that meant anything. "Who was that pair?"

"Tinman and. . . ."

"Tinman! He's the bum that pulled the stunt at Jericho!"

"You know about that?" says the judge.

"Oh, Tinman's dead. I guess there ain't any harm in talking about it now!"

"Not a bit."

"Sure, I knew about it."

"Is it straight that he killed both the old folks?"

"Yep, he croaked the two of 'em," says I, sort of proud that I could tell a gent like the judge anything. "He spent the day in the cellar and come up through the trap door that night when they was asleep. He told us about it afterward. You got Tinman, eh? Who was the other one?"

"Lefty Peters."

"Peters!" repeats I. "The one that killed. . . ."

"He had a long record," says the judge.

I begun to get some new angles on the judge. Peters and Tinman was so dog-gone bad that even the rest of the yeggs steered clear of them. They ran together because nobody else would play in with 'em. Their way of cracking a safe was to start making things safe by murdering the watchman. A killer ain't popular even among hobos. The getting of either one of 'em was enough to make a reputation for a whole posse, but for one man to get the two of 'em after they'd tackled him behind and dropped him was pretty near too much to believe. I begun to understand why the judge's eye was so straight. He needed a straight eye.

"Well," says I, "I'm mighty glad that I met you, Judge! I didn't even know that Tinman and Peters was dead."

"Neither did I until a month ago. It was a year back that I

tackled them, but only the other day I turned up some evidence that established their identity. Did you know Peters, too?" He looked at me, interested.

"Did I? He nearly knifed me once, because he stumbled over me when he was drunk."

"Ah?" says the judge. "How did you get away?"

"Threw a handful of sand in his face and blinded him."

"Hmm!" says the judge. "You seem to be able to take care of yourself."

"A traveling man has to learn how to do that."

The judge coughed. "You ran away from home, I suppose?"

"I suppose not," says I. "Mother and Dad were dead . . . Aunt Maria gave me a job, not a home."

He laughed. He had a fine laugh that come clear from his stomach. When a man laughs up in his chest, you know he's no good. That's the way a woman laughs. Speaking of women . . . but the judge says it's better not to speak of 'em. I'll let that go.

"Where are you bound this morning?" he asks.

"I was just collecting some dope," says I.

"What?"

"Just talking."

"With my nephews, eh?"

"Yes."

"Did they tell you what you want to know?"

"They laughed at me."

"That's why you fought?"

"Nope . . . it takes more than a laugh to make me fight. I ain't proud," I explains to him.

"Oh, well, what was it you wanted to know?"

I didn't want to tell him. Being laughed at by the kids wasn't so bad, but I figured that it would hurt if the judge laughed, too.

"Why," says I, "it was nothing much, I guess. It was about . . . er . . . about Christmas."

"Ah, yes. What about it?"

I doubled up my hands and looked him square in the eye. "Well, what *is* Christmas?"

The judge looked at me a minute like I'd hit him. Then he stepped over quick.

He's going to laugh, too, says I to myself.

But he only picked up a stone and chucked it at the fence. There wasn't no sign of even a smile when he looked up again.

"What is Christmas?" says the judge, sort of to himself. "You never had it explained?"

"Never put in time in a school," says I, feeling mighty awkward with my hands and my feet when I said it.

"Oh," says the judge. He seemed to be thinking of something else. Finally he says: "Most people don't have to go to school to learn what it is, you know." Then he busts out with a frown, getting a little red: "It's the birthday of Christ, my friend."

He had me floored again, but I was too foxy to let him know it. I'd heard that name used for the inside lining of some fancy swearing, but in no other connection.

"Oh," says I, "is that all?"

"Is that all?" says he, speaking sort of quick, as though I'd pinched his watch. "Isn't that enough?"

"Don't get sore," says I.

He give his chin a rub and stared at me. It looked like I was getting deeper with everything I said. I offered him the makings of another cigarette, but he didn't seem to see or hear me. His mind was on something else.

"Do you know when Christ was born?" he asks me.

I had a quick think, then I took a chance. "Sure," says I. "Before the war?"

IV

"The Judge Confides in Me"

The judge begun to walk up and down the yard, kicking stones out of his way. I seen that I'd answered wrong.

"If He was a friend of yours . . . ," I starts.

He cuts me off short. "Boy, boy! He was born more than nineteen hundred years ago!"

What a boob I'd been as a guesser. The judge waited a little longer: "What's your name?" he asks.

I would have said John Smith, or something like that, but he popped it out at me so quick, that I told the truth before I thought.

"Lew Maloney."

"Lew," says he, "d'you know nothing more about Christmas than this?"

"No," says I.

The judge stopped walking around. "I won't try to tell you all about Him now, only this . . . that He gave His life for the rest of us. A terrible death, Lew. You can understand that much of it. They stretched Him on a cross of wood, and they drove nails through his hands to hold Him up, and a spike through His two feet. He died by inches, for the sake of other men."

I tried to think of man dying like that. It took my breath and made me sick.

"That's why," says the judge, "we keep Christmas every year. He gave so much for us that on this Christmas day, we give little things to one another to help us to think about what a good man, what a brave man, what a generous man He was . . . because He gave his life, do you see?"

"It's the finest thing I ever heard of," says I, and I felt it. It gave me a queer tingle clear down to the toes. It made every man I'd ever seen or heard of seem mighty small. "Was this here Santa Claus some relation of His?"

The judge bit his lip—to keep from saying something or to keep from smiling. I couldn't figure which.

"Ah," says he, "Santa Claus is another story. I was saying that we give things to one another . . . but Santa Claus is an old man who gives things to everybody!"

I thought about this for a while. "Judge, excuse me for contradicting, but you're wrong there. He never gave me nothing."

"Of course not. Because you never asked him to."

That floored me.

"Look here," I says, "d'you mean to say that, just for the asking, he gives things away?"

"Exactly that."

"It ain't nacheral," says I. "I got to have that proved, Judge."

"Didn't you, just now," says the judge, "give me a cigarette simply because I asked for it?"

"That's different," says I. "What's a cigarette?"

"Well," says the judge, "Santa Claus gives away things just like that."

"What's his plant?"

"What do you mean?"

"What's his scheme? What's his layout? What does he look like?"

"I can tell you. He's a very old man with a long white beard and long mustaches. Usually he wears a red coat trimmed with white fur, and a tall hat of the same red cloth and white fur. He has thick gloves on his hands, and his trousers are wrapped around his legs with cord to keep him warm, because he rides around in the cold air, drawn by reindeer. . . .”

“Wait! Wait!” I says. “Did you say he drove around in the *air?*”

“Exactly. He has a big sleigh loaded with gifts. When he comes to a house where he intends to leave presents, he stops the sleigh on the roof and comes down into the house through a window, or even by a chimney. . . .”

“Hold on, Judge,” says I. “D’you expect me to swallow that? Driving through the air . . . stopping on the roof? Whoever heard of anything like that?”

“Why not?”

“Not even a feather can ride in the air very long!”

“Lots of strange things can happen in this world,” says the judge. “Is Santa Claus and his rides through the air any harder to understand than a telephone?”

“Why, a telephone is easy!” I tells him.

“What is it, then?”

“Why, you know! Some wire, with electricity in it, and. . . .”

“But what’s electricity?”

It stumped me. I tried to think it out, but then I gave it up. “I don’t know,” I admits. After a minute I went along: “Are you handing this to me straight, Judge?”

“This very night!” says the judge.

I watched him mighty close, but he kept a straight face. He was serious all the time.

“Such as what?” I asks.

“Whatever you want.”

“Suppose I asked him for a pair of shoes?”

“You’d get ’em. Think of something more. Tell Santa Claus the thing you want most in the world. He’ll get it for you, if you really are willing to believe in him."

It made me sort of dizzy. I leaned against a tree and blinked.

"Suppose," says I, talking slow and watching the judge to see if he was about to smile and give the game away, "suppose that I was to ask him for a .32 six-shooter? One of them straight-shooting little guns that can't miss hardly. I suppose you mean to tell me that he'd give me even that?"

"You want a gun, eh?"

"Want it?" It choked me, thinking how bad I wanted that gun.

"Well," says the judge, "all you have to do is to write that out in a letter to Santa Claus. . . ."

"I knew there was a catch," I says, and it made me sick inside. "Yep, I knew there was a catch!"

"Where's the catch?"

"You see, Judge, I never put in no time at school. Aunt Maria tried to teach me, but I . . . I never learned to write."

The judge kicked another stone that rolled clean to the fence. He seemed madder than ever. Then he thought about it, but, after a while, he told me that the thing might still be managed. He said that Santa Claus was a simple-minded guy, so old he was getting childish. If somebody else wrote down that letter for me and signed my name to it, he'd probably never notice that it wasn't my handwriting.

He offered to do the writing for me, pulled a piece of paper and a pencil out of his pocket, and asked me what I wanted to say. I told him I thought it ought to start out with his name and address, so's it would get to him. The judge allowed that was a slick idea. He wrote it down and read it to me: "Mister Santa Claus, Greenland, Northern Hemisphere."

It sounded pretty fine. I told him what to say, and he wrote the letter.

Dear Mr. Santa Claus: It ain't likely that you know me, but, if you'll give me a look tonight, I'll be glad to see you. And when you come, if you happen to have any old .32 caliber six-shooters on hand, I could sure use one. I mean the kind that the Denver Kid was packing the last time I seen him. It's about the right weight for me. I'd be mighty obliged.

Yours very truly,
Lew Maloney

I told the judge that Santa Claus might not see his way to giving as much as that to a stranger. The judge said he thought Santa wouldn't mind, but he said that I'd have to be in a house, because Santa didn't stop his sleigh except on a roof. I was stumped by this, but the judge said that I could come around to his house that night and wait for Santa Claus there.

It all sounded pretty spooky, but the judge seemed to take it pretty serious, so my hopes begun to rise. We added this to the letter:

You'll find me at the judge's house. If you don't want to give me the gun, I'd be glad to just have the loan of it.

I asked the judge if that was enough of an address for Santa Claus to find me by, and he said it was, because when he was a kid, the old man used to visit him regular, every Christmas. After that, I said I'd mail the letter, but the judge said that wasn't the way. He picked out a match and lighted the paper and watched it burn up to a crisp. Then a breath of wind came and floated the ash of the paper up till it was out of sight. The judge watched it sail away.

"Everything that burns up, Santa Claus reads," he says.

"Even old newspapers?" says I.

"Of course," says the judge. "That's how he keeps so well posted on things that are going on."

It was queer, any way you looked at it, but it was the judge that led me on. I couldn't help believing him.

"This here Christmas must be a happy time, then," I says.

The judge allowed that it was, for most folks.

"But you act like you had your coin on the wrong horse," I tells him. "Ain't you wrote a letter to the old boy?"

The judge pulled in a long breath. "There's only one thing in the world that I want," he says. "And Santa Claus can't help me."

"Something too heavy for his sled?" I asks.

The judge grinned. "Santa Claus is a bachelor," he says. "He doesn't keep any women in stock."

That took me back a lot. I got to admit that I lost half of my faith in the judge right then and there. I'd seen old women and young ones, but I never yet seen one that amounted to nothing. Between you and me, what's a woman good for? She can't run faster'n a little kid. She can't climb a tree, even, or throw a stone twenty yards. I've seen 'em jump on chairs and squeal when a mouse come into a room. That's a fact! The only use I ever had for 'em was to work 'em for a hand-out, and that was always a cinch. And here was the judge talking about wanting one of them!

"Judge," says I, "I dunno what you want with one. Here's a guy that'll give you a gun if you ask for it, but still you want to waste time asking him for a . . . well, it beats me, that's all. What's the good of 'em?"

"I'll tell you how it is," says the judge. "I agree with you about all the girls in the world, except one. The rest of them aren't worth a snap of your fingers. They're silly. They're weak. They talk too much. They're nothing that a man wants to have around him. But between you and me, there's just one girl that I could be happy to have."

"What would you do with her?" says I.

The judge put his hand to his throat and pulled his collar a little looser. "I'd use her to warm my heart, boy," he says real slow-like. "I'd take her inside my life and use her to warm my heart the rest of my days. I'd cherish her like a bird come in out of a storm. I'd put her where I could look at her, because just the lifting of her hand, or the turning of her head, or the least word she speaks, or even the memory of her smile is enough to stop your heart! Roll together everything you could wish . . . a gun, a horse, a dog, a house, a million dollars to spend . . . and still all of that wouldn't make up the price of one of her smiles!"

He said it all in a way that put a shiver in me. I couldn't find no ways to say what I felt. I felt that there was things in the judge that would never be in me. It was like seeing mountains and wondering what was on the other side of 'em. Then he gave himself a shake and managed to smile down at me.

"Come tonight, Lew," he says to me. "Come tonight. About this girl talk," he went on, "heaven knows why I said what I have said! But it's between you and me."

"Partner," says I, "it's buried. I've forgot what I heard you say."

We shook hands, and the judge went back toward the house, walking like an old man with his head sunk and his back bowed. I stood there watching him go, and I felt as though I wanted to die for him.

V

"The Lady in Furs"

I went back to the jungle with the wind beginning to yell and tear. When I got there, I found Missouri Slim, but the three other hobos were gone. Instead, there was a little, square-set man and a tall, skinny one, leaning together over the fire and talking very soft and fast. They both looked like old-timers, and I knew that there was business in the air.

After a while, I found out that these were two-hundred-percent yeggs. The sawed-off guy was Whitey Legrange. The tall one was an old second-story man that had turned safe-cracker; his name was Murphy, but they called him Skinny. He'd just done a stretch, and his hair was still short and stuck out like bristles all over his head. He had the prison look, too, and the prison way of talking fast and soft out of the side of his mouth. It was enough to give you the shivers to watch him.

They'd planned a job for that night in the town, and they'd run the three other hobos out of the jungle because they wanted to be alone to talk things over with Missouri Slim. They had some sticks of powder along with 'em, and after a while they begun to cook them to make soup. After it was ready, they poured it into a flask, so I knew it was a job of blowing a safe. They had their doubts about me, at first.

"What about the kid?" says Whitey.

"He'll do," says Missouri.

Skinny caught me by the collar and dragged me around in front of him. He looked at me with his rat eyes.

"Kid," says he, "d'you know what happens to anybody that blows a game on me? I cut their livers out and feed 'em to a dog! That's me!"

"Lay off the kid," says Missouri. "I tell you, I know him for five years. He's got a head like a man on his shoulders. He could work the outside for you, if you want."

"There ain't any call for an outside man," says Legrange. "But if the kid is handy, let's see what he can do. We need some chuck. I haven't had a real square for two days. We need some yellow laundry soap, too. Can the kid get the stuff for us?"

"You hear what's wanted," says Missouri to me. "Go try your hand. I'll give you an hour. Mind you, Lew, if you ain't back with the stuff inside of an hour, I'll give you a tanning you'll never forget!"

I went back to the town. It would have been dead easy to batter doors and beg the stuff. Along about the time it's getting really cold, folks hand out pretty near anything you want to ask them for; but I didn't have the nerve to try the doors, because the judge or one of his nephews might've seen me. I snooped around until I located the grocery store, and I sneaked up to it through the back yard. I worked back the catch on a window with a bit of hooked wire, slid inside, and grabbed what was wanted. I took an old flour sack and dumped in enough chuck to feed twenty men. Then I put in a few bars of yellow soap, got back through the window, closed it, and even locked it again behind me.

When I got back to the jungle, Whitey snapped his watch shut.

"Forty minutes," says Whitey. "I guess this kid will do!"

Slim was the cook. We laid around and ate a big meal. Then everybody turned in, and we slept, or tried to sleep, but it was hard to do because the wind was thickening up with snow now, and the flakes come whistling through the trees and stung when they landed. We moved the fire close to a shelter, but, when we got near it, the smoke choked us, and, when we got away from the smoke, we started freezing. They kept nursing the flask of nitroglycerin all the time, seeing that it didn't get cold, because when the soap gets cold it just explodes—and there's an end to you and your troubles!

After a while, we gave up trying to sleep. The wind was acting crazy, tearing at the trees, poking at us like fingers of ice, and roaring and shouting through the woods. They begun to tell yarns about what they'd done. Missouri Slim led off with some man-sized lies about his fights.

Take him by and large, Missouri was the biggest liar that I ever listened to. He was the best and the safest, too. He always started with facts and then changed 'em a little and then a little more. He talked like he was being cross-examined by a flatty. He gave all the little details, so's you could have sworn that he was telling the truth. He'd start out like this: "I recollect back in the Big Noise when I met up with Sam Juisinsky. That was when he was wanted for killing the copper out in the Bronx. I was over on the west side, walking down Tenth Avenue with Joe Bertran and Ollie McNear. It was one of them thick, hot nights when you could hardly breathe. There was faces up in the windows. There was kids trying to play in the streets, throwing water at each other, and a crip on the corner was playing 'Sally' on his fiddle. 'Look there!' says Ollie. 'Damned if that ain't Juisinsky!' "

That's the way Missouri told a lie. He took his time about it, and it was mighty fine to hear him talk, even when I knew that he was lying every minute. After he finished his yarn, the other two took their turn. They didn't lie. They didn't have to—they'd both done things that might have been in a book.

Skinny told how he cleaned out the upstairs of a house

while a wedding was going on downstairs. Whitey told how the detective, Marks, trailed him for five months and followed him clean to Australia and back; and how he and Marks met up in a joint and had it out with their bare hands, because neither of them happened to have a gun handy. He killed Marks in that fight, and, when he'd finished telling about it, I was sick and pretty weak.

It was getting dark now, and the three didn't plan to go ahead with their work until quite a while later.

"When everybody in town is full of turkey," they says, "and when they're pretty sleepy, then we'll come and get ours!"

But I was thinking about Christmas and Santa Claus and the judge. I told 'em that I would meet 'em wherever they said and whenever they wanted, and it turned out lucky enough that they was going to meet in a barn right next to the judge's house.

When I got back to the judge's house, my nerve begun to get weak on me. The place looked mighty big and black to me. I went around, trying to work up my nerve. The back yard was as big as a building lot, but that wasn't a patch on the size of the rest of the grounds. He had great big trees everywhere; there was stretches of level that must have been lawn, although the snow was all packed and crusted over it, mighty thick. There was a pool with a statue of a lady in the middle of it, with the snow piled upon her head till it looked like a mass of white hair. There was rows of big trees and little ones. There was acres and acres of grounds, with a driveway winding around through 'em up to the house. The more I seen of the place, the more sicker I got about going up to the door and telling them that I'd come to see the judge.

I went back and had another look at the house. How any one family could use a place as big as that beat me. It might've done for a hotel, pretty handy. I shinnied up a drainpipe from the eaves and got to a big window with the shade down on the inside, but through a crack to the side I could see slits of what was inside.

There was a whole fir tree standing in there covered with shining stuff like snow, but brighter than snow. There were strings of colored lights that throwed patches of red and green and blue and yellow on the ceiling. There were things that looked like rubies and emeralds and diamonds dripping from the branches. But that wasn't all. The whole room was strung around with twists and streamers of green stuff, and there were fir boughs and pine boughs standing in the corners. I could guess that that room smelled pretty slick, and somehow I knew that this was the place that was got ready for Santa Claus to come to.

You've no idea how much nearer I seemed to be to that gun I wanted after I seen the room. Still it seemed like it would be pretty hard to go into a place like that dressed the way that I was dressed. I would've give an eye for a new suit of clothes before I had to show my face.

After that, I sneaked back to the ground and took a look up at the roof. It wasn't hard to see everything. The last of the day was gone out of the west, but it was a clear night. The snow had stopped falling. There was too dog-gone much wind for any clouds to be in the sky. Every star was shining, looking so cold you wouldn't believe it. I could see the snow on the roof, heaped up thick, with a shining line along the top and blue shadows along the sides. Somehow, it didn't seem hard to believe now that Santa Clause could drive through the air with a sleigh and reindeer. I begun to strain my eyes with watching, expecting to hear the bells jingle and see the horns of the deer tossing. I figured that he'd stop the sleigh right where the roof branched out on two sides and made a cross. That would give a support for the runners.

I was thinking this all out, when I seen something move along beside the hedge that fenced in the path near the house. Then a figure stepped out and went up toward the house. I followed it quick, because by the way it moved I knowed that it was a sneak of some kind. You can tell when anything is hunting—anything from a cat to a man.

When I got up close and had this here shadow between me and one of the windows of the house, I seen that it was a woman. She was all dressed up in a long fur coat with a great big collar that was folded up over her head and a big fur muff to keep her hands warm. I could tell by the hang of the coat that it was a woman. A man's coat slants in at the bottom because his shoulders are so broad; a girl's coat fans out.

I dropped behind a bush and let a handful of snow slide down my neck without stirring an inch. I was curious now. By the way she was moving, I figured that she was after some sort of loot, but when I seen that coat, I had to change my mind. It was the kind of a fur that you see the ladies stop outside of windows to look it. The wind kept ruffling it around, swinging it into folds and out again, and, when the light from a window hit it, it slid over the arm of that coat or over the hood, like oil over water. It was the kind of fur that the wind parts so's you can look way down into it, but, no matter how deep you look, you never see the skin, just more hair underneath, short and thick-growing, and fine as silk. It was the kind of fur that Missouri Slim said had no price—it just cost as much as you wanted to pay.

A lady that could afford to wear a coat like that couldn't afford to be a burglar. That was easy to see. But then, what was she doing there? She tried to get high enough to look into a window, couldn't make it, and turned around again. Then I stepped out from behind the bush, and she gave a little squawk when she seen me.

"Tommy!" she gasps, and then turns and starts to run. I got in front of her.

"It ain't Tommy," says I.

She stopped short and out of the shadow that the fur hood made over her face I could feel her eyes watching me. She asked me who I was and what I was doing there, but the best thing I could think of was to ask her the same questions.

"The east-bound train is two hours late," she says, "and I have to wait for it. I simply took a walk through the village to kill time."

"You never was here before?"

"Certainly not," says she.

I might've told her that, if she'd never been there before, she wouldn't have called out—"Tommy!"—but I didn't have the nerve to say it. She had a voice as soft as her fur coat. I never heard nothing like it. The harder I listened to it and the deeper I got into its softness, the more I felt like standing there and begging her just to talk.

The wind had dropped away as quick as the snow had stopped falling; and just as quick as the wind stopped, the cold dropped around us, thick and quiet, and biting through the clothes like teeth.

"And you?" says she. "Why are you here, little boy?"

"I ain't little," says I.

She begun to laugh, and that laugh took the frost out of the air. It was as light and as easy as the sound of water in summer when you lie on the bank and wonder whether it's better to sit up and start fishing, or just to lie still and watch the sky through the leaves and feel the air in your face—and go hungry!

"I'm the watchman for the judge," I says, because I couldn't think of nothing better to say. "He put me out here to keep strangers from busting in.'"

She laughed again. "You haven't even an overcoat," she says. "You must be stiff with cold! Tell me true, are you . . . are you waiting here because you're cold and hungry, and because there's so much warmth and light in that house? Is that the reason?"

I seen that there was a chance to make a haul. "Lady," says I, "that's the real reason."

"Poor child!" she says. She fumbled for a minute in her muff. Then she brought out some paper money and give it to me. The hand that touched my hand was as soft as silk and was as warm as a puppy.

"You're mighty kind."

"Merry Christmas to you," says she, and starts to leave.

I tried to stuff the money into my pocket, but my hand couldn't get it inside. "Wait a minute!" I calls after her.

She came back. "Well?"

What happened to me then, I dunno. But something snapped in me so loud that I could almost hear it. It made me sort of dizzy. Before I knew it, I'd made her take back the money and I'd told her that I was a cheat, that I wasn't waiting out there because I was hungry, that I'd just had all the chuck I could swallow, that I'd fooled her, and that I was sorry I done it.

She listened to me and didn't break in till I was done. Then she says: "You're a queer boy. You're a very queer boy. There's fifteen dollars here. Do you really mean that you don't want it?"

That took my wind, of course. Fifteen cold simoleons all for my own, fifteen plunks that even Missouri Slim couldn't never take away from me! Why, it was like being rich all at once. Yet I couldn't quite close my hand on that haul.

You've had that nightmare where you try to run with all

your might, but a chill gets into your legs and you can't work 'em? That's the way it was with me. I wanted that money. I could think of twenty ways of spending it. I could figure it up as big as a mountain. A dime would buy a meal, if a guy knew how to spend it right. There was ten dimes in a dollar; but how many dimes there was in fifteen dollars was more than I could work out. Still I couldn't take it, quite.

"When the judge was a kid like me," asks I, "d'you think that he would of took money like this?"

And she cries out: "John take money? Oh, dear, no!"

VI

"Getting Inside"

That let the cat out of the bag. She wasn't no traveler coming through, like she said. She was there on purpose. This fitted in with the name she'd called me, taking me for one of the nephews of the judge. She knowed all the folks in that big house. She was one of their own kind. I could tell that by her voice—and by her kindness. Her being silly and being took in by my lies didn't matter very much, seemed like.

I hate a man that's a boob. If he gets trimmed, let him take what's coming to him, but I can't say that I like these here sharp women that can't be beat and that have two hard words and two hard tricks for every one of your own! I never knew it before I talked to this lady, but she opened my eyes. I felt like laughing at her for being so simple, but just the same she tickled something in me by being so silly. I part wanted to laugh and I part wanted to cry, which is mighty queer.

She was trying to explain away what she'd said. "Of

course, I mean he wouldn't take money now, because he's a man. But at your age, if he were poor, of course, he'd take it! Why not?"

But I'd heard her the first time, and I told her so.

"And does the judge keep you from doing this?" she asks, very interested. "Are you imitating the judge?"

"Lady," says I, "I'm shy about ninety pounds. If I was that big, though, I'd try to step where he stepped, but he's got a long stride!"

"Does he know that you're his pupil?" she asks me.

"Nope."

"Are you going to try to be like him in every way?" she says.

"If I could," I says, speaking right out from my heart, "I'd be so like him that folks would think that we was brothers!"

"Then you'd have to be very proud."

"Is he proud?" I asks her.

"The very proudest man in the world, the hardest, the sternest, the most unforgiving!" cries she, all in a breath and with her voice shaking.

It made me stare to hear that. "I guess you hate him," says I, feeling mighty sorry for her and also for the judge, them both being fine folks.

"I hate him! Yes," she says, "I do, because I have cause to . . . oh, what am I saying?"

"I dunno that I would put money on anybody, having real cause to hate the judge," I couldn't help telling her. "What's he done to you?"

"What has he done to you, to make you so fond of him?" she asks right back at me.

"He treated me like I was his age and his size," I explains, trying to figure out just what he *had* done. "He talked like I could understand easy anything he had to say. He was square

121

as a gun with me. Dog-gone me if I ever met such a man!"

The lady had come a little closer, so's I could see through the dark beneath the hood the shining of her eyes.

"Yes, yes!" she was saying over and over. "Yes, yes! I quite understand. So gentle, so simple, so kind. Dear John. Oh, dear, dear John."

"Lady,"—I was plain flabbergasted by this way of acting—"one minute you call him names . . . the next minute you say he's the king. What *do* you mean?"

"I don't know," says she, in a sort of a whisper. "I'm afraid that I don't know, except that he's kind on one day, and hard as stone the next! But tell me, what he has done for you?"

I told her that he'd explained this Christmas business to me, and I told her about this friend of his, Santa Claus, that was calling at this house that night.

At this, she puts her muff up to her face, and I was afraid that she was going to laugh, like other folks, but, when she spoke, she was plumb serious.

"I'm very, very glad that you're to meet Santa Claus," she says. "He's such a kind old man!"

"But sort of queer, ain't he? Think of a guy running around the country giving things away!"

"Have you asked him to bring you something?"

"Yes."

"I do hope that he will," says the lady.

"There ain't much doubt, I guess," I tells her. "The judge said that he was sure to get my letter. The judge wrote it for me, you see. I'm to go into the house and meet Santa Claus there."

"In that case," says she, "I imagine you're right."

I told her I'd been watching the roof to make sure, when he come, I'd be in the house in time, but she said that it might be a good idea not to wait until I saw the sleigh, because sometimes it was hard to make it out. If I didn't hurry, he might come and go before I got into the house. That idea gave me a start.

Then a window or a door was opened, and we heard the tingle of voices laughing inside the house.

"How happy they are!" says she. "How happy everyone in that house is today!"

"Except the judge."

"What do you mean?"

Just what I meant, of course, I couldn't tell her, the judge and me having talked it over private. I was stumped for a minute, then I says: "It don't do him any good to write letters to Santa Claus for himself, because the old gent can't bring what he wants."

"Is there anything in the world that he really wants and can't have?" asks the lady.

"There is."

"I'd give a great deal to know what it is."

"It's between him and me," says I. "You'd never guess, looking at him, what it is that he wants."

"More money," says she.

"You're wrong."

"To be a higher judge, then."

"Still wrong. Seems like you can't guess any more than I could, lady."

"He wants. . . ." She stopped and took in her breath, like you do when you dive into cold water.

"Well?" says I, thinking that she couldn't come any closer.

"He wants a . . . a wife!"

It made me blink. Who would have thought that she was so smart that she could see right through to the right answer? I begun to think that she was pretty smart or else I was a good deal of a fool, because I'd never been able to guess it.

Then the lady come up close to me. She took me by the shoulders and turned my face into the light that come out from a window where the shade wasn't pulled down.

"Tell me! Tell me!" she says.

"You're right," says I. "Dog-gone if it don't beat me, how you could know it!"

There was a little sapling near her. She leaned against it with her head down, mighty sick.

"It's Alice, then," says she, sort of to herself. She went on after a minute: "He . . . he's to be married soon?"

"Look here," I says, "I've give him my word of honor that I wouldn't tell a soul what he told me. Here I've let you know, but now that I've spilled the beans, I might as well go on and tell the rest. Nope, he ain't going to be married soon. You see, not even Santa Claus can give him the girl that he wants!"

Well, you'd have been surprised to see how she changed. If I'd give her a horse and a wagon, she couldn't have straightened up so quick.

"He can't get her?" she says. "John can't get the girl he loves?"

"Nope. It can't be done."

"Oh, no," says the lady. "He could win a queen, if he chose to try."

"Chose?" says I. "Well, I've heard him talk about her as though she was the moon and the sun and the stars throwed in. She's the whole cheese to him, lady! He talked about her . . . why, he talked about her as he'd talk about . . . about a gun!"

Then I seen, when I said that, that even a gun wasn't enough. He wanted that girl of his even more than I wanted my gun!

"I got to go in," I tells her. "D'you think that I really got a chance to get the six-shooter?"

"If the judge has talked to Santa Claus for you," she says, nearly in a whisper, "of course, you will get it!"

"Stay here. I'll be out in a minute and let you know," I says.

"Yes," she says. "I'll stay. I wish you luck. What is it?"

I hung around on one foot. There was something I had to do before I left her. When she asked me, it popped into my head. I had to see her face.

"Ma'am," says I, "d'you mind me seeing your face?"

It didn't seem to please her none. She waited a minute and then says: "Why?"

"Because," I says, "I heard you talk, and I've listened to you laugh, and I figure that if you match up with your voice, seeing your face will be something to remember. Besides, you know. I won't tell nobody about you."

"You very strange boy!"

But all at once, she stepped back into the light that fell from the window and threw back her fur collar that curled over her head.

How can I tell you what I seen? It was like a match being struck in the dark. She seemed to shine and grow dim and shine again, while her smile went in and out around the corners of her mouth.

Suppose I put down the particular parts. About her hair—it was like the copper that's been beat up with a hammer, so's there's a lot of burning places and places of shadow mixed up together. She had the biggest eyes I ever seen, and every time she looked up at me, my heart jumped. But what's the use talking about one thing at a time?

To give it to you all in one lump, with that big fur collar rolling around her face and away from her face, she was like a pearl in a velvet case. Then she pulled the collar up again and she was like a light going out, once more.

"Hurry," she says. "I think Santa Claus is in the house! Hurry! Hurry!"

I turned and ran for the front door of the place, but, when I got to the steps leading up to it, I sort of lost my nerve again. By the time I was in front of the door, I was feeling pretty wobbly and weak. The door was about three times as tall as me, d'you see? And there was a pane of glass in the middle of it, with a light shining behind it, and over the top of the door there was an arch like the arch of a bridge. I waited, trying to get up my courage.

Down the main street of the town come a bunch of cowpunchers riding, yelling. I looked away from the house, and in a gap of the trees I could see the 'punchers riding across a lighted window. I could see the glitter of their slickers. I could see the glisten of their sombreros blowed straight back into their faces by the wind of their galloping. They was riding to beat the band, whoopin' it up.

I wished I had been with them instead of standin' there on the porch, wonderin' how I'd be able to look the fine folks in the face if I ever got inside.

Then I thought about the gun. So I went up and banged the knocker. There was steps on the inside right away. Then the door was opened, and I looked up to see the face of a big black man about seven feet tall. He give me a look from head to foot.

"What foh you come heah, white boy?" says he to me.

It sort of peeved me to have him talk like that. "I got a message from the President," says I. "That's why I'm here."

He drew back one foot, like he wanted to kick me off the porch, but I done what I often seen Missouri Slim do when he got into a pinch. I put one hand into my pocket and stuck out the fingers so's it might look as though I'd grabbed a gun or something like that. The man stared at that bulgin' pocket and stopped moving his foot. He didn't think that I had a gun, but he wasn't quite sure. He wanted to slam me right off that porch, but he figured that there was just one chance in ten that I might have a chunk of lead under my fingertip. I didn't blink an eye.

"Come along, sonny," says he. "If you-all's hungry, jus' trot aroun' to the back door. The cook's feedin' everybody today."

"Go call the judge," says I. "I can't waste no more time talkin' with a low colored servant."

His long fingers started working. He sure was mad.

"Call the jedge to talk to a piece of poh white trash like you?" says he. "Git out of that doorway, sonny, before Ah close the door!"

There wasn't no time to waste. There wasn't no time even arguing about it. Inside that there house was the gun that should belong to me. Between me and that gun was a long pair of legs and a mean Negro. I didn't hesitate none; I just closed my eyes, hoped that I wouldn't break my neck and that he wouldn't fall on top of me, and dived for his legs.

VII

"I See Santa Claus"

Did you ever watch horses in a corral? It ain't always the big ones that are cocks of the walk. The sassy ones are the ones that do the bossing most of the time. Once, I seen a mean little sorrel cow pony back up to a great big draft horse, and they started exchanging kicks. The big horse kicked so dog-gone' hard that her shots went wild. Her hoofs kept shooting above the back of the sorrel, and, when she dropped her hoofs between kicks, the sorrel would plant her—*Crack! Plot! Biff!* You could hear those hoofs landing a half mile away.

Pretty soon the big mare had enough and went off, squealing and shaking her head. After that, she didn't have nerve enough to drive a yearling away from her feed box. Mind you, that sassy little sorrel wasn't aiming to take any licking. If one kick had landed on her, she'd have run lickety-split to get clear. She just fought while the fighting was good, and *happened* to win.

Well, that's the way with me. I don't mind taking a chance, but I don't hang around when I see things going against me. I dive for that colored gent's knees. He was standing with his legs a little apart. My head went through the gap. My shoulders hit his shins, and he sat down with a yell. He missed my head when he sat down. Before he could get up, I was on my feet and had hold on a big round-headed cane. I grabbed it in both hands.

"If you make a move at me," says I, "I'll bash your head open."

He got up, groaning—he had twisted an ankle when he went down. "The jedge'll have you in jail for this!" says he.

And there stood the judge himself! He was laughing so hard and so silent, that the shaking of his body kept the whole floor trembling.

He says to the servant: "Sam, I'm sorry this has happened. I suppose you were both at fault. Go back to the kitchen, and have another piece of turkey." Then he turned around to me, while I was putting up the cane and looking mighty foolish. "Son," he says, "you've seen football games, I presume?"

"Nope," says I.

"Well," says he, "that was one of the finest tackles that I've ever looked at. Come on with me!"

I went all cold and sick. "Judge," says I, "can't it be between Santa Claus and me? Do I have to go in there and face the rest of the people? Look here, I'm . . . I'm as ragged as a scarecrow, and . . . ."

"You are," says the judge, not making no bones about it. "But I'm going to change you. Tommy has a suit he's never worn that's a shade too small for him. It would do very well for you, I think."

Well, can you imagine that? A whole new suit of clothes! He took me upstairs, and, while I was diving out of my clothes and sliding through a bathtub full of water, the judge himself was laying out the clothes. I got into 'em in a jiffy.

When I was all through, you never would have knowed me. I looked just like any rich boy. My shoes was shined so bright that I could see my face in 'em; they was so stiff and so squeaky that I could hardly walk in them. My trousers come down to the knees and buckled there, so's there was a little pull at the hips every time I took a step. I had a white shirt to put on with a mighty stiff collar that folded down across the collar of the coat.

"Jiminy, Judge," says I, "you don't think I'm no dog-gone girl, do you?"

The judge only laughed. He told me to go ahead and do what he said. I done it. It was hard, but I kept saying to myself that it was my chance to get a gat for myself and make myself a name later on. With a gun in my pocket, I'd see if Missouri Slim or any other man in the world—or leastwise on the road—could bully me! Well, I had to get a blue necktie tied in a bow knot that flopped and flowed around as big and dog-gone near as bright as a ribbon in a girl's hair. It made me pretty sick.

"Judge," says I, "are you trying to make a fool out of me?"

He only laughed which worried me a lot. He put the coat

on me. It had a belt around the outside and fitted in pretty snug. Then the judge himself started to work on my hair with a comb and a brush. He worked a long time, mostly on the crown of my head where the hair stuck straight up. He said that my hair was stiffer than bristles, but even so he'd make it behave. And he did. Pretty soon he made me stand up, and he looked me over.

Well, sir, at the same time I got a chance to look past him, and I seen the whole picture in the mirror. It was a shock, I tell you. What I seen in the glass I felt like walking up to and pasting on the jaw. I looked like a dog-gone sissy. Of course, I was pretty brown, which helped some, but I looked mighty skinny, and with that big, white collar and with that blue tie I was a ringer for a Sunday school prize winner.

"Judge," says I, "when Santa Claus sees me, he'll give me a knitting needle, instead of a gun!"

Yes, sir, I was all gone! They called me Oklahoma Lew on the road, and I had the rep of being one of the shiftiest that ever hit the pike with anything, from my dukes to a knife. You never would have guessed it when you seen me dolled up like I was. The long man-trousers, cut off so's they'd hit me between the knees and the ankles, was gone. They'd always give me a sort of growed-up, dignified look, I figured. The old hat with the brim loose halfway around was gone. The shirt that used to be blue, with one sleeve in and one sleeve out, was gone. The coat with canvas patches sewed onto it with twine to make pockets, that was gone, too, and so was my shoes. With them old shoes, I could wiggle my toes in the open air any time I wanted to. These new ones made me terrible cramped and nervous. I would've give ten dollars to wiggle my toes just once. I felt as though something was dead, and that it would take a lot of trouble to ever bring Lew, the Oklahoma Kid, back to life again.

"How d'you feel?" says the judge.

I was mighty disgusted with the way the judge had made me do all of these things, but I wasn't saying nothing about what I thought to nobody until I had my hands on that six-shooter that might be coming my way. For a square guy and a good sport, the judge was sure acting bad.

"How do I *look?*" says I to the judge, instead of answering.

"Very well," says he. "Like a million dollars, Lew."

"If I look like a million," says I, "then I'm glad that I ain't like I look. If having a million means living in clothes like these, why say, Judge, I'd a lot rather go to jail in my old clothes than live in a fine house in such-like things!"

"What's wrong?" says the judge, biting his lip.

"What's right?" says I. "They choke me . . . I couldn't run in 'em . . . I ask you, man to man, what chance would I have of climbing a tree in togs like these here?"

The judge begun to laugh, and that made me madder'n ever.

"For the love o' Mike, Judge," says I, "don't make me go down and face nobody wearing this here fancy tie!"

The judge kept right on laughing. He took me by the hand and made me go downstairs with him, and I got to admit that my opinion of the judge was sinking with every step that we made along them stairs. When we come down below, he brought me through the hall, where that mean servant was standing again. The fellow looked at me, and bugged out his eyes at me, but he didn't recognize nothing. I looked so different that it scared him—he turned from brown to yaller.

We went on through a door and into a great big room where the tree was standing that had the strings of light all over it. There wasn't no other lights in that room. All the walls was spotted with soft colors. The stuff that looked like snow on the branches of the fir tree was full of rose and green.

Even the rug, which was about three inches thick and which kept my new shoes from squeaking, was spilled across with colors. They was on the folks that was sitting around, too.

There was about a dozen in that room. Four of 'em was kids, two being Tommy and his brother. The rest was growed-ups. Old and little, they all had a lot of contraptions around them. There was boxes of cigars, whole boxes of slick, long, black-looking Havanas, I could tell by the smell. Missouri Slim used to smoke 'em with both hands when he was smoking 'em. Never would play cards, or drink, or even swap lies when he was smoking 'em, because he said that they was enough to take all of a smart man's mind. And here was stacks and stacks of them same smokes. I thought I might swipe one of them boxes, but then I knew that Missouri Slim would just plain die of joy if I did!

Cigars wasn't all. They wasn't even the beginning! There was silver stuff lying every which way. There was smoking jackets and fur coats; there was heaps of books in bright leather bindings; there was everything that you could think about. Take the two nephews of the judge, for instance; I tell you that they was swamped in things. They was all piled around with sleighs and little steam engines that would *go*, and picture books and other books, and one of 'em had a little bull-terrier pup as white as chalk that looked like it would start talking any minute. The other had a young goat with a beard just beginning to grow out.

Well, sir, you wouldn't believe it, those two kids had so much loot lying around 'em. But when I come by pretty close, what d'you think? Tommy looks over the top of his sleigh and whispers to me: "Croow! Them's my clothes you got on!"

I turned around, and I give him a look. I picked the place where I wanted to hit him, but, of course, I didn't do nothing, and the reason why was that right here in front of me was the old gent himself that was such a pal of the judge. There was the guy that brought all this stuff to this one house. How he could have loaded enough on his sleigh to visit that many places like this beat me hollow. But there he was, and all the doubts that I had was kicked higher than a kite.

The judge hadn't been wrong about one thing. I could tell that him and Santa Claus must've been old pals, because he'd described Santa so close. He had on the red coat and cap with the white-fur trimmings. He had the red trousers tied around with cords to keep them from blowing. He had the brightest red face that I ever seen. You'd've wondered if you could have looked at it. His eyes was snapping and shining to beat the band, and there was snow on his shoulders, and the wet of the snow around his boots, and there was even snow tangled in his long, long white beard.

Well, sir, he was good to look at. You could see what a kind old man he was by the red of his face, somehow. He could hardly talk for laughing, he was so happy to give away all of them things. Every time he handed out anything, he said something, and just at that minute he'd took up a little package.

"Alice Pell! I heard you wish for this, Alice," says Santa Claus. "And, because you've been a good little girl, I brought it along to you."

She wasn't little at all. She was pretty tall. She was more'n twenty years old. She had black hair and black eyes and a long, dark-skinned, mighty handsome-looking face. She had long, thin fingers, and they untied that box in a jiffy and opened it, and then she pulled out of it a string of pearls. She held 'em, and they slumped into her hand and looked creamy and dull in the shadow. Then she looked right up—not at Santa Claus at all, but straight at the judge.

"Oh, John!" says she. "Oh, John, you dear! You extravagant, extravagant man!"

She shook a finger at him, but you could see that she was busting with happiness about it.

"You see, Alice," says the judge, "that I have nothing to do with it, but Santa Claus keeps his eyes on good little girls!"

Everyone looked at the girl; and the girl looked at the judge.

Rats, I says to myself, *this is what the girl told me about outside. This is the one he's going to marry. This here is the girl that he wants to marry!*

Well, she was mighty fine-looking, but she didn't mean much to me. She had an eye like a cat, always hungry.

Everybody begun to exclaim about the pearls, and everybody had to handle 'em. The ladies said they was too darling for words, and the gents allowed that they must have cost a pretty penny. All of this here talk without so much as a word or a look to Santa Claus, that had brought the whole shebang to 'em. I begun to doubt even the judge. He was standing there with sort of a silly, pleased look, like he'd bought them pearls himself and given 'em to the lady.

Poor old Santa Claus, like a good sport, didn't seem down-hearted because he wasn't thanked. He went on laughin' and nodding, and now he picked up a package that was pretty near the last of the lot.

"Well, well," says he. "Here's something for a man who's a stranger to me. Here's a package for Lew Maloney. Is he here?"

VIII

"In the Garden"

Was I there? If I'd been buried twenty feet under the ground, for the hope of what might be in that there package, I'd have come up like a shot and found old Santa Claus in the house of the judge. Still, it wasn't so easy to step out into the center of the room in front of all those faces. They was already staring at me hard enough, but I thought of what the gun would mean, and it made me able to walk right out and stand in front of Santa Claus.

He looked down at me and made a rumble and a grumble in the middle of his stomach, it sounded like. "Ah," says he, "are you Lew Maloney?"

"You put your money on that," says I. "I'm Lew Maloney, Mister Claus, and I'm mighty glad to see you."

I put out my hand. Santa Claus give a look around the room like he was sort of took aback. I heard them chuckling, sort of behind their hands, and I knew that I'd done something that was all wrong. But he shook hands with me and then he says: "You're a stranger to me, Lew. I dunno that I ever heard of you before. This time the judge has spoken to me about you, and I trusted to his word and brought along something that I thought you might want. But just how can I be sure that you're Lew Maloney?"

"Easy," says I. "There's one trick that everybody on the road knows me by. I'll show it to you, and, if you can find anybody else that can do the same thing, I'll never ask you to give me nothing, now nor never!"

135

I pulled out my knife. It had a four-inch blade that snapped open and locked. There was lead in the handle. The blade was steel that would cut steel. There was an edge of it that melted through things without no weight nor strength being used. I weighed it for a minute in the palm of my hand. Then I chucked it across the room so fast that it made just a wink of a flash.

They only had time for the ladies to squeal and the gents to grunt. Then there was no more knife in the air but only the top of the tree waving backwards and forwards, slow and easy. The judge stepped out and pulled the knife from the tree, where it tapered up small, not more'n two fingers thick. He pulled the knife out, looked at it, and give it back to me

"That's my proof," says I to Santa Claus. "If there's anybody else that can do that, aside from Missouri Slim, lemme know his name and I'll go where I can call him a liar."

Santa Claus seemed sort of rattled. "Good heaven!" says he to the judge. "That knife would have gone halfway through a man!"

"It would," says the judge. "But go on, Santa!"

Old Santa Claus looks at me again. "I guess you're Lew Maloney," he tells me. "And if you are, here is a gift for you."

He gave the box he'd taken up from the foot of the tree. First of all I was sure that there was no hope, because it didn't seem like the box was heavy enough to have a gun in it. Then it seemed a pile too heavy. But finally I sat down cross-legged and worked that box open, and then I seen it lying right there under my nose.

It was the gun that I'd dreamed of having—a neat little .32 that looked like a toy alongside of the big .45 Colts that the cowpunchers wore. But while it was light, it carried six shots, and, while the barrel was short, it would kill at thirty yards as dead as a Winchester. It was a beauty. It was all shine and polish. I picked it up, and smelled the fine oil that it worked on.

"Do you know that gun?" the judge asks me.

"Know it?" says I. "Know it?"

I had to laugh, and my voice was shaking and crazy when I laughed. Know that gun? When young Purvis was with us in New Orleans, he used to let me have his gun to play with. I used to keep it clean for him. I got so's I could take it to pieces and put it together again plumb easy in the dark, or blindfolded.

"Sure, I know it," says I to the judge, and still looking up to him and laughing up to him, and shaking because I was so happy, I stripped that gun quicker'n a wink, and then assembled it again, and spun it over my fingertips, and tossed it in the air, and caught it again. "I know it better'n I know myself," I tells him.

But I wasn't forgetting Santa Claus. I went up to him and says: "Mister Claus, giving away a big thing like this to a gent you never seen before looks mighty fine to me. I dunno that I can pay you back right away, but, if you ever should get in a pinch, just let me know and I'll go the limit for you. The judge says that your hometown is Greenland. I dunno where that is, but, if there's a railroad running into it, I'll beat my way there to be on hand!" I says this as earnest as I could.

I figured that was pretty smooth, that speech, but it didn't seem to please none. They stood around and begun laughing at me so hard they couldn't stop.

"What the deuce *is* this, Jack?" one of the men says to the judge.

"Wait," says the judge. "Wait a while, Steve. It's better than a book when I tell you all the facts. Lew," he says to me, "come along and have a word with me on the side." He starts taking me out when a fat-faced lady leans over and says:

"What a bright little boy!"

Now, wouldn't that eat you? After seein' me sling a knife and make a gun talk, to get something like that crack throwed in a gent's face? I turns to her and says: "Lady, I ain't so small, but I ain't begun to put on weight yet. I still want to keep moving!"

She was built along the lines of a tub, and that shot settled her. She sat down, puffing something about impertinence, but the judge dragged me on into the hall.

"Look here, Lew," he says, "you'll ruin yourself with one of the richest old ladies in the county, if you make another remark like that."

"Rich or poor, she's a sap," says I.

"She happens to be an aunt of mine," he says, but he grinned at me when he says it. Then he went on: "What are your plans now?"

"I meet some friends of mine at nine," says I.

"Where?"

"Not far off."

I couldn't help sighing, because I figured out what the judge would think if he knew just what sort of gents I was to meet that night at nine.

"And what are your plans later, Lew?" says the judge.

"To hit west," says I.

"And with the gun?"

"I'll make the gents along the road see that I'm a man, and not a kid!"

"Lew," says the judge, putting his hand on my shoulder, "if you were to shoot another man, do you know what would happen to you?"

"Sure. Lights out," says I.

He waited a minute. He seemed about to say some more about the same thing, but he must've changed his mind.

"It may be that you'll grow tired of this life you're leading, freezing in the winter and burning up in the summer, starving one day and eating like a camel the next, associating with criminals and liars and traitors. If the time ever comes when you *do* tire of them, then come back here and come straight to me, Lew, because I'll have a place for you."

That was pretty fine talk for a gent like the judge. I told him he was the salt of the earth and that there was nobody that I thought more of. But as to coming back to him, I couldn't never do that.

"Why not?" says the judge.

"Because sleeping inside where the air chokes a man ain't good for me . . . it gives me bad dreams," I tells him.

He frowned at me for a minute after this, and then he patted my shoulder again. "Poor old Lew." He sighed.

"Why poor?" I asks him.

"You'll wander all your life and never find happiness," says the judge. "But wherever you go, I think you'll keep a clean heart. Well, Lew, if you have to go, I can't keep you here . . . but you'd be surprised if you knew how much I want you."

Him being so mighty friendly, I begun to think that I might have the nerve to say to him something that was pretty heavy in my mind.

"Judge," says I, "you've just tried to give me some good advice. D'you mind if I try to give you some, too?"

"Fire away, Lew. By all means."

"Well, there's a lady in that room, named Alice. . . ."

The judge frowned. "Whatever you have in mind, son," says he, "remember that a gentleman can only say certain things about ladies."

"I ain't going to say much, Judge," says I, "but, between you an me, ain't it true that you know another girl that could give this here Alice all the aces in the deck and then beat her?"

He was starting to be pretty mad, but now he seemed sort of surprised. "What under heaven are you talking about, youngster?"

"I figure you've guessed it, Judge."

"Do you know . . . but you can't! She's not within a thousand . . . Lew, what are you talking about?"

"There ain't much I can say. I'm bound to keep quiet, you know."

He was excited now. He started for the door, then he come back to me. "You've seen something?" he says.

"I ain't saying nothing."

"Lew, I'm guessing at the most wonderful thing that could possibly happen to me. Tell me if I'm right!"

"There's nothing I can say."

"You've seen a woman tonight."

"Maybe."

"Where?"

I shook my head.

"For heaven's sake, Lew!" says the judge. He was shaking like a leaf.

What could I do? "Tell me what she looks like?" says I.

"Copper hair, blue eyes, and nothing but goodness, gentleness in her face and. . . ."

It took me off my feet. "That's her!" I says. "She's outside in the garden now. . . ."

It was like touching off a train of powder. He was through the front door before I could turn around.

"He'll never find her," I says to myself. "Not in this dark and with her behind the hedge. . . ."

But when I got outside, I seen the judge on the far side of the hedge with something huddled into his arms. I sneaked away, because I didn't want her to know that I'd let him find out from me. It was the second thing that I'd let slip that day when two folks had talked mighty private and confidential to me. But I didn't hear her telling him in no loud voice to go away, although she'd told me that she hated him.

That seemed queer to me, so I sneaked along by the hedge and dropped into the snow and waited. What I heard was something like this:

"Nell, dear Nell."

"How did you know?"

"I only guessed."

"It was that boy?"

"God bless him."

"I didn't come to hunt for you, you know that, John?"

"Of course, I know it."

"I only . . . I only came to peek through the window. I . . . I wanted to see your happiness, John. I didn't mean to interfere."

"Hush, dear. Interfere? There's nothing in my life except this one moment."

"No, no! You're to marry her when you. . . ."

"Never, by heaven! They've lied to you about me. They've always lied."

"If I could only believe it!"

"I swear to you, Nell. . . ."

"John, for the sake of your manliness, don't lie to me, because, just now, I can't help believing you."

"Heaven has had a hand in bringing you to me. Do you think that I could lie to you now? I've only waited and waited to see you. I couldn't hope that you'd understand or believe my letters."

"What letters?"

"The dozen . . . the dozen or more letters I wrote after you left on that terrible night."

"John, there hasn't been a line from you."

"What . . . ?"

"It's true. Not a syllable."

"Then they've interrupted my mail. They know my hand-writing. They were afraid that even in letters I could explain. Oh, the cowards! Don't you see, dear? They've always hated me. They always wanted you to marry a happier man and one who is more polite. I was too rough. They hated me for that. Heaven knows I've never dreamed that I was worthy of you. . . ."

"Hush, John. You're worthy of a queen."

"Will you let me tell you what I wrote in the first letter, and in the others?"

"If you wish to tell me, but. . . ."

"You would doubt me anyway?"

"Not that. Not that! But I don't care to hear. I think there's no more doubt left in me. I've been so wretchedly unhappy, John. Tell me anything, and I'll believe."

"Believe first, last, and always that I love you, that I've always loved you, Nell."

"Oh, if that's true, then nothing else matters."

"I swear it's true. Come in with me. You'll die of the cold out here."

"I don't dare to face them."

"Face them with me to tell them that you are to marry me tomorrow and make me the king of men, because you are truly like a crown to me, dear. You are beyond my hopes and my dreams. You are all that I wish for come true."

"John, when you speak that way, I feel like a foolish girl and a very simple one."

I didn't hear any more. The clock in the hall of the house begun to strike nine. I could hear it plain, because the front door was open. Then someone called from the house, and I heard the judge answer. The last I seen, as I hurried off to meet Missouri Slim and the rest, was the shadows of them two crossing the snow and then walking into the light and up the steps of the house with the light glowing on the hair of Nell. It all made me sort of dizzy. I didn't see how a man like the judge could talk so foolish to any girl.

IX

"Underground Work"

When I got to the stable, I found that Missouri, Whitey, and Skinny were already there. They was standing under a shed at one side of the barn, talking soft. When they seen me come, Whitey says: "Well, Missouri, you win. I figured sure that the kid had blowed the game on us."

"There's no yellow in the kid," says Missouri. "Are you ready?"

They said they was, and so we all went into the barn. Skinny had an electric lantern with a shutter. He pulled it open enough to let one ray of light start working. He showed us the way around the old stalls. There hadn't been horses in 'em for years, it looked like.

"The house used to stand right close up to the barn," says Whitey. "That's how I got my hunch, and the hunch worked out. We're going to make it rich tonight, boys."

He pulled open a door to what was once the grain bin. In the middle of the bin, where the wood was all polished and smoothed from the rubbing of sacks, he raised a trap door. By the light he sent down below, we seen a lot of cobwebs covered with dust and broken by the wet that had soaked in from

143

the sides during the winter. There was a flight of steps, but Missouri wouldn't go down first.

"Suppose one of them spiders was to drop down my neck . . . ," says he, and broke off, gagging.

By that, I knew he'd been drinking too much. Whenever he got full of booze, it used to start his imagination working, and he always talked as though there was spiders crawling around ready to bite him. He said that once a fortune-teller had told him he'd die from the bite of one. Anything that crawled made Missouri Slim sick. So Whitey begun cussing him out for a coward and went down the steps first himself. Skinny went next, then me, and Missouri Slim went last.

It wasn't very much fun going down them steps, and, when we got below, Skinny opened up his lantern, and we could see everything plain. It was an old tunnel about three feet wide and seven feet high. It had joists—big four-by-six timbers—every six feet along the two sides, and it had been walled up with big oak planks, too, but the wet of the underground had rotted the oak, and the pressure of the dirt on the outside had caved 'em in and made 'em fall all across the passage.

There was the smell of that dead wood, and the reek of the old water that had dripped in and soaked in through the sides, and the cobwebs hung down from the tops of the place. Missouri was so scared that he doubled clean over to keep from brushing against the cobwebs as he walked.

We come down to the end of the passage, where it took a short turn to the right, and there we leaned up against a wall of bricks.

"Now, boys," says Whitey, "here's where we do a little work. Gimme the bar, Skinny."

Skinny took out a little crowbar, sharp at one end, and with a hook at the other. It was about two feet long, and made of the finest steel you could get hold of. Whitey threw off his coat, and, with Skinny holding the light, he begun to work fast. He gouged the mortar out from between the layers of the bricks, and then, after he'd been working about fifteen minutes, he loosened a brick and got it out. After that, the rest was easy. He took out brick after brick, by bashing them down with the butt end of the bar. Pretty soon he'd eaten right through the brick wall, but there was still wood on the other side.

"We've got rotten luck," says Whitey. "It's a cinch to cut through these here boards, but we got to do it so's there'll be no noise."

It wasn't so hard, though, because when Missouri put his shoulder against the right-hand board, it loosened off with just a little groan. In a jiffy we had two more boards off, and there we was on the inside of the room on the other side of the wall.

That room was just sheathed with wide boards tacked on to a molding. There wasn't no strength in the wood. It was just a mask across the face of the brick. The room was about ten feet square. In the middle there was a big safe with a circular door in it. It looked like you could drop that safe a couple of miles onto solid rock and still you wouldn't bust it, but they didn't plan anything like that. All in a minute they was at work, and I seen what they wanted Missouri so bad for.

Now and then along the road I'd heard talk that Missouri Slim in his palmy days, when he was just a kid, had done a lot of work as a safe-cracker, and they said that he was jim-dandy at that work, so smooth that nobody ever got to him. He could crack a safe while the family was eating soup in the room over him, they said, and they wouldn't even see the soup wiggle in the plates when the shot went off. I guess that was handing some frills to the story, but anyway it showed what the regular profession thought of him.

I watched him now. So did Whitey and Skinny. They just stood back and eyed him to see what he'd do. And it was a sight!

Missouri begun to tremble like a bull-terrier pup when it sees raw meat or a chance for a good toothful of fight with a dog that'll stand plenty of chewing without yelling for home and mother. He begun to lick his lips, and them little eyes of his rolled in his head.

"Gimme!" he says. "Gimme."

"What?" says Whitey, like a kid taking orders from his dad.

"Soap, you fool," says Missouri. "Soap, blockhead. To think that I should be working a gentleman's game with a pair of ham-egg bums that couldn't work even a can opener. Soap, you little runt. *Pronto!*"

I thought that Whitey would soak him for talk like that, but Whitey didn't say a word. He just fished out the soap that I'd swiped, and which they'd worked up to the right softness for the job. He handed it over quickly.

Then Missouri started making the mold that would run the soap around the door. He worked like lightning. I never seen a man's hands move so quick and do so much. While his fingers finished one thing, his eyes was wandering off ahead, looking at something else that was next to be done.

"I knew it!" says Whitey to Skinny. "They all said that his nerve was busted and that he'd never work again, but I knew that he was ready for the stuff if he once seen a job ahead of him. Look! You'd think that he was painting a picture!"

It *was* something like that. Missouri was growling like a cat that's hungry, but that wants to play with the mouse before she bites its head off. He run the mold, and then he got the soup ready.

"Whose house is this?" I asks Whitey.

"I dunno what that's got to do with you, kid," says Whitey, sort of sharp. "Thing for you to do is to keep your eyes and your ears open and watch out what's doing. When you get a mite older, you can use what you're learnin' now. I was near growed up before I was lucky enough to have the chance that you got tonight."

"Lay off the poor kid," says Skinny. "Lay off of him. What harm does it do if he knows? This house belongs to a sap that's a judge in this here county, Lew. His name's. . . ."

I didn't want to hear the name. It all hit me in a heap. It was the judge's house! I seen that I was a sap not to have guessed it before, because that passage run from the old stables straight to the house. Maybe it was used in the old days. I found out later that there used to be an old house between the place where the judge lived and the stables, and this was a way of getting handy into the stables in a time of a storm. Once it had been dug out for drainage. When it wasn't used for that, they just lined it up with planks and let it go for the tunnel.

I should have thought of it before, but somehow it didn't come into my head that, while the judge was having all those people in the house and making them happy, the way he'd made me happy, other folks could be down in the basement of his house trying to rob him.

I let out a sort of a yell. Skinny clapped his hand across my mouth, and Missouri looked around to me with his rat eyes. But I wriggled away from Skinny and stood back by the tunnel.

"Stop the job, Missouri," I says to him. "I know this judge, and he's white!"

Missouri Slim snarled at me, with all his yellow teeth. "Stick a knife in the little skunk, Whitey," says he. "Here's a

147

chance to get rich, and he's queering the game! Stick him in the hollow of the throat. He'll make no noise then. Here, let me do it!"

He fetched out his knife and turned around to me, but I jumped to the edge of the passage now, and I gave 'em just a glimpse of me.

"If you try anything," I tells Missouri, "I'll let out a yell that'll bring 'em all down here after you. The judge is a fighter, and his house is full of gents that look like trouble was their middle name. Don't start nothing, Slim, or I'll bring 'em all right here after you!"

Slim was so wild that he hung in his tracks, swinging to and fro and slavering, he was so keen to plant that knife in me. It made me sort of sick to see his face. I knew he was no good. I'd known that for five years, but after all the time we'd been together, and all the times I'd taken care of him when he was sick, and all the times I'd kept us from starving by singing and begging and giving him everything that I got, I couldn't believe that he'd turn on me like this.

Then I remembered what the judge had said of the folks I was herding with. It was all true, I saw. I had the picture of the judge in the corner of my eye, for comparison—the way he stood back on his heels and the way he looked down into your eyes, and the way he shook hands, and the way he smiled. He was clean, and these were all dirt. I begun to feel crawly myself.

Whitey was the real boss of the gang. He took charge now. "Put up that knife, Slim, you fool," he says. "Kid, you know Slim was only joking. We wouldn't hurt you. Us? Why, we're all pals, ain't we? When we make this here haul, we all split it up four ways." He had a piece of broken brick in his hand. "If this was all gold, we'd split it both ways, Lew," he says.

"You can't soft-soap me," I tells him.

"This is straight," he says. "D'you know there's twenty thousand dollars in that there safe, and that it's all cash, and that the four of us will have five thousand dollars . . . each one of us, five hundred ten-dollar bills!" He patted the brick with each one of the words.

"If you was to give me half of it," says I, "I'd see you all in blazes before I'd let you rob the judge."

Whitey groaned. "You try to talk reason to the little fool," he says to Slim, and he turned his back on me.

"Listen to me, kid," says Skinny. "There ain't nothing that you need to worry about for the judge. He's rich. He's got a cow ranch and some lumber acres. He's got a salary and a big house. All we're doing is taking some of the fat off'n his bank account, so's he won't have the cash to worry about . . . you know . . . where he'll invest it and. . . ."

I didn't hear the rest of what he said. I'd come half a step out of the passage and that was what Whitey was waiting for. He seen me out of the corner of his eye, and then he whirled around like a top and threw the brick. I saw him whirl and tried to dodge, but he threw that brick as though he was a pitcher on the mound, serving up a strike.

At that distance I didn't have a chance. Just as I turned, the brick caught me in the back of the head, and I went down on my face. I was clean out, and plunged into blackness before I hit the floor.

X

"The Open Road"

When I come to, it was like I was trying to pull myself up a long rope that had no ending. Above me, there was light; I was dragging myself up out of the dark. Then, all at once, a door seemed to open, and there I was in the day. It wasn't the day, though, for there was only a sort of a twilight from Whitey's torch.

I looked around to the side, without stirring my body. They had the job all finished. The mold was made, and the soup poured in. They was running the fuse now. Missouri was still managing things, and the other two yeggs was helping. I got the feel of my legs to see if I could act quick and trust to them being strong enough. They felt mighty shaky, and one eye was closed with the blood that had run down from my cut head. Then, too, my head ached like I was going to die. The blood was still running. I thought I *would* die, but as long as that was going to happen, I thought that I'd try my hand to do a turn for the judge before my end come.

So I ups with all my strength and starts away down the passage, and the minute I gets to my feet, I lets out a yell at the top of my lungs. It was so loud and pitched so high that it scared even me. The echoes of that noise crowded all around me. Before they died out, I heard the crooks, cursing and groaning.

"The brat has queered the game," yells Whitey. "Clean out, boys, and get away if you can."

Then I heard them coming, running down the passage.

They showed the light ahead of 'em, and I stumbled over the wreckage of the old, rotten boards, but they kept gaining on me. I reached the end of the passage. They was close behind me. Skinny yells: "Knife the squealin' kid as you go by, Slim. Finish the little quitter!"

"I'll have his heart out!" yells back Missouri Slim.

But here I was with the light from the electric torch showing on the steps just ahead of me. I bolted for them and run up to the top and shoved up against the trap. My heart turned to nothing inside of me! The door stuck. There had to be some secret way of opening it, and I couldn't manage it at all!

They was coming fast behind me. I could hear Missouri Slim snarling like a dog, and running first, so I knew that he meant what he had said and that his knife was in his hand. Well, I had seen him use that knife of his before, and just as I was about to give up and hope that the first stab would kill me and put me out of pain, I remembered the gun that Santa Claus had give me. I yanked it out.

"Keep back!" I says. "I got a gun, and, if you crowd me, I'll use it! Keep back, or I'll shoot to kill."

"I'll wring your neck!" says Slim, panting as he come on. "I'll cut the gizzard out of you, you little rat."

He swung around to the steps, and I pulled the trigger. Slim gives a yell and drops back, throwing up his hands.

"Are you hurt bad, Missouri?" shouts Whitey.

"Nope. He missed me clean. But what'll we do, boys?"

"Go on and get him. He can't drop more'n one of us, and, if we stay back here . . . ah, there they come now!"

Right down the passage I heard the shouting of men. Then I heard the judge's voice: "Keep back, boys. Let me go first. Come behind me as close as you please, but this is my party, and I go first!"

It gave me a lot of heart to know that he was nearby me. Seemed like it would be a pile easier to die. I got a hold on the gun and got it ready.

"Judge!" I hollers. "Quick!"

Then I seen the three come in a lump. There was Slim in the lead. I took a bead, but not at his body. I didn't have the heart for that. I fired at his legs, and I seen him go down with a hiss like a snake, and wriggle on the floor. But the other two come on like tigers. I fired right at Whitey and heard him curse and knew I'd hit him. But he picked me up with one hand and slung me against the wall. My head hit a joist, and I was out for the second time. It was a long time, too.

When I woke up, I listened for the wind and the feel of the winter night, but there wasn't any. My hands was on cool sheets. There was a white ceiling above me, and there was a sweet smell of flowers around me. You'll think that it was stupid, but my head wasn't all clear.

"Hush," says someone. "I think he's waking up."

That brought me back halfway to good sense. I calls out: "Judge!"

But it wasn't the judge that I seen first. It was a head of copper-colored hair. There was Nell standing over me. She dropped down on her knees, and it brought her face just beside mine.

"D'you know something?" says I to her. "The closer a guy gets to you, the better you look!"

"Hush!" says she, smiling at me. "You mustn't talk yet . . . not till the doctor says you may. You've been terribly hurt, Lew. Those devils incarnate. . . ." She couldn't finish it. She could only shudder. "John," she says. "He wants you."

There comes the judge. He sat down on the other side of the bed. "Dear old partner," says he. "How are things coming?"

"Slick," says I. "What happened to 'em?"

"We have them all," says the judge. "Two of them are living. The rabid cur named Missouri Slim . . . the one who stabbed you . . . fought till he died when we tried to take him."

That was the end of Missouri. He'd got to his knees after he had seen the other two run up the steps and break open the door. He knew that the men would catch him. So he crawled up the steps and got to me. He wanted to finish me before they come to him. He put his knife into me, then they swarmed over him. How he happened to miss his stroke, I dunno, but his knife just slithered along my ribs and didn't get at my insides at all.

"The safe didn't blow?" I asks the judge.

"Safe and sound as a fiddle," says the judge. "Lew, you've brought my lady to me . . . you've saved my property . . . how can I repay you?"

"By not tryin' to," I tells him. "I didn't know they was planning to break into your place. I'm a crook, Judge, but when I seen that they was aiming to. . . ."

"Let it go," says the judge.

"We're friends?" says I.

"To the limit," says the judge, and took hold of one of my hands. Nell took the other.

You would have laughed to see the flowers that folks sent to me. You would have laughed harder if you'd heard the newspaper story that Nell read to me one day when I was lying out on the porch, being mean and nervous and eating everything I could get my hands on. That's what they call convalescing.

That paper called me a hero and a lot of other bunk. It said that the judge wanted to adopt me, if he could persuade me. I asked the judge about it, and he said that was what he wanted to do. He said Nell and him would be mighty happy to have me in their family, but, after I'd thought it all out, I told him that I was a Maloney, and that I could never be anything else so long as I lived.

He didn't say no more, except that he respected my wish. That was the beginning of a queer life for me. I got to navigating in the next month. Then I was started to school, wobbly on my pins, but still able to lick any two of them common kids that went to the school in town. I lasted that out for three weeks. At the judge's house, I had everything my own way. The judge give me a room all for my own. I had a fishing rod, a rifle, a pair of shotguns, and a whole little rack loaded with revolvers. I had more clothes'n you could name, and a horse all of my own to ride. I had a shelf full of my own books, and the judge said that someday I'd be able to read them all. This was the time we talked about getting this story all wrote out, and he told me to tell the whole truth—with a wink.

Maybe that was what took the heart out of me. I didn't ever go into my room without seeing those books. Every time I seen them, my head ached, thinking of how I'd have to put all those words through my mind. Still, I didn't have no idea of what I was going to do. It just popped into my head all at once.

I was lying in bed one evening with the moon dusting in through the window and beginning to sneak across the floor. Away off in the distance, I heard a train whistle for a station, and that whistle brought me up out of bed. I went to the window. It was cold as ice, but the wind was full of the pines. The moon hadn't drowned all the stars. The mountains walked away north and south against the sky. An owl hooted, sailing over the trees. Everything was moving outside in the night. Everything was bound somewhere, and here was I sitting still, waiting for things to come to me. Just on the other side of that range, I figured that there was a fine time waiting for me, even if I didn't know quite what.

I went to the closet. What I got out was my own old clothes, and, when I jumped into 'em, I knew that I was starting back to real good times again. When I had those clothes on, I wondered how I could tell the judge of what was in my head. So I took some of the books and piled 'em on my bed. Then I put my best clothes beside the books, with the shoes that I had to shine every morning alongside of them. Then I got a piece of charcoal from the fireplace and wrote the first word and the only word that I'd ever learned to write. I wrote it big on the pillow: **No.** The judge would understand. I was sure of that.

After that, I slid out the window and hit the ground running. It was like having wings. It was like being out of jail. In five minutes I was down at the railroad yard. A big engine had just come in, and she was standing there, panting and shaking and sending out steam with a *hiss* and getting ready to take her rest at the end of the division. She was good enough for me.

By morning she was snaking me east through the mountains, and me snugly lying out on the rods of the second boxcar.

I ain't never seen the judge since, but I keep him tucked away in the back of my head. He showed me where to find Christmas. I've had ten fights since with smart guys that say there's no Santa Claus. Can you beat it, how some folks will argue? Even with me, after I seen the old boy with my own eyes and got a gun out of his hand.

Well, I've had my bunkie write this out just the way the judge said I should. These are all facts, just the way I tell 'em, of how I turned around the corner and found Christmas.

Sometimes I dream about the judge and Nell, and want mighty bad to see them again, but I never go back because I know that it would be too hard to say good bye again.

The Peril Trek: A Reata Story

This, the final entry in the Reata series begun by Frederick Faust five months earlier, originally appeared as "Reata's Peril Trek" in the March 17, 1934 issue of Street & Smith's *Western Story Magazine*. The seven-part series was written under Faust's George Owen Baxter byline. The first story in the saga was "Reata," which was reprinted in THE FUGITIVE'S MISSION (Five Star Westerns, 1997). The second, "The Whisperer," is to be found in THE LOST VALLEY (Five Star Westerns, 1998). The third, "King of the Rats," is to be found in THE GAUNTLET (Five Star Westerns, 1998). The fourth, "Stolen Gold," is to be found in STOLEN GOLD (Five Star Westerns, 1999). THE GOLD TRAIL (Five Star Westerns, 1999) contains the fifth, and "The Overland Kid" appeared in the book of the same title (Five Star Westerns, 2000). In "The Peril Trek," Reata again finds himself under the thumb of Pop Dickerman when he decides to help out Bob Clare, a stranger to whom he feels a kinship.

I
"The Slide"

As Reata crossed the side of the mountain, he did not look up toward the height. He simply knew that there was no cover in that direction from which a rifleman could get a good bead on him, and below him there was a long flume of danger that took all of his attention, a flat-bottomed valley with walls as straight and polished as though they had been chiseled out by hand. Perhaps a glacier with a few hundred thousand years on its hands had done the stone cutting. When Reata entered that cañon, he knew that he was entering the mouth of peril. It might be for this very moment that the agents of Pop Dickerman had been waiting before they struck at him. Perhaps there were a dozen of them lying somewhere up there on the rocks, safely ensconced with repeating rifles, ready to blow him into the next world.

Already they had turned him twice during his desperate effort to break away from the country that was under the actual domination of the junk peddler. He was halfway through Glassman Pass when a storm of bullets hailed about him. He owed his escape to the warning that his little dog, Rags, running ahead, had managed to give him at the last instant. That and the thickness of the twilight had saved his body, although there were half a dozen bullet holes through his clothes.

Again, when he was above timberline, in the white wilderness of the Ginger Mountains, forms had risen at him out of the thickness of a storm, and he had fled as he could, with

Sue, the roan mare, stumbling and sliding and slithering over the impossible terrain. The wise, fuzzy head of Rags had given the first warning of that danger, too. How worth Dickerman's while it would be to poison the tiny mongrel, that pocketful of wisdom and mischief!

Reata thought of that as he patted the head of the dog that had its usual place in front of the saddle. But, staring down into the narrows of the cañon beneath him, the brown face of Reata clouded with trouble. In just such a place the hired devils of Dickerman might be waiting. But even before he came to a definite decision, the urging of his blood told him that he would take the chance and try to pass through the gorge.

Presently he was descending into it over the difficult terrain, letting Sue take her own way, because he knew that he could trust that ugly head of hers at the end of that long ewe neck. With her skinny sides and her upthrusting hip bones and long-lipped face, she looked like a small camel, but brains and legs and heart make the horse, and Reata knew that she had all of these.

He was well inside the walls of the cañon, therefore, without ever glancing up toward the danger that might come to him down the slope. It was Rags, again, who saw the thing, and snarled and shuddered in a sudden terror that made Reata look back.

Riding behind him was one of those Devil's Slides that one finds here and there among heavily eroded mountains. This was not a smooth slope of gravel and sand, but rather an accumulation, a junk heap of broken boulders that graduated, toward the top, into the usual smaller drift of rock and pebbles.

What Reata saw at first, he took to be a wisp of white cloud caught against the forehead of the mountain. But after a moment a small rumbling, like wheels over a bridge in the distance, told him what was happening. There was no thunderhead above the horizon from which that noise could be pouring across the sky. It must proceed from the white fluff far up the mountain, and now, as he watched, he saw the dust cloud grow, and before and beneath it was a movement as though a herd of horses was rushing down the slope, forms leaping and rolling and bounding recklessly down with a speed that increased momentarily. Then he understood perfectly. For perhaps a pair of centuries that slope had remained there, growing more and more unstable, more and more crumbled to the point of dissolution, and now, at the exact moment when he was trapped inside the walls of the cañon at the base of the slide, the whole mountainside was dissolving and rushing down at him.

He turned the head of the mare, thinking for a moment that he could ride her out of the cañon walls to safer ground above, but he saw instantly that there was no time. She was as swift as a bird, almost, but against her was matched the speed of a flung stone. The great forehead of the slide was already spreading wide and growing in enormous bulk. It was a wave that gathered head and power until it tossed into the air boulders that weighed tons, and caught them again in a carelessly back-tossed hand, and hurled them forward once more with redoubled speed. No, he could not escape by retracing his way. The good mare, pricking her ears, bravely faced that danger, ready to run straight toward it in spite of her instinct, so perfect was her trust in the brain of her master, but Reata swung her about again and sent her shooting down the ravine.

Could he distance the slide, which was sure to lose momentum as it struck the floor of the valley? No, for that valley floor was sharply inclined downward. Like a flume it had seemed to him, even from a distance above it; it was even more like a flume now that he was enclosed between its walls, and he knew that, when the avalanche struck the ravine, it would shoot far forward, for a mile or more, perhaps, like a wave that beats on the slant of the shore and slides suddenly far up the sands. In that forward dashing of the landslide, he would be caught and overwhelmed and buried.

There was only one possibility, and that was to find some way up a side of the cañon. But, at first glance, not one appeared. No, over to his right he was suddenly aware of a crevice, the sides of which were like two broken flights of steps. It seemed that nothing could mount it—and yet he had to try.

Instantly he had the mare at the bottom of that giant's stairway, and, flinging himself out of the saddle, he began to upward climb, only pausing to snatch little Rags from the saddle.

Perched on the shoulder of his master, the tiny mongrel barked furiously, throwing his challenge at the overwhelming mass of rocks that now roared down the mountain. Reata, with a side glance, could see the vast wave rushing. Behind it was a flying mist that towered into the sky, and from that boiling mist he saw great birds fleeing, sliding down the limitless arches of heaven while the man, like a poor, scurrying little ant, clambered up the steps, the broken ways, the difficult inclines of the ravine crevice.

The mare? She was following, incredible to say. Like a mountain goat, she was leaping from side to side, and always up. Her long training among the uplands helped her now, and that wise brain of hers, and, above all, the sense that she could always do whatever her master asked for. So she came up, striving mightily, and Reata barely kept above her.

He saw, from the corner of his eye, how the landslide spread wider and caught a huge fold of virgin pine forest, a mighty growth, and mowed it down with a stroke, and tossed up the glorious trees like playthings among the leaping fury of the boulders. Then the thundering tumult reached the smooth of the valley and plunged into it. The senses of Reata were overwhelmed. No longer striving to climb, he clung close to the rock, for the immense reverberations of the slide threatened to break his eardrums; the mere weight of sound stifled him, squeezed the breath from his body. Against his face he felt the warmth of Rags pressing, while the small dog shook with a mortal terror.

All in an instant the danger was flooding on him. Huge stones, flung out before the advancing wave, streaked through the air and landed far away down the ravine. A ten-ton boulder smote the opposite side of the side crevice in which he was climbing, and smashed out a great chunk of living rock, and itself exploded into a million bits. But none of those flying particles, dangerous as fragments of an exploding shell, touched the three breathing creatures in the crevice.

The huge forefront of the slide now swept past the crevice, and through the mist of dust that poured with it, the hurling trees, the dancing rocks, seemed to be sentient things that were rejoicing. The end of the world would be like this—then a wave with its roots in the abyss and its tongue licking heaven might carry in its front such vast and entangled living shapes as those which Reata thought he saw in the heart of this maëlstrom. Missiles of incredible size cleft the air, which hummed with their passage. Into the bottom of the crevice flooded the destruction, and piled up almost to the feet of Reata where he stood on a narrow ledge, overwhelmed. The mare was beside him. Terror bowed her knees, and she pressed her head against the breast of her master. He threw his arms about that ugly head and held it hard.

He and the dog and the roan mare, they seemed one blood

and spirit in the storm. Then Reata was aware that the uproar had lessened; it was traveling forward. The far blue walls of the sky seemed to be repeating the thunder in vast, vague echoes.

After that there was stillness. Miles and miles of quiet began to roll in on Reata. He could breathe again. Nearby he heard weighty stones occasionally settle downward, embedding themselves with grinding sounds, like the crunching of bones. Still the echoes flew, but fewer and fewer, and thinner and thinner. The thick dust cloud was ripped apart by the wind. Huge white billows lifted and sprawled across the sky, and were gone from the face of the blue. And still the quiet poured in upon the shuddering soul of Reata.

He could not find the taste and relish of life for a moment. He had not the strength of a child. In body and spirit he was still crushed, and now, peering around the edge of battered rock that had shunted away from the three of them the hurling dangers of the avalanche, he saw the side of the mountain laid bare, all virgin, shining rock. In the midst of it, something leaped and glittered. It was a spring that had been given birth out of the breast of the cliff. The small waters of it would soak down through the boulders of the ravine. Gradually they would form as a running stream, and that little rivulet, partnered by infinite time, would gradually carve ten thousand times more greatly than this avalanche of the moment had done. The river would wear the stones away and wash their dust into the far-off plains. It would clear out and widen the valley. It would bring life into this wilderness of broken rock.

Reata, lifting his head with that thought, saw three white columns of smoke rising from the head of the mountain, and, near them, a bright eye was winking. He understood. He drew a great breath. The awe left him. For it was not the blind hand of nature that had stuck at him, but the malice of man again. Up yonder were the agents of Dickerman who had seen their chance to start the slide that might bury him, and now the white smoke columns, the flashing eye of the heliograph, joyously told, at last, of their great success. Reata began to laugh softly. For this time the sun talk would be telling a lie that would vainly warm the heart of Dickerman, that king of the rats, far away.

II

"Gold Rush Town"

Rafferty Hill lies in the fork of Tumble Creek and Tin Can Creek. Tumble Creek got its name naturally, Tin Can Creek from the fact that some tins were lodged, one day, in a sand-bar near its junction with Tumble. The town of Rafferty Hill was so called because there is a mound of earth some fifty feet high in the middle of it, and because Jack Rafferty was the prospector who first struck gold on the edge of Tin Can Creek.

The gold rush started blindly for Rafferty Hill. All gold rushes are blind. One man in ten is a miner. The other nine are exploiters of labor and treasure—they are gamblers, saloon-keepers, thieves, fugitives who wish to bury their heads in a new human deposit, scoundrels, sightseers, gaping tenderfeet, riff-raff of all sorts. A lot of gold was coming out of the black sands along Tin Can Creek, and a lot of it passed over the bars in the town.

Rafferty Hill was loud with a noise that began with the dawn and continued almost to the end of night. There was only an hour or so of deep silence in the course of every twenty-four, and then it seemed that the beast was asleep, or that, growing human, it had paused for a little, appalled, to think over its crimes of the day. Then, rousing, it began to bury the past in an orgy of whisky and gold.

Reata came down into the town at its gayest moment, the twilight, when the men whose hands were sore with labor wanted to forget the day, and when the men whose hands were full of gold wanted to make the night memorable. The two elements combined perfectly to start the uproar. In the mob, the sightseers drifted slowly, idly, staring, and the thieves moved with sinuous ease, and the gamblers strode with accurate, piercing eyes.

Into that mob descended Reata. He was happier than men who had made fortunes this day, or who had at least uncovered the face and the promise of great wealth. He was happier than they because he had something better than gold to rejoice about. He had life!

The saying went, in that world from which he had come, that no man could avoid the reaching hands of Dickerman. Time and distance did not matter. Dickerman, reaching out from his junk heaps at Rusty Gulch, would surely get his man sooner or later. But he, Reata, had reversed the old saying. He had ripped out of the hands of Dickerman the stolen wealth of the old master of theft and murder. He had restored that stolen money to the hands of its owners. He had, in this manner, struck the king of the rats in the face, and then he had melted away into the mountains.

Back in Rusty Gulch, Pop Dickerman, by this time, was rubbing his grimy hands together, and then smoothing the fur of his long, lean face and contenting his heart. His hate and his revenge were being fed full by the thought that, after all, Reata had been taken and smashed as other fools had been overwhelmed by Dickerman's agents. All had gone down, every man who strove to stand out against the dark will of Dickerman. And, among the rest, Reata was gone—buried under the endless tons of rock in the Ten Mule Ravine.

But, while Dickerman rejoiced, Reata would be dipping into life again, and there could not be a better place for him than Rafferty Hill. It was not that he wanted to throw up his arms and shout and get drunk. That was not his goal. He simply wanted to rub shoulders with many men, no matter of what sort. He wanted to see and feel about him endless life, of which he was miraculously still a part and a portion.

So he went down into Rafferty Hill and put up his horse at a livery stable, and then, with Rags, he went out into the twilight world.

It was only his bad luck that took him into Texas Charlie's saloon. If he had gone to any other place, Bob Clare would have died that evening, and his name would never have sounded in the ears of Reata, perhaps. But chance—or fate—led Reata and Rags into Texas Charlie's.

Of course, it was going full blast, for Texas Charlie's was the best saloon in Rafferty Hill. Through the crowd, Reata drifted from the long bar where the six bartenders were laboring, wet to the elbow in the splash of liquor, and then through the dance hall, where the music was beginning to hum and squeal and bump, and so back to the gambling rooms, which were really the most famous part of Charlie's establishment.

Perhaps there were other honest lay-outs in Rafferty Hill, but the honesty of Charlie's faro table and roulette wheel were known to be proved. That was why men who had lots of money to spend were sure to spend the greater part of their time at Texas Charlie's tables. There, Reata saw Bob Clare for the first time. There should have been some warning in

Reata's blood. There should have been a thrilling and an icy touch, benumbing his very soul, and telling him that the face of this man was to turn him back into all the dangers which he had left buried in the distance.

But no voice, no murmur in the spirit suggested to Reata the things that were to be. Instead, he merely laughed pleasantly. He wanted to see life, and Bob Clare was life. He was the symbol of it. He was the smile, the flash in the eye, the heat in the blood of human life.

It made every man feel good to see Bob Clare on a rampage, and he certainly was on a rampage this night. They say that Bob Clare was not over six feet tall, but he looked more than that. Some men are not measured in inches. Even physically they seem to belie their actual proportions. And Bob Clare, as he moved through the crowd with his Stetson pushed well back on his head, stood among the other men like a moose among elk, like a wolf among dogs, like a blood horse among mustangs. He was handsome not because his features were regular, but because there was such a strength and brilliance about his face. He was rather dark, with brown eyes full of light, and he was always smiling.

At the moment when Reata saw him, he had just left the faro table with both hands full of money. He stuffed one handful into his pockets, and, since there seemed to be no more room in his clothes, he tossed the other handful of greenbacks into the air. There was a shout, a flourishing of hands. Men leaped up to grasp at that rain of wealth. Good bills were ripped in two as rival hands grasped for them. A great roar of laughter made the room tremble.

Reata, according to his nature, having seen a fool in the midst of his folly, should have passed on. But it happened that just when the uproar was the greatest, through the forest of the reaching hands he had a glimpse, in the face of Bob

Clare, of a devastating weariness. The smile remained, because it was always there, but it was the smile of a man playing a part, sticking to a rôle in spite of an agony of fatigue. What was the matter with the fellow?

Now, when that question came into the mind of Reata, he still continued in his first direction across the big gambling room, but he turned back a moment later to examine the face of Clare again. He surveyed the man idly. The whole look of the spendthrift and the daredevil was in Bob Clare. One hardly needed to ask questions about him. He was simply one of those who burn brightly but for a very short time. Yet there was that shadow in the midst of the illumination, so to speak, and that was what baffled Reata. There was something that suggested that the fellow was aware of his own follies. Then why did he persist in them?

"Who's the fellow in the middle of the big noise?" asked Reata of a gray-headed man with a sour face.

"Him? That's Bob Clare," said the other. "The worst fool and the best fellow that ever come into Rafferty Hill. There ain't a drunk or a deadbeat or a bum that he ain't staked. And there's a lot of other gents that have got their chance to work and make a strike because of him."

"He's got a big mine, has he?" asked Reata.

"Him? He don't need no mine. Luck's his mine. And he never works it dry. He can't lose. You watch him, and you'll see."

Reata watched—and saw.

Bob Clare, at the roulette wheel, was playing the red. A thousand dollars. He lost. He doubled. He lost. He doubled. He lost; he doubled. Four thousand dollars over the shoulder, like that. Now eight thousand to be risked—and he won. And again, a thousand on the red; and he won; doubled; won; doubled; won. . . .

The crowd began to shout and to laugh.

"How does Texas Charlie stand it, with this fellow Clare winning all the time?" Reata heard a tenderfoot ask.

The answer was: "What difference? Sure, Clare wins, but that makes everybody else feel lucky . . . and, after watching Clare win, the suckers step in and lose. Twenty of 'em will lose as much as Clare wins. Besides, he gives away most of what he collects. It all gets back into the game sooner or later."

Reata saw a sample of that. A man muttered at the ear of Clare, who instantly thrust half a dozen bills, without counting them, into the hand of the stranger. The fellow melted off into the crowd with a grin of fox-like gratification.

A strange impulse moved Reata. He stepped to the side of this man Bob Clare, and said: "I'm broke, Clare. Take a chance on me?"

Bob Clare answered—"Sure!"—without turning his head. He was extending the money when his eye fell full on Reata's face, and then he started a little.

"I know you, do I?" asked Clare.

"You never saw me before."

"Well, take as much as you want," said Bob Clare. Suddenly he hauled out a fortune and held it heaped in his hands.

Reata picked out a one-dollar bill. "I like the color of your money. Thanks, Clare," he said. He felt the bright, steady eyes of the other upon him.

"Look here," said Clare.

"I'm looking," said Reata gravely, his gray eyes piercing into the brown.

"I'll be seeing you later," said Clare.

"You will," answered Reata. And it was only then that something clicked inside him and told him that he might be lost.

III

"The Lariat"

That almost unconscious warning was sufficiently strong to make Reata go straight to the bar and put three fingers of whisky down his throat. While the fumes filled his brain, he told himself that it was no business of his, if fools threw themselves away. Neither did he care what mental torment compelled Bob Clare in this foolish path of his. Men have to take care of themselves.

But something drew him back into the game room. He told himself that it was merely because he wanted to try his hand at roulette and see his money go with a flash and a gesture, or double and quadruple itself. But he was barely inside the room before he heard a voice cut through the tumult. It was not the voice of rollicking Bob Clare. It was not pitched high and shrill to edge its way through the waves of noise that still rolled away from the place where Clare was playing. It was the harshness, the dull flatness of the voice that gave it way, because it was so out of place.

The voice was saying: "This here game is crooked! It's a fake."

Suddenly the rest of the room was stilled. Men pulled back, pressing close to one another, and Reata found himself not far from a table where a tall, frail-looking man with the stooped shoulders and the forward-canted head of a student was rising from a poker table as his five companions looked foolishly up at him with frightened faces.

Perhaps there *had* been crooked work at that table, but

probably it was simply the despair of the loser that had operated like an evil magic on the brain of the tall man. He was white. The pull at the corners of his mouth was not a smile, but it had the look of a caricature of a smile. The evil grin was something to remember long afterward with nightmare horror. He had twitched back a hand and brought out the glimmering, blue length of a gun. But no one shrank from the gun. They shrank, instead, from the white distortion of the face.

"A dirty . . . robbin' . . . fake!" said the tall man, staring into the upraised faces of his companions.

They said nothing. Plainly they were too frightened to move in their chairs even to flee, for fear lest the first move, misunderstood, might be the last. For that white-faced man was too obviously ready for anything.

Then another voice cut across the silenced room, and it was Bob Clare speaking in a tone full, mellow, easy. "You can't talk like that about a game in the place of my friend Texas Charlie," Bob Clare was saying. "You'll have to eat that talk . . . and get out," he said.

There was something like relief in the look of the tall stranger who had just risen. His grimace of a smile changed a bit, almost softened and gentled, one might have said. He had found a target, and that was clear. "I'm goin' to eat my talk, eh?" he asked.

"Right here and now," said Clare, "and you're going to start by putting up that gun."

"You're goin' to make me put it up, are you?" asked the tall man.

"I'll make you put it up . . . or eat it," said Clare.

If the losing gambler was content, there was no mistaking the pleasure in the voice of Bob Clare. He was almost laughing as he walked straight across the room toward the stricken tableful of gamblers and that one tall, leaning figure. That pain, that pretense were gone from his features, Reata could see. He was all reality, now. He advanced as a man might have come forward to take a drink, or to shake the hand of a friend. There was an instant readiness about his manner that made Reata see that, instead of fearing death, the fellow would actually welcome the end of everything. It staggered Reata.

Then, bursting through his ears and shattering his brain, he heard the tall man bark in that same husky, flat voice: "You fool . . . you fill your hand!"

The muzzle of the gambler's Colt jerked up to a level with his target.

Bob Clare? He simply laughed and strode forward, rejoicing. And death was a whisper, a breath, a gesture, a second away.

Reata acted. Out of his coat pocket came that forty feet of coiled lariat, slender as a pencil, rawhide-covered, or perhaps rawhide all the way through, except that leather alone could hardly give it such a weight. The noose loosened and freed under his rapid fingers.

"Stop . . . or . . . !" screamed the loser at the table.

Out of the hand of Reata, with a subtle and under-arm gesture, the lariat shot forward. It struck down over the head and shoulders of the tall fellow, and the jerk with which Reata pulled it taut brought the other headlong over the table, spilling the cards, the stacked chips in a rattling, rolling shower across the floor. But even as he was falling, that tall man managed to fire, and at his shot the back-tilted Stetson leaped from the head of Bob Clare.

At the figure of the tall man, writhing and twisting on the floor, a dozen men rushed.

The voice of Reata stopped them. It was not a very loud

voice. It seemed as though the careless good humor of it arrested the others. Besides, they saw that the speaker held the end of that rope which was hardly much thicker than substantial twine. He was the doer of the deed, and he had the right to dispose of his prey. Perhaps that was the chief reason that the crowd held back.

Reata, to their amazement, loosened the noose of the lariat and actually helped the fallen man to his feet. The fellow was loose on his legs, staggering. He needed the support that Reata gave him. A moment before he had been sober enough to knock the hat off the head of Bob Clare with a bullet that would surely have brained his man, except that Reata had intervened with the magic of his rope. But now he seemed too drunk to stand. Little, bubbling, horrible sounds came out of his throat with every breath that he drew.

He said: "What's the matter? What's happened?"

Reata answered: "There's the fellow you might have killed. The one with his hat off."

"It's Bob Clare!" said the stranger. "I didn't. . . ."

"Get out of here and stay out," answered Reata. "There's a lot of angry men in this town, partner, and one of them might want to take a fall out of you. Get out of Rafferty Hill as fast as you can get. There's the door yonder. Start!"

The fellow who had been so close to a murder, without reply, went wavering toward the door, and outside, and pulled the door weakly to behind him.

After that, the talk began in a double wave, from each side of the room, and closed in a roar over the head of Reata.

He had coiled up his rope, however, and now he was withdrawing. Those fellows in Rafferty Hill wanted to pick him up on their shoulders and give him a cheer and provide certain rounds of free drinks at the bar. It was not only because he had saved the life of Bob Clare. It was rather because of something in his manner of doing the thing that they were profoundly moved.

We know a good actor from an amateur by his manner of taking the stage and doing the simplest things. We tell him by the way he walks and sits down and rises, before he has parted his lips to speak. We discover the perfect dancer by the first few steps, simple, plain, gliding, by something of exquisite balance and unpronounced rhythm in the stepping. And so the men of Rafferty Hill were able to see in Reata the man who had handled death before, taken it intimately up into those slender, active fingers of his, and disposed of it with just such lightning-fast gesture as they had seen him use on this day. The thing had been impossible until he had done it. Then it was simply, ridiculously easy, the sort of a thing that every man should be able to do—but which no other man in that place would have dared to attempt.

That was the major reason why they wanted to flatter and cheer and make much of Reata. Most of the things that other men do to distinguish themselves make us a little jealous because they are barely above our own talents. A step more and we should, we think, be able to accomplish them. But sometimes there is a voice that silences jealous prejudice. The men of Rafferty Hill had heard that voice.

But the man they wanted to cheer disappeared from beneath their eyes. While they were reaching out their hands for him, he glided away from the touch of their fingers. He was here, he was there, and suddenly he was lost in the throng of those who had just poured in from the barroom and had not witnessed the thing that had just happened.

A moment later he was out in the street, cursing himself. For he had done the very thing that he had sworn he would not do. He had stepped out before a crowd and drawn all eyes upon himself. How long would it be, therefore, before the

fact of his existence was brought to the attention of Pop
Dickerman, from whose bright and rat-like eyes he had just
buried himself? Messages that traveled by the sun talk of the
heliograph by day or through the winking of mountain-built
fires by night would swiftly convey, across the great wilderness, to the brain of Pop Dickerman that the man he wanted
was still alive—and in Rafferty Hill.

That was why Reata gritted his teeth. He could have done
the thing in any other way, being among men who were
strangers to him and his past, but the use of the slender lariat,
thin as twine and heavy as lead—thin as a string but strong
enough to hold a horse—that was the feature by which he
would be identified. Pop Dickerman was sure to learn the
truth, and perhaps before the dawn gleamed over the next
day.

Reata, having paused in the darkness in front of the place
of Texas Charlie, started down the winding street. Shortly he
was aware of someone following him with long strides.
Already? he wondered. Perhaps already one of the men of
Dickerman had spotted him, for those men were to be found
everywhere, and everywhere the description of Reata, the
arch-enemy, must have gone abroad.

A wide beam of light struck out through an illumined
doorway. On the verge of that light, on the farther side of the
bright wedge of it, Reata whirled suddenly about, the subtle
noose of his rope in his hand. He saw that it was tall Bob
Clare who followed him. And Clare, hooking his arm through
that of Reata, suddenly whirled him around and took him
striding down the street.

IV

"A Shot in the Dark"

"That was fine," said Clare. "Not what you did, but the way of it. You surely saved me. Now, partner, why did you do it? Because I saw you were hating the doing of it as soon as the tall fellow was sprawling on the floor!"

Reata could have laughed. It was not fair that this reckless gambler, this gamester at life and death, should possess, also, a penetration so deep and so instant.

He said nothing, in answer, because he found no answer that would be easy to make, and Clare went on: "We're going up the hill. I've got a cabin up there. You're going to come up there and talk to me, partner."

Still Reata said nothing, but he walked along, keeping step with Bob Clare, rather dizzily conscious of that premonition which he had first felt when he looked into the brown, bright eyes of this stranger. Something hooked them together. He had known other men for whom he had felt a liking suddenly. But never before had his heart gone out to another man as it went out to Bob Clare. That was the reason for his silence, and perhaps similar reasons were the cause of the speechlessness of Clare all the way up the little hill to the cabin that stood on the top of it, and into which Clare brought Reata.

The ramshackle stove in the corner was lighted, and so was the lantern on the wall. Coffee was made in the same silence through which the eyes of the two men crossed each other, from time to time, clashing and falling away like swords from thrusts and parries.

Across their cups of coffee, the two stared frankly at one another.

"Now," said Bob Clare, "what's the matter with you?"

"I was going to ask you the same thing. What's the matter with you?" asked Reata.

"With me?" said Clare, surprised. "Why, there's nothing the matter with me. Everybody in Rafferty Hill knows that I'm simply a fool for luck. What could be the matter with me?"

"You're in hell," said Reata. "That's what's the matter with you."

Clare stared at him, and swallowed down his coffee. Reata followed that example. He needed that hot drink more than he had needed whisky in the saloon.

"What makes you talk like that?" demanded Bob Clare.

"What made you walk up on the fellow with the gun?" asked Reata.

"I didn't think he'd shoot," said Clare.

"You *hoped* he'd shoot," said Reata.

Clare rose suddenly from his stool.

Reata said to him: "A man can't lose money . . . not when he's already in hell. That's what your luck amounts to, Clare."

Bob Clare rubbed his knuckles across the top of the table. "What's your name?" he asked.

"People call me Reata. I'd as soon be called Smith or Jones, just now."

"Smith, who put you on my trail?"

"Chance," said Reata.

"Chance never does anything," said Clare, scowling.

"The queer look in your eyes," answered Reata. "I can't help pitying the poor devils who pretend that they're having a good time."

Bob Clare did not smile. After a heavy moment of silence, he said: "You see too much, Smith-Jones. Anyway, it's about time to turn in, from the look of you. You've been traveling a lot more than miles, lately."

Reata turned in, accordingly, with a fairly clean blanket to wrap around himself, and a straw tick to lie on, filled with sweet-smelling, sun-cured grass. He was so tired that even the problem of Bob Clare could not hold him entirely. He saw the red blink of the dying fire in the stove, shining through one of the wide cracks. He sniffed at the smell of coffee fumes and wood smoke that thickened the air, and then he was asleep.

He had no dreams. Men who have ridden as Reata had ridden that day, men who have found security deep and profound and suddenly have walked out of safety into the firing line again, are able to sleep in no matter what peril they may lie.

When he was awakened, it was by the loud report of a gun. Across his stomach dropped a wet, warm weight.

He got out of the bed to the floor, sliding away from the loose burden. It was a shadowy figure of a man with a knife still gripped in a loose, dead hand. Then he saw Bob Clare, vaguely illumined by the glint of red light from the stove, crushing another man into a corner, mastering his hands, lifting a hatchet to smash out his brains.

Talking and shouting would do no good. There was no time for that. A man in the killing humor of Bob Clare could not be checked by a word before his slaying stroke was completed. But the whisper of Reata's ever-ready rope was better than speech. The lariat slid with a faint hiss of speed through the air and neatly surrounded both men, and jerked them crashing to the floor.

Reata picked the weapon out of the hand of Bob Clare.

"You fool!" shouted Clare. "They were going to. . . ."

"Look at that *hombre* over there on the floor and see if he's dead," said Reata.

He himself put his knee on the chest of the second assailant. He saw a broad, red face, a powerful jaw—a face contorted now as when a man faced a firing squad, about to have the bullets drive through his flesh.

"Harry Quinn," said Reata. "I'm sorry it had to come out of your hand!"

Harry Quinn said: "You know, Reata . . . hell, you know!"

"Yeah. I know," answered Reata. "Get up and sit down on that stool, there in the corner."

His practiced hands took from Quinn a revolver and a knife. Quinn obediently got up and moved to the stool slowly. He sat down on it, facing Reata.

"Head of this *hombre* is all blood, but he seems to be alive," reported Bob Clare.

"Light a lantern," suggested Reata.

Clare did so, and Reata saw a man with long black hair lying on his face beside the bunk that he himself had recently occupied. The knife the murderer had been about to use was lying still near his unclosed hand. There was a red furrow across his head. Plainly the shot of Bob Clare had glanced from the skull and merely stunned the other.

"Who's that?" asked Reata.

"You wouldn't know him," said Quinn. He added, with a slight suggestion of humor: "You wouldn't wanna."

The man on the floor stirred, groaned, tried to sit up.

"Tie his hands," ordered Reata. "Wash the blood off his head and tie half his shirt over his sconce for him."

Bob Clare obeyed without a word, and presently there was seated at the table, on the second stool, a man who looked like an Indian or a half-breed, his dark skin now a little yellow. He swayed somewhat from side to side, but the natural fire was beginning to come back into his eyes.

"You travel around with some good-looking fellows," said Reata to Quinn.

"You know," answered Harry Quinn. "What Pop wishes on a gent, he's gotta take up with."

"Sure. I know," responded Reata. "What his name?"

"Sam."

"What else?"

"There ain't any more. That's all there is."

"Knife work, chiefly?"

"Yeah."

"In the back?"

"Yeah."

"Nice boy," said Reata. "You're nice too, Harry."

Harry Quinn said nothing. He lowered his head a little and stared at the knees of Reata.

"You're damned nice," said Reata.

"Go ahead," said Harry Quinn. "I'll take it. I'd take it even if I didn't have to. I'll take it because it's coming to me."

Bob Clare, who stood opposite to Sam, turned his head a little.

"Old friend of yours, eh . . . Jones?"

"Call me Reata," said the other. "These boys knew me well enough to call on me. You might as well use the name."

"I meant . . . old chums of yours, Reata, eh?" said Clare. "I woke up and saw the shadow of that dog . . . Sam, they call him, eh? . . . leaning over your bunk. I saw the flash of the knife in his hand. The other hand was feeling at your chest. But I sleep with a gun under the pillow. I let him have it. I must have aimed high. I'm sorry," said Clare, looking again into the dark, expressionless face of Sam.

Reata turned his back on Quinn.

"Look out!" exclaimed Clare.

"Harry won't try anything more," said Reata.

He stepped to Sam and put a hand under his chin and jerked up his head so he could see the face in the full. The black eyes glared back at him.

"You're a pretty boy, Sam," said Reata, and drew his hand away.

The head of Sam remained tilted back; the glare continued to be fixed on Reata.

"Are you pretty good with a knife, Sam?" asked Reata.

The breed grinned mirthlessly.

"I'll open the door and call in some of the boys," said Bob Clare. "They'll put these two snakes right out of their pain." He went to the door and pulled it wide.

"Wait a minute," said Reata.

Clare turned slowly back toward him.

"Stand up, Sam," said Reata.

The 'breed rose.

"Walk out of that door," said Reata.

Sam went to the door, cast one glance behind him, and then, throwing out his hands to help his speed, leaped away into the darkness.

"Stand up, Harry," said Reata.

Harry Quinn rose.

"Get out," said Reata.

But Quinn remained where he was, his head hanging a little, his shoulders swaying a trifle.

V

"A Doomed Man"

This picture remained for a long moment. Bob Clare, with the discretion of a gentleman and the restraint of a man of self-control, had seen the 'breed exit with only a slight gesture toward his hip. He waited by the door, now, without a single word.

But when the silence had continued for another instant, he said harshly: "Quinn . . . if that's your name . . . you've got your orders . . . jump!"

Quinn made a queer two-handed gesture, with the palms of both hands turned up, a gesture that would not be expected from a hardy fellow of his type, because, somehow, there was a sort of Oriental surrender in it.

"You dunno nothing about it, Clare," he said. "Reata . . . I was done for, and he saved my neck. I had about twenty-four hours to go, and he risked his hide, and he pulled me out."

He stared vaguely toward Bob Clare, who started a little, and swore under his breath.

"And so you come in here and tried to . . . ," Clare checked himself.

"So I came in here and tried to help a 'breed stick a knife into him," filled out Harry Quinn. He got a step forward toward the door, but, coming to the little table in the center of the room, he leaned his two hands upon it, and rested his weight on his hands.

Bob Clare stared fixedly at him. Then he went to a corner range of shelves, took down a bottle, and poured a stiff drink of amber-colored whisky into a glass. He shoved it onto the table in front of Harry Quinn. The gray eyes of Reata, all this while, never stirred from Quinn. There was pity in his look, not hatred.

"I come and try to get him, and he pulls you off when you're about to brain me," said Quinn huskily.

"Drink this, you poor fool," said Bob Clare.

Harry Quinn took the drink and poured it down his throat. He coughed, made a gesture against strangulation, and then turned himself slowly around toward Reata.

"Give it to me now," he said. "I'll get it sooner or later. Maybe from a greaser or something that ain't got the right over me. I'd rather have it now . . . from you. You got the right. Go ahead and give it to me, Reata."

Reata said nothing. Bob Clare stepped discreetly back and obliterated himself among the wall shadows.

"Go on down the hill," directed Reata finally. "But wait a minute. I might want to see you a while later. Come back in an hour, will you? And how about that 'breed?"

"Him? Aw, he comes when I whistle."

"All right. Keep an eye on him. So long, Harry."

"So long," said Harry Quinn. He made a sudden gesture with his hand toward Reata and then drew it back. "Hell!" he said, and pulled himself together, and walked out of the little cabin with his head held high.

Clare closed the door behind him and turned to find Reata sitting on the stool where the 'breed had been. A drop of blood had fallen from the poorly bandaged head of Sam onto the tabletop. Reata seemed to be studying the red sheen of it.

After a time, Clare said: "Have a shot of this." He poured some more whisky into a glass and pushed it toward Reata.

"Thanks," said Reata, "but it wouldn't hit the spot."

"I'll take it, then," said Clare. "I need it." He tossed off the liquor, filled the glass, emptied it again at a great swallow.

Since Reata remained staring at the drop of blood, Clare went to the stove, kindled the fire, put on a pot of coffee, and actually brought it to a boil, and still Reata had not spoken. Silently he accepted the cup of coffee that Bob Clare offered to him. He rolled a cigarette, and, blowing puffs thoughtfully toward the ceiling, he sipped the coffee. Clare remained in a corner, withdrawn from the field of thought.

"Sit down," said Reata.

Clare pulled up the second stool, filled a second cup of coffee, and sat down opposite this smaller man. He had thought Reata was very young. Now he began to find the pleasant brown face much older than he had thought. Not with years. Time doesn't matter.

"Now, talk," said Reata suddenly.

"Sure," said Bob Clare agreeably. "I know how you feel, sort of. What line shall I talk about, Reata? Dogs . . . or men?"

"Yourself. Talk about yourself," said Reata, still staring at the drop of blood.

"I'd rather not do that," answered Clare.

"Don't be a fool," said Reata. "You need to talk."

He waited. After a silence, Clare said: "About everything, eh?"

"About everything," answered Reata.

"My father liked the booze and the high spots," said Bob Clare, in a casual, cheerful voice. "He hit most of the high ones, one time or another. Once he opened the ground up and pulled a stack of gold out of it. He knew he wouldn't keep the stuff. He left it all in trust for his son. His son by his second wife. He had another son by a first wife. That fellow is still alive, he and his mother. She's Inez Clare. Her son is Antonio Clare."

"Mexican?" said Reata.

"Mexican. I'm of age next month. I'm not going to come of age. That's Tony's idea."

"I see," said Reata. He began to tap his fingers on the table, drumming them rapidly around the little drop of shining blood. Then he expounded the theme in brutal words. "Your father was a carefree, young *hombre*. But he was right. The right sort of a fellow."

"My father," said Bob Clare, with a deliberate consideration and in a very quiet voice, "was the finest man that ever lived."

"I knew he was," answered Reata curtly, as though he objected to being interrupted. "The point is that he lost his head about a pretty Mexican girl and married her. Eh? And he had a son, this fellow Antonio. But, afterwards, things went wrong for him and his wife. He divorced her."

"She went crazy mad with jealousy and divorced him," said Bob Clare. "He was queer. He wouldn't have gotten the divorce otherwise, I don't think."

Reata raised his hand, protesting against these suggestions. "Then he married your mother, who was the finest woman in the world. And they had for a son a rattle-headed fool named Bob, eh?"

Bob Clare was silent.

"Your old man, whatever his front moniker was," continued Reata rudely, "saw that he wasn't going to last long, the way he was stepping. He left the gold mine he found in trust, with you in mind. He made only a small settlement for his first son."

"He left Tony plenty, but it was spent," said Bob Clare.

"And the poison in the Mexicans," continued Reata, "is still boiling. You get your father's money that was left in trust until you're twenty-one. You're twenty-one next month. The greasers will see you dead before they see you rich with that coin. They're going to bump you off."

"Don't call Tony a greaser," said Clare sternly.

Reata lifted his hand again.

"Somehow, Tony has the bulge on you. You know that you can't keep him off. You know that he'll have you dead. You know there's no chance in the world of your living another month, eh?"

"There's no chance in the world," agreed Bob Clare.

"That's why you were ready to chuck your money away . . . and your life after your money?" suggested Reata. "Well, what has Tony got that's so sure to put out your lights?"

"LaFarge," said Bob Clare.

Reata jerked erect. "LaFarge?" he murmured.

"And all LaFarge's crooks," said Bob Clare. "I suppose they sold me to LaFarge. If I die, of course, the money goes to my stepmother and Tony. It's an easy deal. Suppose they give LaFarge half the loot when I'm knocked over. You see?"

"How much loot is there?"

"Half a million."

"Half of that? Yes, that might buy LaFarge. Just about," said Reata.

"Well, I've talked," said Bob Clare. "I swore that I never would. Not after I decided that the police could never protect me."

"No, the police would be no good. Not against LaFarge," said Reata. "They wouldn't have a chance to keep you away from him."

Bob Clare nodded.

"I've got a few days left. Any part of a month left. It's going to be a good time, and you're going to be in on it," said Bob Clare.

"And close your eyes and see you laid in Boot Hill, eh?" said Reata.

"Any way you want it," answered Bob Clare.

"You go back to bed," said Reata. "I've got to think. I knew that I'd want to talk to Harry Quinn again."

"What about?" asked Clare.

"Don't bother me," said Reata angrily. "Go back to bed and don't bother me!"

Clare stared for a moment and then followed that advice. He was, in fact, sound asleep when nearly an hour later a hand tapped gently at the door of the cabin.

Reata went and opened it. He saw Harry Quinn's wide shoulders and short body before him. Overhead were the mountain stars with the summits pricked in sketchily against them. There was the good, sweet savor of the pine trees in the air. But there was no sweetness in the heart of Reata.

He said: "Harry, how long to flash word to Pop Dickerman?"

Quinn muttered: "I dunno. By morning, Reata?"

"Get word back here by the morning," said Reata. "Have it here by the dawn. Send this message to Pop. Tell him that I'll sell out."

"Hi!" gasped Harry Quinn. "*You* sell out? To Dickerman? You'd rather die, first!"

"Shut up!" said Reata. "Are you listening?"

"I'm listening, chief," said Quinn humbly.

"Tell Pop Dickerman that I'll sell out, but that my price is as high as the sky. If he wants to go that high, get the word back to me by sunup."

VI

"Reata Rides"

The sun was not half an hour high above Rafferty Hill when a light tap came at the door of the cabin. Bob Clare slept a wink more lightly than a wildcat, and yet he was not sitting up from his blankets before Reata was already opening the door on the wide, red face of Harry Quinn.

Harry Quinn was nodding as he said: "Pop will pay the sky for you. But he says . . . 'What sky?' "

"The top sky," said Reata. "I've got to see him and talk the thing over. What's the fastest way of getting to him, Harry?"

"With relayed horses," said Quinn.

"There's no line of relayed horses between here and Rusty Gulch," reminded Reata.

"There wasn't any line, till Pop reached out his arm for you. There's plenty of nags in that relay now."

"It's a hundred miles to Rusty Gulch," said Reata.

"There's ten or twelve relays to take you there," answered Quinn.

"I can make it by night, then?"

"Sure you can, if you're all made of steel and whalebone," said Quinn. "And I guess that's the stuff you're built of."

"Pass the word along that I'm starting," said Reata. "I'll be down the hill in no time."

"Wait a minute," growled Harry Quinn.

"You're going to tell me that maybe it's only a frame on the part of Pop and that, when I come to him, all he'll say to me is going to be heavy lead. That may be, too. But I've got to ride. It's one more chance. I hope that it'll be the last one I'll ever have to take." He waved down the slope. "Run along, Harry," he commanded.

He went back to Bob Clare, who had begun to pull on his boots.

"Something up?" asked Clare, looking keenly at Reata.

"I'm on my way," said Reata. "So long, Bob. Have to make a jump that'll take me a couple of days or less. Then I'm coming back here. You're going to take a rest till this evening. Mind you, you're not going to step outside the shack, and you can spend the spare time cleaning up your guns, and working some of the nerves out of your hand."

Clare watched him silently.

"You've had too much booze aboard every evening for a long time," said Reata. "You're sobering up now."

"Anything you say," answered Clare, his lips tightening a little. Then he broke out: "But what's the main idea, Reata?"

"You were sitting down and waiting for your finish, weren't you?"

Clare nodded.

"Now you're standing up and getting ready to fight," said Reata.

"But hold on, old son."

"To a finish, you and me against the crowd," said Reata.

With that he went out quickly from the shack, smiling a little as he thought of the staring, startled eyes of Clare. Then he went down the hill with Harry Quinn. At the very livery stable where he had put up Sue and left Rags, he found a big, clean-limbed bay tethered near the door.

"That's a Dickerman horse," said Reata.

"How come?" asked Harry Quinn.

"Because nothing but crooks and kings rate horses as good

as that one, and there aren't many kings in Rafferty Hill," said Reata.

"Hi, Reata, there's nobody like you." Harry Quinn chuckled. "That's the horse you'll start with on your ride. Here's a chart of the whole way you'll travel, and the points are described where you'll find the other stations of the relay. I want to know what . . . ?"

"So long," said Reata, and sprang into the saddle. The keeper of the livery stable shouted: "Hey, get out of that saddle. That horse belongs to. . . ."

Harry Quinn had to dive at the excited man to keep him from reaching for a gun that would have been out before he received Harry's explanation, and it was in this way that Reata managed to ride the tall bay out of the livery stable.

The bay was strong, the way was hard, and an hour and a half and eight miles later Reata dismounted at the mouth of a blind ravine. At his shout a little man with a face so thin that it seemed only half of a countenance, a twisted face under a broad, noble forehead, led a small mustang blue as mud and ugly as sin out of a tangle of brush. He stood turned to stone at the sight of Reata, his mouth agape and his right hand frozen on the half-exposed butt of his Colt.

Reata snatched the reins of the mustang and flicked himself aboard. For three torrid minutes, the horse butted holes in the sky and knocked chunks out of the hard rock. As it quieted, Dave Bates shouted: "Reata, are you back with us?"

"I'm only at the entrance to the rat hole," said Reata, "but I suppose that I'll get all the way inside. So long, Dave."

He left Dave Bates half laughing and half dumbfounded, and headed into the heart of the mountains. The blue was a wearier and a wiser broncho before ever they passed the ravine angle and came to the head of a long, easy valley, six miles and one hour away. A staggering, bleeding, frothing little horse was what Reata turned over to a tall young Negro who had led out to him, in answer to his call, a good gray mare with the sort of long legs that a man wants to have under him when there is level going to ride across.

The gray and then a tough brown bucking mustang got him through the easy miles of that long valley in all of its windings; and then under the full glare of the powerful sun he took a roan horse, and then two fire-eyed buckskins, to lope over the burning desert beyond. A black horse and a gray and then a short-legged mountain climber of a low-geared runt of a pinto to bring him through the hills, and last of all a tall bay gelding, blood brother, it seemed, of the one on which he had left Rafferty Hill that morning, carried Reata into Rusty Gulch in the later heat of the afternoon. For he had ridden a hundred miles in ten hours.

His body cried out in protest, but his lips, which had grown thinner, smiled. There was an ache up his spine, where pounding blows had been absorbed all during those hours. But well ahead of the time he had planned, he was drawing rein at the entrance gate of Pop Dickerman's junkyard, on the edge of Rusty Gulch.

He could remember when he had first entered that place. It had not been so very long before, for that matter. But he had been a child, then. All men were children except those who had known Pop Dickerman. And heaven help those unfortunates.

As he looked up to the long, high roof line of the barn that Pop used as warehouse and living quarters, he saw a cat sitting on the top, calmly washing its face in the sunshine. The cat stopped its work, and, with one paw still raised, it yawned a red yawn and showed Reata the delicate little ivory needles just inside its mouth. Then it went on working, but to Reata it was as though even the cats of Pop Dickerman were laughing when they saw the slave return to the master.

Reata led the tired bay horse into the long shed and tethered it in a stall. In that very shed he had found the roan mare, Sue, and begun his partnership with her. That had not been bad. But everything else that had come to him from Dickerman had been evil.

He stepped out into the junkyard and ran his eye over the rusted heaps. They always baffled and amazed him. The hours that Dickerman spent in collecting this stuff from broken-down, failing ranches and the sincerity with which he bargained for it and sold it again, struggling over every five cents of profit or loss, seemed to indicate that the man was a total miser. Yet he was a man who also dealt in thousands, in tens of thousands, taking long chances, risking fortunes like a mighty gambler with a heart of steel. He had, some men said, hundreds of thousands deposited in various banks. What could the junk business be, then, except a mask and a blind? Or perhaps there was a truer explanation. In junk he dealt at Rusty Gulch. Outside of it he dealt in criminal lives and criminal actions; he was the receiver of stolen goods. And these things were junk, too—junk of broken laws and ruined lives.

He went on to the big sliding door that gave access to the huge mow of the old barn. It was ajar, and he stepped inside. A big old bronze bell hung from a joint nearby. He struck it twice, heavily, and then three times more so that a rapid, running echo fled after the two booming notes.

After that, he looked about him, at the familiar bundles of old lamps and lanterns that hung at the ends of ropes fastened from the rafters. He moved slowly forward. The heaps on the ground, the bundles hanging in the air charmed him, and yet there was a sort of horror that followed him. It came, perhaps, from the scent of perfumed tobacco that hung in the air, left there, no doubt, by the fumes from Dickerman's water pipe.

He came to the central space where Dickerman's legless couch was in its old place, covered with its greasy, time-marked brocade. The big double-burner lamp still hung above that central place of business conclave and small bargaining. And on either side of the lamp was suspended—like grisly decorations for a candelabrum—two huge bunches of knives. There were stilettos, hunting knives, Bowie knives, common steel kitchen knives, penknives, knives of all the kinds that a person could readily call to mind, and the torsion of the rope from which they hung kept the two bundles turning a little, very slowly, so that the eye could always find something new.

Reata lighted a cigarette and lay flat on his back on a deep heap of rugs that stood on the floor just opposite the couch of Dickerman. That flat position eased and soothed his body. He seemed able to breathe in a new manner, which threw less strain on aching muscles. The relief was so great that he could have groaned a little with every breath. He blew long, thin streams of cigarette smoke high up among the shadows, and waited.

He knew from old experience that it would be useless to watch, for Dickerman would never appear from an expected quarter, and, when he came, it would be with a soundless footfall.

So he tried not to be surprised. He tried not to be shocked when suddenly, beside him, appeared the tall form of Pop Dickerman clad only in undershirt—sadly dirty—and trousers, and the two bright little ratty eyes looking down at Reata out of that furred, long, grizzled face.

"Well, well, well," murmured Pop Dickerman in his deep and husky voice that always seemed to proceed from frayed-out vocal chords.

"Damn your welling," said Reata. "Go cook me something to eat, and then come and tell me when the stuff's ready."

"It's ready this minute, Reata," said Dickerman.

"You mean they heliographed to you as I got near? They sun-talked the news to you, eh, all the way across the hills and the curse of that desert?"

"No. They only gave me the hour you left Rafferty Hill. I knew when you'd come. I added it up . . . the hours it would take any other man to ride that distance . . . and then I subtracted two hours from the lot, and, you see, I got just the right time for you, Reata. Come along, son. I got some of your favorite things out there . . . some roast pork, and Mexican beans, and corn bread yaller as gold, that'll melt in your mouth, and I got some chicken soup that you'll want a quart of to start with. And there's cheese crackers to eat with the soup, and there's some sweet things, because I wouldn't forget that you like sweet things, Reata. No, sir, I been and baked you a pumpkin pie big enough for ten, and I've made my special coffee that'll make you sing like a bird. And I've got a fine lot of honeycomb for you that smells like the whole month of May. I've got hold of some Mexican wine you'll have with the roast pork and them things. Why, I've laid out just the dinner for you, Reata, and you're the boy that can eat it!"

Reata was in fact the boy that could eat it. He devoured a mighty meal, smoked one cigarette, and then went back and stretched himself on that pile of rugs and slept for two hours. It was still only the red of the sunset time when he wakened.

VII

"The Agreement"

The sweet smell of the Turkish tobacco, specially scented, was in the air, and, as Reata sat up, he saw the junk dealer sucking with closed eyes at the mouthpiece of the long rubber tube. It was the first time that Reata had ever seen the eyes closed and the suggestion of weariness in the face of Pop Dickerman, but now the man looked very old and tired. It was nearly possible to pity him, until the eyes flashed open again. But then their brightness and their eternal youth put out all other thoughts in the mind of Reata.

He made another cigarette. There was a scent of coffee, and he found a steaming pot that Dickerman had just brought. What had made that devil of a man understand the exact moment when Reata would awaken?

Well, if one started asking questions about Dickerman's strange intuitions, there would never be an end of them. Reata poured out a cup of the coffee and tasted it. It was thick and strong, but it was not bitter. Instead of being black, it was a profound but not very clear brown. The taste of it was not like the taste of other liquids. It was to be drunk straight, out of little cups hardly bigger than eggshells. They held one perfect mouthful at a perfect temperature.

"What a cook you would have made, Dickerman," said Reata.

"And what a cook I am," insisted Dickerman.

A black cat climbed onto his shoulder. He put up a hand, and the scraggly creature began to rub itself against the fur along the side of Pop's face.

"Aye, you're a cook and other things," said Reata. "Now we talk about the price you're going to pay for me."

"Aye, aye," said Dickerman. "I'll have to pay a price for you, Reata. But I've already paid a price for you! Think of what I've paid out!" He held up a finger. "A hundred and eighty or two hundred thousand dollars of gold out of the Decker and Dillon Bank, back there in Jumping Creek. I have it. It's mine. It's in my hands. Then you come and snake it away and take it back to Decker and Dillon. Why, I could pretty nigh hate you for that, Reata!"

"You hate me, well enough," said Reata. "And the thing you hate most about me is that you can use me better living than dead, eh?" He looked at Dickerman with a glimmer of that yellow light coming into his gray eyes.

Dickerman saw the change and noted it well. "Aye," he answered frankly. He always knew how to appear frank, and that was what seemed, to Reata, the most detestable characteristic and power of this detestable man. "Aye, you're more to me living than you are dead. But, as I was sayin', you've cost me aplenty already, Reata. There's the gold of the Decker and Dillon Bank, but that ain't nothing compared with what gents know you've been and done to me. You've tied my plans into knots, and you've got off with a hide that ain't been scratched. There was a time when the gents that know me . . . there ain't so many of them. . . ."

"Not with their pictures in the papers . . . no, not many of them," said Reata.

"There was a time when they hated worse than a gun at the head to back-chat to Pop Dickerman. But maybe things is goin' to be changed, since you've showed that I can be slapped in the face and keep right on livin'."

"Maybe I won't live long," said Reata.

"Who's goin' to tell about that?" asked Dickerman.

"How many men have you got at the doors, waiting for a whistle from you, Pop?"

"How many?" said Pop. "There's only five, Reata. But they all shoot terrible straight."

Reata smiled. "It would be a pretty good thing for the world if I threw the noose of my rope over your scrawny neck and hanged you up to a rafter, here, Pop."

"Aye," said Pop Dickerman calmly, "that would be a good thing for a lot of folks. And now, we was talkin' about the way you've made a fool out of me, Reata. I ain't a proud man . . . I'm a kind of a humble poor sort of a gent. I dicker around with junk, and I put a price on rusty chains, and things like that. But still there's a little mite of a flicker of pride in me, too. And you've sort of shamed me, Reata."

"I nearly shamed you for the last time at Rafferty Hill," said Reata.

"I never shoulda sent out Harry Quinn on your trail," said Dickerman. "He's got an idea that he can't ever handle you, and the idea is what sure enough beats him. But the 'breed was a promisin' sort of a young gent, I thought. What did you think of him, Reata?"

"As good a man as you could find . . . for your sort of business," agreed Reata. "He looks like murder and he acts like murder, and he *is* murder. No, you didn't make any mistake about him. He would have finished me off, but his trouble was that he didn't pay enough attention to the other fellow who was in the room."

"I've got him wrote all down," said Dickerman. "Bob Clare. I'll be knowin' things about him before long."

"Sure you will," said Reata, "because I'm going to tell you. He's the high price that I'm talking about."

"Him?" cried Dickerman, and suddenly his dark eyes

flamed. "You ain't able to handle him yourself? You want help to get rid of him, Reata? A little cuttin' of the throat . . . is that what you mean?"

"I mean the other way around," said Reata.

Dickerman sighed and settled back in his place. "Yeah, and it wouldn't've been the way I tried to guess," he said. "It wouldn't be nothin' as easy as that. You mean . . . to *keep* his throat from bein' carved?"

"Yes."

"Who wants to carve it?"

"LaFarge."

It was seldom that Pop Dickerman permitted himself to show either great surprise or dismay, but he showed them both now, and finally, stretching out both his long arms, he turned the palms up, as if asking the gods to witness the height of the impossibility that he was required to perform.

"LaFarge?" he echoed at last.

"LaFarge has to die," said Reata.

"Then go ahead and do the dirty work yourself," said Dickerman. "You killed Bill Champion. If you killed him, you can kill anybody."

Reata smiled.

Suddenly Dickerman shouted: "I won't have nothin' to do with it! I got a respect for LaFarge. I sort of . . . er . . . like him. I wouldn't touch him, not for ten like you!"

Reata kept smiling. Pop Dickerman pulled out a big bandanna and mopped his furrowed brow. His eyes kept dodging from side to side as though he were hunting for a way of escape.

"You don't know LaFarge," he said, his voice bubbling lower and more huskily than ever. "You don't know nothin' about him or you wouldn't talk foolish like this, Reata."

"I only know," answered Reata, "that LaFarge is one of

the chief devils, like Pop Dickerman. I only know that he's got his hand in a lot of fires. I know that LaFarge is doing twenty things at once, from running Chinamen over the Río Grande by night, to peddling hop in Chicago. I know his men are sticking up stagecoaches in Montana and crooking the cards in Tucson. I know that LaFarge has kept so far behind the curtains that he's only a name. Nobody knows so much as his face."

"And you're asking me to wipe him out?" asked Dickerman, leaning forward and rapping his knuckles against his bony breast. "You're askin' old Pop Dickerman, down here in his junk heaps, to step out and wipe the great LaFarge off the earth? Why, you fool, I ain't even tempted."

"You're afraid of him, Pop," said Reata. "But just balance against LaFarge what you can do with me. If you help me to smash LaFarge and make Bob Clare safe, I'll be your man."

"Aye, forever!" said Dickerman.

"No, for three months . . . after LaFarge is dead."

"Three months?" screamed Dickerman. "You're goin' to be my man for only three months . . . is that any price for LaFarge?"

"Think it over," said Reata.

Dickerman actually rolled his eyes toward the doors, but then, sinking back on the legless divan, he began to comb his furry beard, occasionally flashing up a bright, ratty look at his guest. Afterward, he commenced to smile, the corners of his mouth curling up and showing red through the fur on his face.

"I'm hearin' you straight, Reata," he said.

"You're hearing me straight."

"Because it means a lot," said Dickerman. "Because now I ain't talkin' with any ordinary hobo. I'm talkin' with a gent that might pick a pocket, but that never broke his word. A promise from Reata is stronger'n toolproof steel, ain't it?"

Reata shrugged his shoulders. He began to sit up very straight.

"If you was to gimme three months of your time," said Dickerman, "you'd do anything I asked you."

"Wait a minute," said Reata. "Not murder, Dickerman. Not that, of course."

"Why not?" rasped the junk dealer. "Why not murder . . . if I want it done?"

"No!" said Reata.

"This here Bob Clare that saved you from the worms . . . you wanna do something for him. Now's your chance. Maybe I can save him from LaFarge. I dunno. I'll try with everything I got, so's it'll be death for me or for LaFarge. I'll take the long chance, the big gamble . . . but I'm goin' to be paid big if I win! Big, big, big as hell!"

Reata took a breath. From air hunger, his heart was fluttering and failing.

"Aye," said Dickerman, "if I have you for three months, I'll make you pick the jewels out of the eyes of the devil in hell! You hear me, Reata? I make no bargain except for all of you . . . for three sneaking little short months! Are you my man to do everything and anything that I ask?"

"If Bob Clare goes safe and free, I . . . ," began Reata.

"Aye, and what's he? I'll manage it, I tell you, or have my own throat cut tryin'. Answer me up bright and strong, Reata. Will you be my man in everything, for three months after LaFarge is dead?"

Reata, sick at heart, put back his head with a groan and answered: "Yes."

"Gimme your hand on it, then!" demanded Dickerman.

"I'll give you my word, but not my hand. My word is good enough for you," said Reata.

"I'll have your hand," said Dickerman, stretching out his grimy claw.

Reata, surrendering, felt that cold and bony grasp crushing his fingers.

"This here young adventurer, he's goin' to have some adventures now!" said Dickerman. "He's wanted trouble to play with, and I'm goin' to give him trouble enough. You're goin' to wish you could breathe fire and handle melted gold," said Dickerman, "and that's about what you're goin' to have to do. I've got your hand on it, and now that hand is goin' to be my hand as soon as I've killed LaFarge. That hand is my hand, that brain is my brain, and the soul in you is goin' to be my soul . . . to throw away, if I feel like it." He laughed. "You drivelin' fool!" cried Pop Dickerman. "This here makes me feel good, I tell you! You're one of them that calls friendship sacred, and I'll tell you that I laugh at you, because, for the sake of this here Bob Clare, I'm goin' to drag you through the bottom of the pit. I'm a man that never had a friend in my life, and I'm glad of it and proud of it. I don't need no friends, and I'm above 'em. And the soft-headed weak-wits like you gents, you're the ones that I line my nest with. That's why I sleep soft and dream of gold . . . and have it! But I've got you, and I'm goin' to use you to be worth more'n millions to me!"

It was as though Reata saw a pit of darkness illimitably deep before him. He lifted his eyes from it and stared at Dickerman. "I've had my life given once, and Clare was the man who gave it," he said. "I've got to pay him back, and this is the only way . . . and God help my soul. Now sit down . . . there. We've got to talk facts. Because I'm starting back for Rafferty Hill before the red's out of the sky."

VIII

"The Trap"

Before the red was out of the sky, Reata had started back for Rafferty Hill. He carried with him a keener sense of the dangers of the work that lay ahead of him, because Pop Dickerman had had much to say, but there were many things which Pop did not know, and above all there was that question of primary importance which Pop could not answer. Who was LaFarge? "He's only a signature on a piece of paper," Dickerman had said. "Maybe he ain't anybody real, maybe he's a shadow . . . maybe he's a corporation! We know what LaFarge can do, but we don't know what he looks like."

It seemed to Reata, as he urged the first horse in the relay up the hills from Rusty Gulch, that he was rushing back to save Bob Clare from something fatal, but unavoidable and nameless as a sliding shadow. Even Dickerman, even that king of rats, had winced when he talked of LaFarge, the light in his eyes shrinking to glittering points of malice, and of fear.

Weariness began to work in the body and the brain of Reata. Where another man would have set his teeth against it, Reata smiled a little. He did not struggle against it; he simply enlarged his spirit until he was above it.

But the way was very far. Measured in pain, the return would be five times more deadly than the journey to Rusty Gulch had been. Yet, when he reached Rafferty Hill, he would be able to use all the wiles and the powers of Dickerman's organization to protect Bob Clare. So Reata maintained his calm and denied the creeping poison of

202

fatigue and spurred on into the cool wind of the night.

There were still long miles of rough country between Reata and Rafferty Hill when that shadowy hand of LaFarge began to reach toward the cabin of Bob Clare. It began to work not long after sunrise, not in Rafferty Hill itself but close to a shanty that lay a bit back from the town in the mouth of a gorge that was choked half with stunted trees and half with boulders, relics of days when the downpouring of the spring floods had been powerful enough to tumble those mighty stones.

Why the shack had been built just here would have been hard to say. It could have been placed on higher ground nearby where the wind would have blown away the mosquitoes of the creek flats. But lodged here in the gorge, it would be well sheltered from the storms of winter. It was big enough to be called a house, because in part it was two stories with an attic above, but it was such a confused jumble of logs that it could not be termed more than a caricature of a cabin. The sides were indented, the roof sagged, but still from the chimney a rising twist of smoke announced habitation.

These things were noted by Jeff Miner with a good deal of care and of circumspection. He had left his mustang back in the brush tangle, well out of view, and now from between a pair of tree trunks he examined the big shack. He was one of those men who seem always frowning because there was a heavy line of black eyebrows ruled straight across his forehead. On the other hand, his cheeks puckered in so deeply that he seemed about to smile. Notwithstanding, frowning was probably more his nature. His long, heavily marked face, his strong-boned and spare body gave him the look of some beast of prey that eats only now and then, and always on what it kills.

After he had studied the shanty for some time, he began to divide his attention between it and his more immediate surroundings. These glances of his were those of a hunter. His head moved in small jerks because in whatever direction he looked, his eyes penetrated deeply among the rocks and trees, sifting through the shadows to find a stir of life.

Even at that, he was half surprised by the sudden appearance of a man on his left, stepping lightly around the side of a boulder. The newcomer was the exact opposite of Jeff Miner. He was not much more than middle height; he looked rather sleek as if with fat—although it might be muscle that covered him so well—and he had a pleasant but almost featureless face, a face that would be hard to remember because it would be easier to remember what it was not than what it was. He came straight up to Jeff Miner, making on the way a quick and furtive gesture with his right hand, like that of a man snapping a black snake. Jeff Miner darkened his natural scowl and made the same sign in answer.

"Who are you?" asked Miner.

"Name of Tommy Alton," said the stranger. "I'm on the job with you here."

"Yeah, and how would I make sure of that?" demanded Jeff.

"The same old way," said Tommy Alton, and took out a wallet from which he carefully extracted a one-dollar greenback. This he did not give into the hand of Miner, but held it close so that Miner could see, scrawled across the face of the note, the signature: **Gaston LaFarge.**

Miner started a trifle. It was plain that he recognized the signature, but he used up a full minute making that recognition perfect before he stepped back a little and nodded at blond-headed Tommy Alton.

"All right," said Jeff Miner. "I guess it ain't the first time that LaFarge has sent his orders out through some kid! But what's up for us to do in the shack there?"

"That ain't a shack," said Tommy Alton, grinning a little. "If you was to look at it right close, you'd see that it's a rat trap."

"Yeah? Is that so? And what kind of a rat do we trap in it?"

"A rat by the name of Bob Clare. Ever hear of him?"

"I've heard of him, and I've heard *him*," said Jeff Miner. "I've seen him, too, and he ain't the sort of an *hombre* that a man would fool too much with."

"Not unless LaFarge said to," said Tommy Alton.

"No, not unless he said to," agreed Jeff Miner. "Look here, when you last seen LaFarge, what did he . . . ?"

"I never looked LaFarge in the eye," said Tommy. "Did you?"

The tall man started a little. "Me? How would I 'a' seen him?" he asked.

At this, Alton stepped a shade closer and peered hard into the eyes of Miner. "I'd lay one buck ag'in' three that you might be LaFarge yourself!" said Alton.

"You talk like a fool!" declared Jeff Miner. But he bowed his head a little so that the dark of his brows quite obscured his eyes. "Would LaFarge be dressed like this?" He swept a hand down to indicate his coarse blue jeans, worn gray-white at the knees, but stuffed into soft, finely made riding boots. His shirt was the toughest and cheapest sort of rough cotton cloth, showing a dull checking in green and gray. His Stetson must have been a model of the first year.

This gesture of Miner's toward his clothes did not seem to convince Tommy Alton very thoroughly. He merely said: "No matter who you are, I ain't fool enough to try to corner LaFarge with questions. But whether it was you that wrote out the orders and passed them under my door at night, or not, I've gotta tell you again what they were. We're to get this here big Bob Clare down to the cabin, and we're to use Inez Clare as the bait. She's inside that shack, or she oughta be."

"What's she? A sister or something?"

"Her?" asked Tommy Alton. "The way I get it, she's his stepmother, but there's a lot more step than mother in her. We'll go in and see."

When they knocked at the door of the house, a woman's voice called out: "Who's there?"

It was Jeff Miner who pushed open the door. He and Alton could see a big kitchen that had fallen into ruin although the cooking stove seemed in fairly good repair, and at the stove stood a woman in blue gingham, a woman with a fat body and a face that had once been handsome but which was now too starved and lean and lined. It might have been the head of a man except for the massive coil of glossy black hair at the base of her neck. In a chair tilted back against the wall sat a big, handsome fellow of not much more than twenty, the dash of Southern blood showing in his olive skin and the dark of his eyes. A silken sash knotted about his hips and the bright metal embroidery on his short jacket gave the Mexican flash to his outfit. A great sombrero sat well back on his head, letting the full fine height of his forehead be seen.

He greeted the strangers by shifting his cigarette from his right hand to his left. The gun on his right thigh gave some significance to that gesture.

" 'Morning, ma'am," said Tommy Alton. "You Missus Inez Clare?"

"I'm Benjamin Clare's widow," she answered harshly. "What about it? What you want?"

"Talk," said Tommy Alton with his small, good-humored smile. He stepped close to her and showed the greenback that held the elaborate signature of Gaston LaFarge.

"Humph," grunted Mrs. Inez Clare. "That's it, is it?" She stepped back a bit to look over Alton, as though the signature that he carried had made him a bigger man, one to be surveyed from a distance of a greater dignity.

The big young man in the corner stood up and stepped with a musical jingling of golden spurs close to the strangers.

"Tony, g'wan out of the house," said Mrs. Clare, without glancing at him.

"I dunno why," Tony said in protest.

"Do as you're told," said his mother. "Get!"

Tony considered the strangers with his head back. He smiled a little and wafted a soft cloud of smoke toward them. His attitude was that of a man who merely waited for the first gesture before taking offense, but since neither Miner nor Alton appeared to notice the abruptness with which Inez Clare had treated her son, Tony strolled to the door, flung it open, and stepped out into the air without closing the door behind him.

His mother went hastily to the door and shut it. Then she faced the two. "Set down," she invited, hooking her thumb toward a pair of chairs.

"We'll talk standing, since there ain't much time," answered Tommy Alton. "You going to do the talking, or me, Miner?"

"You talk," said Miner. "I was always a better hand at listening." He stood back against the wall, and from the shadows of the corner of the room he kept his eyes flashing under his heavy brows as he glanced from one face to the other.

"News," declared Inez Clare, "is what I want, and that's what I hope you got for me,"

"I got an idea that oughta turn into news," answered Tommy Alton. "Bob Clare has to die . . . is what I hear."

"He oughta be dead already," answered the woman fiercely. "I been waiting . . . but I never hear that he's dead."

"There's a whole lot of him to die. I guess you know that," replied Alton. "But now the time has come to bump him off, and the place is here."

"Where? This house?" asked Mrs. Clare.

"Right here in this house," said Alton.

"It ain't going to be here," she answered. "That'd look pretty good, wouldn't it? Bob Clare found dead in my place? Bob Clare . . . and Tony the next in line to get the money of Ben Clare? That'd look so good that they'd hang us for it."

"All right," said Alton. "I ain't here to argue. I was told what to say and what to do. That's all. I'm through, unless Miner has something more to say."

"I got nothing to say," answered Jeff Miner slowly, thoughtfully. "Except that, if Missus Clare is going to make the winnings out of the killing of her stepson, she oughta take part of the trouble."

"Have him killed right here in this house?" said Mrs. Clare. "I ain't going to have it!"

"All right," said Alton. "I guess we slope along then, Jeff."

"Hold on!" barked the woman. "You mean that LaFarge is pulling out of the job?"

"I dunno," said Alton. "I dunno nothing about it. I ain't LaFarge to know his mind."

He turned toward the door and waved to Miner to follow him. Big Jeff Miner strode heavily across the floor, but Mrs. Clare stopped them both, exclaiming: "Listen here! How would Tony take it? What would he think? He ain't like . . . I mean, he's a queer kid. He wouldn't mind shooting it out with his brother, but he wouldn't stand for no funny business, I guess."

"Look," said Tommy Alton with a casual gesture that put

everything up to Mrs. Clare. "Here's the two of us. The deal is all set. Bob Clare can die today. But you keep on blockin' things. You can make up your mind, if that's good business, but it ain't part of my show."

"Well," she said, "what's the scheme?"

"The way I got it is the way I pass it on to you," said Tommy Alton. "It sounded pretty easy to me."

"Start talkin', then," she said.

"Well, you ever been chummy with Bob Clare?"

"Never! Who says I ever done that?"

"I didn't. But I say you're goin' to start chummin' today."

"I'll not!" exclaimed Mrs. Clare.

"You're goin' to write him a letter," said Alton. "You can write a letter, can't you?"

"To him? Yeah, if the letter was boiled in oil and poured down his throat. I could write that kind of a letter."

"You could set yourself down and write a letter to Bob Clare telling him that you're sorry for the bad feelin'. You remember he's his father's son. You wanna have good feelings more than you want Ben Clare's money. You want. . . ."

"Would I have to write a letter like that?" asked Mrs. Clare.

"You sure would. And you say that you want him to come down here and see you, and then you and him can square up the bad things that've happened and all the bad feeling."

She groaned. "Writing a letter like that would burn the fingers off my hands."

"That ain't for me to say. I show you the way, and you take it or you don't."

"He wouldn't come," said the woman.

"Sure he'd come. The idea is that Bob Clare is kind of a fool romantic dummy, you see, and, if he gets a letter from any sort of a woman askin' him to come, real important, what can he help do but come to her just the way that the letter says?"

Mrs. Clare jerked back her head and closed her eyes. A pan of beans, heating on the stove, began to burn. The odor blew unheeded across her face. At last she said: "Yeah, and his father was that sort of a fool, too. I dunno . . . maybe this would work, and he'd come. Then what?"

"Then what? Why, it's pretty easy, I'd say. I take your letter up to him, and I ride back with him to this here shack. I come in the door after him, and inside the house there's my friend, yonder, steadyin' a sawed-off shotgun. I guess that would fix Bob Clare, all right!"

"But then," said Mrs. Clare, "there'd be all the blood . . . all the blood all over the floor . . . all over everything. I've seen what a sawed-off shotgun would do."

"This house ain't your house," answered Alton, "and there ain't very many people that know you're livin' in it. After Bob is dead, wouldn't this here shack be right dry and fine for the starting of a fire that would burn him to an ash?"

Mrs. Clare looked around her rather wildly. Then, suddenly, she had made up her mind. "Wait till I fetch me some paper and a pencil, and I'll write him a letter," she said.

She was soon seated at the kitchen table, at work, her face viciously set and eager.

Jeff Miner, who had not spoken for a long time, suddenly suggested the contents of the letter, saying: "Write to him that the seein' of your boy, how dog-gone like he is to his father, and how like that makes your boy to him . . . write him that lookin' at your boy is what makes you scribble to him, hopin' to get together one happy family, sort of."

Mrs. Clare, at this, stared fixedly at Jeff Miner, for a moment, and then nodded.

"You," she said huskily, pointing her pencil at Miner,

"you got brains. You got the real kind of brains that keeps hell full and runnin'."

The letter, written with a rapid pencil, with a pressure that dug the lead deeply into the paper was soon finished and signed with a flourish.

"It'll fetch him," said Mrs. Clare savagely. "That idea that Miner had . . . that's what'll fetch him. A happy family, eh?" And she put back her head and laughed.

"You ain't holding back now, are you?" asked Tommy Alton, rather in curiosity than in disgust.

"Holding back? Now that I've made up my mind, I can't wait to see the thing start working," she answered. "Go on, and go fast. But when you talk to him, remember that every Clare, though they may look damn' stupid and careless, has got brains under the surface."

Tommy Alton went to the door. He said to Jeff Miner: "Remember to shoot for the middle, eh? If you brought that riot gun with you, the way the thing was planned, Bob Clare is just as good as dead right now.

IX

"Half-Brothers"

Tommy Alton rode up to Rafferty Hill to get Bob Clare, who was just as good as dead—and still miles separated Reata, reeling with weariness in the saddle, from the mining town.

As Alton jogged into the town, he could survey the stir of life up the creek, and then the swirlings of the main street until he got up the little hill itself to the cabin of the man he wanted. Tom Alton dismounted and tied his mustang to the rack in front of the cabin. Before he tapped at the door, he gave a glance around him at the sunlight, and the trees, and the shadow, and the big white clouds that floated through the blue of the sky, and Alton considered this beauty and this freshness with a great deal of thought because he knew that he was going in to face a man capable of thinking quickly and shooting straight.

For that matter, Alton was a sure and rapid shot on his own account, but he had fought with guns so many times that he was always ready to credit the other fellow with enough skill to make the day precarious. He tapped at the door and was told to come in. The interior of the cabin was shadowy, when he pushed the door open, but he could see well enough the big fellow with magnificent shoulders who sat at the little central table. There was a rifle leaning beside his chair, and he wore revolvers. It seemed to Alton, all in all, that he had never seen a better picture of a fighting man.

A brown-eyed, smiling man stood up from the table. "Are you coming in, or am I coming out?" asked Bob Clare.

Alton liked that. Tommy Alton was the sort of a man who could appreciate a friend. He liked the way Bob Clare looked, he liked the way he talked, but he was not one whit less determined that Clare was to die. So he said: "I was just bringin' you up a letter. You know Inez Clare, don't you? Well, it's a letter from your mother."

He put that word in with malice aforethought. It would qualify the thoughts that Bob Clare might have about the Mexican woman who had been trying for his life in order to wipe him out of the path of his half-brother. Mother is a word that has a certain value, even if it is only a false one.

Bob Clare seemed not at all startled. "She's writing to me, is she? Then there must be the devil and all in her brain," he commented.

"She's a hard one, all right," said Alton. "The funny thing is that she sure used to give you the rough side of her tongue, all right. But she seemed to've changed sudden."

Bob Clare looked earnestly at him, asked him to sit down, and then opened the letter. Alton was already smoking a cigarette when his host looked up from that reading. "She says . . . you know what she says?" asked Clare.

"Sure. She read it to me. She wondered could I put in any better words," answered Alton frankly. For he knew that a man can tell a better lie when there are grains of truth in it.

"What I wonder is," said Clare, "that the old girl could ever think that I'd be fool enough to come down to her place." His brown eyes glared with yellow fire as he added: "She doesn't think that I've forgotten a pack of things, does she?"

"Aw, I don't know what she's forgotten," answered Alton. "You know how it is. She told me that she wanted the best blood out of your heart, most of the time, but lately she'd taken to changing her mind."

"She'd never change her mind," said Bob Clare. "A wildcat might stop hungering for red blood, but Inez would never stop hungering for my life."

"Yeah? Is it as tough as all that?" asked Alton carelessly. "Well, I'll be sashaying along then."

He got to the door, and, as he stood in the brightness of it, Clare called to him: "Wait a minute. D'you think that she's really changed?"

"Why, I dunno," answered Alton. "I ain't particular familiar with her."

"What reason is there for her changing?" demanded Clare.

"Her? I dunno. Except that she's pretty sick. Kind of caved in."

"She is? Really ill?"

"You know how it gets the Mexicans. They go quick when the consumption knocks into them," said Tommy Alton.

The brown, fine eyes of Bob Clare widened, and he came out quickly through the door into the open. Hatless and half-dressed as he was, with moccasins instead of boots on his feet, still he seemed larger than the normal man, there was such a greatness of spirit and stir about him.

"Consumption?" muttered Clare. "You mean she's got that?"

"Yeah. She's kind of all caved in," said Alton. "Well, so long, Clare. Damn me if I blame you for not wanting to see her. She's sure a sight, just now."

"Hold on. Stop a minute!" commanded Clare. And he laid the grip of his powerful hand on the shoulder of Alton.

What Clare felt startled him decidedly. For the digging tips of his fingers sank not into pulpy fat, as the rounded outlines of Alton suggested, but they slipped and slid over a big, rubbery cordage of muscles, hidden under the skin. Alton looked like an overly fat man, almost a weakling. That touch revealed him as a giant of prodigious strength.

"If she's really sick," said Clare, all the gentleness in his nature rousing to the call, "I'll be glad to see her. I'll *want* to see her. But what could be in her head to send for me?"

"It's the kid, I suppose," said Alton. "I dunno, but I guess it's the kid. You know how it is. You're a pretty tough *hombre*, Clare. And she's raised up Tony to hate you. Tony ain't a bad kind of a fellow. The minute his ma is dead, he'd be apt to make a beeline for you and start a fight, and I guess she knows that. She wants you two to be friends before she passes out. There's something like that in her old head, I suppose. She's dying, d'you see, and death sort of softens up the hardest of them."

214

"Dying? I thought she'd live forever, like the devil!" exclaimed Bob Clare. Then his mind was made up. "I'll be with you in two minutes," he declared.

He moved fast, kicking off his moccasins, jumping his boots onto his feet. The activity of the man was such that Alton, shrewdly observing, made out that there was never a moment during this process of dressing, when he would have Clare at a complete disadvantage. Otherwise, it would have been a great temptation to jerk out a Colt and finish the job on the spot.

However, Alton was the sort of a man who, like a hunting beast, prefers surety to chance. Now big Bob Clare was out of the cabin and, quickly, on the back of a horse which he took from the shed behind the shack.

That was the way they rode across Rafferty Hill and over the hollow and up the gorge to the shack where Inez and her son were staying. They dismounted before the door, and the horses were tethered to the old, eaten beam of the hitch rack with deep hollows under it that had been pawed out by horses of two long generations of men.

"Oldish kind of a place," said Bob Clare, as he looked up along the front of the house.

There was no suspicion in him. Tom Alton noted this with a grin of amusement that did not appear in a single line of his face. People had found it hard to circumvent Bob Clare, but the gunman wondered a bit at the reputation of the big fellow. Clare might be both strong and brave, but certainly he was not cunning in any sense of the word. When he saw Bob Clare before the door, he stepped swiftly in behind him, keeping a bit to the side.

When that door opened, according to the plan, what should greet Clare was a frightful blast of fire and lead that would lift him, at a single blow, across the threshold of his life into the long eternity. And Tom Alton would be just as sufficiently near to catch the backward falling body and cast it forward so that the blood would flow on the boards of the kitchen floor. And then fire would lick up, with its greedy mouth, both the boards and the blood that soaked them afterward.

It should be a perfect crime. There was nothing, it seemed to Alton, to prevent the thing from going through, but he was not too confident, and he was not blind. Only he could hardly have been prepared for the thing that followed. No man could have been.

For when the rap on the door came, instead of a voice—that of Inez Clare—the door itself was suddenly opened, and on the threshold stood none other than tall Tony Clare. When he saw Bob Clare, his half-brother, before him, realization took him like a flame in one tenth of a second that simply enabled Tom Alton to see, over the shoulders of Tony and Bob, the sinister form and the ready shotgun of Jeff Miner in an obscure, opposite corner of the kitchen.

Then Tony with a yell cried—"It's you!"—and he grabbed for a gun.

Bob Clare had no time to do anything but reach for the gun hand of Tony, who pitched hard back to pull himself away from the restraining grasp. That pull jerked the fighters over the entrance into the room. Alton, running in behind them, had a glimpse of Inez Clare seated at the table, motionless, grinning wide and sour, with her elbows on the table and her chin in her hand.

Bob Clare must have seen enough to know that the message that had brought him here was utterly false. At any rate, when he was tugged forward into the room by a grasp that he dared not relax, he tried for freedom by whipping over a short, hooked right that landed neatly on the chin of Tony. It was a pretty punch, well devised and cleverly landed. The trouble was that Tony had a jaw of steel and was going away from the blow. All it served to do was to redouble the force with which Tony was diving backward.

He pulled Bob with him. They struck the floor and rolled over and over against the side wall, which was struck with a heavy blow. It was Bob who happened to hit the wall, and there he lay on the floor, stretched senseless, while Tony gathered himself to his knees.

"Get out of the way, kid," snarled Jeff Miner, "while I finish the bastard!"

Tony jerked his head about and saw the executioner standing ready with the gun.

"Put down that shotgun, you fool!" he shouted. "This gent is goin' to die, but it's me that's goin' to do the killing, and the fight's gotta be fair and square! Nobody so much as point at him. He's my meat!"

X

"Reata's Return"

Not long after Bob Clare fell senseless in the shack, Reata came into Rafferty Hill. The bright bay mare that carried him was a-foam from the fierceness of his riding. Reata was so tired that he kept smiling constantly. In the back of his brain, in the base of it just above the spinal column, there was a steady ache, a numbness that spread forward through his scalp and stretched a band of coldness across his forehead. Below the knees and hips there was a constant ache, and the middle of his body was taut with the pain of ten thousand torsions as the wild mustangs had bucked and twisted and fought their way through the wilderness, carrying him.

As he slanted into Rafferty Hill, he looked back and saw on the brow of the western hill a quick flickering of light, a thing almost imperceptible except to an understanding eye. But the glance of Reata found the thing and understood. Pop Dickerman's messages were flying through the air. The long arm and the ratty, bright brain of Pop Dickerman now fought on his side! He got a savage comfort out of that, and he was rallying a little as he sent the bay mare pounding into the stable from which he had started in the first place.

Broad-faced, thick-necked Harry Quinn came out of the shadows, muttering as Reata dismounted and threw the reins to a stable hand. With Harry Quinn moved another man, slenderly built, beautiful to see as a cat, and with an air of feline strangeness and pride about him.

The stable boy who took the horse away looked back with a grin, for it was early in the morning to see a man drunk, and drunk was what Reata seemed to be, with Harry Quinn supporting him powerfully on one side and that slender, sleek-stepping fellow on the other.

"Look-it, Salvio!" said Harry Quinn. "We could take and tie him in knots. There ain't much to Reata just now."

Gene Salvio glanced over the drawn face of Reata and said nothing, but there was a half-hungry gleam in his eyes nevertheless.

"If there was danger in us," said Salvio at last, "he wouldn't be here, I guess. And if he was here, he'd have us both inside the loops of his rope."

It was a strange admission from the lips of this proud and fierce Gene Salvio, and Reata said: "Quit the talking, Gene. I'm glad to be on your side of the fence. When I was on the other side of it, it was dreaming about you that used to wake me up in the middle of the night with a cold sweat on my face."

"Yeah?" Salvio said, much pleased. "Aw, well, that's finished. Only I'd sure like to know what sort of a deal you had to make with the old man to get him to switch over to you."

"I had to pay high. I had to pay as high as the sky," said Reata. His legs were still sagging under him at the knees. They would gain more strength later on. "Get the mare and the dog for me, will you?" he said to Quinn. "Get Sue and Rags, Harry. We're going over to look in on Bob Clare. There's where our job is."

Quinn went off. Reata slid down on a sack of crushed barley and leaned his shoulders against the wall. He started to make a cigarette, but the paper tore in his trembling fingers that had been tugging and straining for so many hours against the hard mouths of galloping mustangs. Salvio, with a queer look, took the makings from Reata and with a single twist of his sure, swift fingers built the smoke.

"How far did you have to go after you left Rafferty Hill?" asked Salvio. "How far did Pop ride to meet you on the way?"

"He didn't ride to meet me. I went all the way to Rusty Gulch and saw Pop with his cats and his rats," answered Reata.

"Hold on!" exclaimed Gene Salvio. "You mean that you been all the way, and back . . . as quick as this? I don't want to call you a liar, Reata."

Reata sighed. "I'm pretty tired, Gene, but don't call me a liar."

Salvio began to stare. He took hold of the sunken eyes of Reata and the steady pull at the corners of his mouth. "Aye," said Salvio. "You've done it. Nobody else would ever. . . . But what the hell? You're always doing what nobody else could do."

Reata looked up at him with vague eyes. The long-bodied roan mare with the ugly head came out, dragging her hoofs across the floor in her long-geared walking step. Little Rags came out from beside her shambling feet and leaped to the lap and then to the shoulder of his master, where he reared up and, with one forepaw resting on top of the hat of Reata, whined and shuddered with his consummate joy. His tail kept lashing and his free forepaw kept making odd motions of ecstasy in the air. As for the mare, with her flattened ears and her head thrust out at the end of her scrawny neck, she seemed about to go for Reata with her teeth, but she merely tried to thrust her muzzle into his face, whinnying softly.

Reata caught her by the mane and pulled himself to his feet, then he swayed into the saddle as Harry Quinn and Gene Salvio mounted their own horses. The three of them rode out of the stable and across Rafferty Hill. No one who looked at them could have suspected that the roan mare was worth ten of the fine, shining, dancing horses such as Quinn and Salvio rode. Certainly no one would have dreamed of comparing the rather small and drooping figure of Reata with the slender and dapper alertness of Salvio or with the thick-chested strength of Harry Quinn.

Reata made no effort. He allowed his body to jounce loosely in the saddle, and with every moment, he knew, in spite of the numb agony of his tortured body, that he was recuperating little by little. However, he would soon be able to sleep. He had only to get back to Bob Clare in the cabin in order to relax completely, with Quinn and Salvio standing guard.

Quinn and Salvio? Yes, and there were others. Two men who passed them slowed up their horses with inquiring looks, but Salvio waved them aside.

"How many of you fellows are there in town?" asked Reata.

"How many of us are there?" answered Salvio. "You gotta remember, Reata, that you're one of us now. Aw, I dunno how many Pop has called in. Plenty, I guess. Because it's goin' to be a big job, Reata, ain't it? Who lies on the other side of the fence now?"

Reata lifted his weary head a little and stared into the handsome face of Salvio. "LaFarge," he said.

He saw the blow strike home into the very soul of Salvio; and they rode the rest of the way in the silence that Reata wanted. Only, now and again, he could hear the hushed murmuring of Harry Quinn, as that sturdy fellow tasted the name again: "LaFarge?" As well speak of the devil in this part of the world!

They came up the hill to the cabin and found the door ajar—sure proof that Clare must be inside. So Reata dismounted and stepped with uncertain foot across the threshold, saying: "All right, Bob. I'm back here with some friends."

There was no answer. The emptiness and the damp cold of the shadows alone had received his voice. He looked helplessly around him, as Quinn and Salvio pressed in at his shoulders.

"Where's he gone?" asked Quinn. "Where's this *hombre* that we gotta look after?"

"Maybe in the horse shed behind . . . ," began Salvio.

"No. He's not here . . . and I told him to stay . . . I told him not to budge," muttered Reata.

He went back to the door. The heat of the sun felt weak as moonlight against his face, and there was a chill in the stir of the thin, pure air. Faint noises, muffled shouts of command, curses, drifted to him from the town and the mines along the creek. "He's gone," murmured Reata in disbelief. "I'm too late. I'm beaten. And that means that Pop's beaten, too. But maybe we can run down the fellows who grabbed him. Spread

221

out, Gene. Harry, get all of Dickerman's agents working. Find out if Bob Clare was seen anywhere this morning. Everybody knows him. If he's been seen, then come back and get me. I'm going to sleep."

At that word, such an aching flood of exhaustion poured over him that he barely made out the voices of his companions answering. He turned into the cabin, dropped face down on the nearest bunk, drew one groaning breath of ecstasy, and then was fast asleep.

The mare started grazing in front of the cabin door, and Rags hopped up on the bunk and lay down at the head of the master. In that way, there was a sentinel placed in front of the house, and inside it. This double system of mounting guard was perfectly well known to both the horse and the dog.

XI

"The Proud Young Man"

More than an hour went by before a rider sped straight up the slope of the little hill toward the front of the cabin. As it became clear that he was headed for this place, the roan mare stamped and snorted. She turned an anxious head and whinnied the sort of a call that would have brought any wild mustang's colt to its feet out of the tall grass. What it accomplished now was to set Rags frantically at work on the wakening of his master. He whined, and he barked sharp and small, but he drew only a groan for a reply. Weary nature had posted too strong a guard over the sleeping senses of the man.

Rags caught at the brim of the hat that Reata had not pulled from his head, but, tugging at the hat brim, accomplished nothing. Rags pulled at the next thing—the ear of his master. He caught it very gently in his needle-sharp teeth and whined as he drew back against the flesh. At that, finally, Reata roused himself and sat up, moaning with exhaustion.

Then, in a moment, hearing the rattling of the hoofs of the approaching rider, Reata mastered his need of sleep, and drove the ache of it out of his brain and winked his eyes clear. He stood up just as Gene Salvio pulled up at the door and flashed down out of the saddle.

"We've spotted a place where he was seen ridin' down close to the creek, headed out toward the gorge," said Salvio. "Come on, Reata, and see if you can pick up the trail for us. We can't make out a confounded thing . . . ground's all covered with rock and small stones."

Reata nodded. His own senses were, ordinarily, some shades sharper and keener than the senses of white men usually are. But sleep had dulled them now. Luckily he could call in an auxiliary force far more acute; he could use Rags. So, first, he took the little mongrel to the horse shed, at the entrance to which Rags quickly was put on the hoof prints of the horse of the missing man. Those prints Rags followed around to the front of the house. He quickly found a line down the slope of the hill.

"He's got it," said Reata. "We can take it easy now, boys. Rags is on the job, and he'll do his tricks for us."

"That there damn' dog," said Harry Quinn who had ridden up to join them, "how many times has he saved your neck, Reata?"

Reata grinned suddenly. "More times than I have fingers," he replied.

"And how many times have you saved *his* hide?" asked Salvio, as the three of them rode after the twinkling form of Rags.

"I don't know," said Reata. "Being partners, we don't keep count of little things like that."

The other two exchanged glances.

"Hi!" exclaimed Gene Salvio. "He's lost it!"

They were coming toward the mouth of the gorge, well away from the town, where the ravine was choked with vast boulders and scattering stunted trees. And here Rags began to run in rapid, irregular circles, cutting plainly for the lost sign.

"He's lost it," said Reata, "but don't push in with our horses and ball up the scent for him. You take a fellow like Rags, and he likes to work out his problems for himself. If you crowd him too much, he'll just sit down and let you tackle the thing by yourselves."

"He's lost it," answered Harry Quinn. "And if there's LaFarge, or any part of LaFarge, at the other end of the trail, I'm damned glad that Rags has missed."

It was a good bit earlier than this that, in the shack where Inez Clare lived for the time being, Bob Clare recovered his senses and found, to his bewilderment, that the man whom he had glimpsed in the cabin had not yet poured lead into him. Right beside him, and over him, young Tony, his half-brother, was arguing fiercely.

"He belongs to me!" declared Tony. "I put him out. I slammed him!"

"The side of the house slammed him," answered Jeff Miner. "That was what put him out. Except for that, he would have tied you in knots, it looked like to me."

"It looked like to you, did it?" said Tony savagely. "And who are you, I wanna know?"

"Me?" said Jeff Miner, his head tilting down and his eyes glittering out of the shadow. "Me? I'm a gent that would like to take you apart and see how the stuffing is packed inside of you."

"You would, would you?" snarled Tony. "Lemme tell you, brother, that by the look of you, I see that you're my meat, and damn' me if I ain't hungry."

"Come on and get your food, then, if you can shoot the venison or even whittle a slice off it with your knife," challenged Miner.

"Right now!" cried Tony, leaping to his feet.

But his mother's grim voice broke in: "Steady, Tony. Steady, son. There ain't going to be no fighting inside of this here shack."

"I'm to lie down and take it, am I?" demanded Tony. "I'm to be a sneakin' sort of a coyote, am I?"

"There's a whole lot of free air and free ground outdoors," said Inez Clare. "And there's a whole lot of time to come. There's thousands of years of it. But we've got another kind of a job on our hands, just now. Back away from that crooked fool on the floor. He's comin' to!"

The announcement caused Tony to swing about suddenly. He turned with a gun in either hand, saying: "You gents behind me . . . don't make no move to throw lead into this *hombre!*" He leaned over his half-brother.

Bob Clare pushed himself up on one hand, and his brown eyes looked deeply into the darker eyes of Tony. Then the half-breed leaned and snaked Bob's gun out of its holster.

"Get up," said Tony. "We gotta do some talkin' together."

Bob Clare rose to his feet silently. With his back to the wall, he looked over the three men, and then he stared at the woman. Oddly enough, it was her expression that made him surrender all hope. The men might be handled by force or by craft, but it would be hard to reckon with the uneasily shifting

225

light in the eyes of Inez Clare.

She came over toward him with a swaggering, slow step, her hands on her hips, and confronted Bob. The excess of her insolence and her hatred made her look him greedily up and down.

"You're the papa's boy, are you?" said Inez. "Well, even if his ghost was to stand up and start yapping for you, it couldn't do no good now! We got you, Bobbie!"

He said nothing to this. He preferred to look away from her toward the faces of the men. She snarled another word or two and then turned away from him.

"What are you waiting for?" she demanded fiercely. "You got him, ain't you? Then why don't you get rid of him?"

"Because I ain't done talkin', and I ain't done thinkin'," said Tony.

"You?" shouted his mother. "Hey, are grown-up men going to be stopped by a young brat like you? Knock him out of the way, Jeff, and see if you can put enough lead inside the hide of that fellow Bob Clare to sink him and to hold him down!"

At this, Tony did a strange thing. He stepped back until his shoulders were against the breast of Bob. He was a shade taller than Bob, but slighter, and a man's strength had not yet toughened in him. More important than all else, Tony still held two guns, with which he was patently willing to cover the other men. He said: "This here has gotta be talked out man to man. You gents understand me?"

Jeff Miner, his ugly face lowering, said nothing. But Tommy Alton murmured: "Aw, what's the use? If the kid's goin' to act this way, we gotta humor him, don't we?"

"Tony! You're talkin' like a fool, and you're acting like a fool!" shouted his mother. "You're throwin' everything away!"

"I ain't throwin' nothin' away," said Tony. "What am I throwin' away?"

"What? Tell me what these two gents were sent here for! Tell me what they're doin', will you? Tell me why I got the great LaFarge into this here deal, will you? To get rid of that . . . that thing behind you. And now you're playin' the half-wit and holdin' up the game. Tony, stand away from Bob and let him take his medicine. You're throwin' away your own chances!"

The eyes of Tony grew a little dreamy, and his head tilted back bit by bit. He smiled on the three, and in that smile there was an increased resemblance between him and Bob Clare.

"I'm throwin' away murder," said Tony.

"Murder?" screeched Inez Clare. "Listen to him! Alton . . . Jeff . . . listen to him! As though Bob ain't tried to have *us* bumped off, a hundred times . . . and now Tony talks about murder?"

"You call it what you want," said Tony. "I won't have no murder. Not in my house!"

"Your house? It ain't your house," said Jeff Miner.

"Nobody else claims it, and, while I'm livin' in it, it's my house," said Tony. "There ain't goin' to be no murder in it!"

They could only stare at him. For obviously Tony was the pivot upon which the entire plan turned. It was Tony who would inherit the money of the dead Clare the moment Bob was out of the world. And Jeff Miner and Tom Alton, no matter how furious they might be, were able to see that Tony would have to be treated with care and even with a certain amount of deference.

Tom Alton suddenly said: "Look here. You can put up your guns, Tony. We'll give you our word. Nothing is going to happen to Bob till you say so. Does that suit you?"

"What are you talkin' about?" shouted Inez to Alton.

"Leave him be. Leave what he says go," directed Jeff Miner, with a knowing look at the woman. "We'll give our word that nothin' happens till the kid says for us to start it."

"That's straight, is it?" asked Tony eagerly.

"Sure, it's straight," answered Alton. "We'll just put a rope on Bob to make sure that he stays in the stall. That's all."

Tony stepped away from the captive. He looked at Bob without kindness, but with a certain relief in his eyes.

"All right," he said. "Hog-tie him, if you wanna. I don't care about that. Only there ain't goin' to be no murder in my house!"

That was why they tied Bob Clare hand and foot.

And because the nature of Tony was proud and stubborn, because he was a thoroughly spoiled young man, Jeff, Tom Alton, and Inez Clare had to argue with Tony till dusk before they could manage to hit on a means of disposing of the prisoner.

XII

"Searching for Sign"

There was small wonder that Rags lost the scent in the midst of the gorge. Even a wild wolf or a hunting wildcat might well have missed it, but not even a starving wolf in winter would have shown the patience of the small dog. Shallow rills of water, washing over the rocks, gave a hundred chances for the losing of scent altogether; and the rocks themselves had been exposed, now, for hours to a burning sun where it seemed impossible that the slightest trace of a trail could remain. Yet

Rags kept laboring.

As for Gene Salvio and Harry Quinn, they were thoroughly discouraged. They knew of many wonderful things that the little dog had accomplished, but this work seemed hopeless. It was the faith of the master alone that remained as patient as the endurance of the dog. It was he who called out softly to little Rags, from time to time, when the mongrel paused, dead beaten from scrambling here and there. When Rags heard the voice, his tail slashed right and left like mad, and he went to his work again with a full zest. Sometimes he would run a few steps with his nose almost rubbing over the surface of the rocks. Again he would lift his head a trifle and seem to be reading messages that rode upon the wind.

This was bitter work to try the will power of dog and man. But whereas both Gene Salvio and Harry Quinn were merely greatly bored, the tenseness never went out of the face and the eyes of Reata.

"Think of it, Gene," he said to Salvio at one point. "While we're inching along this trail, maybe Bob is being rushed a hundred miles away from here."

"You like that gent. You like him a whole lot," said Salvio. "How much cash do you get out of this job, Reata?"

"Cash?" said Reata vaguely. "Not cash, old son. It only gives me a chance to . . . well, to pay off part of a debt."

"Yeah, I know," growled Salvio. "There ain't anything practical about you, Reata. There's Harry Quinn with a rag around his head from the night when he tried to stick you in your sleep. You don't seem to carry much of a grudge ag'in' him. There ain't much hate in you, Reata. But that gent Bob Clare, that dropped Harry . . . why, you'll spend the rest of your life tryin' to pay him back for a thing that any decent partner would do for a friend, if he could. There's too damned much gratitude in you, Reata. It kind of softens you up."

Reata said nothing. He considered this remark for a time, and then, as he often did when he came to a thing which he could not answer, his idle fingers pulled out from his coat pocket the slender length of that rope, pencil-thin, harder than rawhide, more supple than water, and he began to make the length of rope form figures in the air. He made it run over the ground in single and double loops; he made the loop rise quivering into the air, spinning with incredible speed; he made it descend again over his head and rise once more until the trembling circle of the noose seemed to be flying on invisible wings. Or, again, with a noose no larger than the grasp of a hand, he caught up small stones and made them fly to a distance, or tossed them into the air and caught them. All of these things he performed with a perfect carelessness, since his mind was occupied with other matters.

It was not that he seriously considered that he was engaged in a work of folly. It was simply because the mention of Bob Clare had made him see the big fellow again, more clearly, the laughing face and the haunted eyes. Once more he saw the handful of bills extended to him; once more he seemed to select a single greenback from the lot—as a means by which he might remember the moment.

That dreary length of day began to close, and, as the evening approached and the fires burned up in the west and then circled the entire horizon, Reata felt the last hope running out of him. Only one thing kept him from surrendering now, and that was that Rags was still busily at work, following the trail for a few steps, losing it, circling for half an hour in a small compass, stepping delicately until he discovered, once again, a fine-spun clue that could be followed.

Then as the darkness commenced to close—long after Salvio and Quinn had demanded that the waiting stop—little

Rags suddenly straightened away and ran ahead through the brush and the boulders, and across the wash of a little rivulet until he brought the men to the verge of a clearing in the center of which stood a two-story shack composed of really crazy log-work.

One eye of light gleamed from a window of the place. There was just enough illumination in the sky to show, rising against it, a pale drifting of smoke that poured out of the chimney. Rags, with the face of this building in view, dropped on his belly and stretched like a dead thing along the ground.

For the first time that day, Reata touched the little dog. He dropped to one knee beside him, and ran the tips of his fingers repeatedly over the hot body. At that caress, a tremor of pleasure ran through Rags. He was rewarded.

Reata murmured over his shoulder: "Get the horses, Harry. Take 'em back into the woods. This is the place, all right, and Rags knows that Bob Clare is in there, dead or alive. Gene, you cut around behind the house and take a look-see. I'm going to try the front of it and make out what's going on inside, if I can. Either of you know anything about this place?"

Neither of them had so much as dreamed that a house existed in this hollow.

"All right," said Reata. "If nobody knows about it, nobody knows anything good about it. Things that aren't known are mostly crooked, I guess. And Bob Clare's in hell right here under our noses. Go ahead, Salvio. Be back here inside of fifteen minutes and tell me what you've found out."

Reata himself, with a whisper, made Rags stay flat on the ground. For his own part, he went straight up to the front of the house. If there were danger inside it, most men would have skulked, but Reata walked as freely and carelessly as though he were approaching home. He did not hear voices until he was almost at the front door of the place.

And then he was struck motionless, for what he heard was the voice of Bob Clare, exclaiming: "I'm not talking!"

An unknown voice answered: "It ain't much talking that you need to do. Don't play the fool now! But the other night there was a gent that pulled you out of a tight fix down there in the gambling rooms of that joint. All I want to know is had you hired that gent to guard your back?"

"No," said the voice of Bob Clare. "I didn't hire him. He just happened to be a there . . . a decent man. Ever meet one, you fellows?"

Someone laughed—it was a woman's laughter. That was the only answer to Clare.

Reata, stepping closer still, found that he could look through the lighted window. It had been boarded over, but there were some ample cracks through which the light was shining, and one of those same cracks gave him a view of what was inside.

The first face he saw was the dark, gloomily savage countenance of Jeff Miner, and, since it was framed alone in the lantern light, at the first moment, it made Reata think of what he had said to Salvio and Quinn. For if this house was playing the part of hell on earth, then the dark-faced man was certainly the chief devil in it.

Moving his head from side to side, Reata discovered most of the remainder of the room. He saw the shrewish, embittered face of Inez, and the strangely featureless head of Tommy Alton. He saw Tony, tall and graceful and brilliant in his semi-Mexican outfit. Last of all, he made out Bob Clare —alive!

He was in danger. Yes, he was tied hand and foot and belt to a chair—the best of all ways of tying a man securely, perhaps—and, although he maintained his habitual smile, his face was worn and his eyes deeply hollowed, as though by exhaustion. Well, he had as much reason, say, as a snow-bogged moose that must stand all day because the wolves have encircled it, waiting for it to sink down.

An insane impulse came over Reata to dash the door open and leap in on the scene. Instead, he turned and slipped back to the place where he had left Rags.

Harry Quinn was already there, on the shadowy edge of the woods, and he muttered: "How is it, Reata? The whole day for nothin', eh?"

Reata pointed to a quick-stepping figure that was approaching them.

"Ask Salvio," he suggested.

Gene Salvio, coming up at a gliding run, breathed: "He's in there, Reata. Harry, Rags was on the trail, all right."

Quinn consulted his thoughts in silence, for a moment, hearing Salvio say: "That ten-headed rattlesnake, that Jeff Miner . . . he's in there, too. And a kind of a gent with a smooth mug. Reata, both of them gents belong to LaFarge, and that means that they're hand-picked. And then there's the young gent. That's three of 'em. Now, how in hell, are we to pry Bob Clare loose from 'em? How are we going to reach inside that house without getting Bob Clare killed the first shot they fire?"

Reata sat down on the ground, cross-legged, with his back to a tree, his hands throwing ceaselessly into the air something that looked like a small and snaky shadow. It was that same thin-stranded lariat that was constantly in his fingers, so constantly that he seemed to think with it.

At last he said: "What's the answer, Harry?"

"There ain't any answer," declared Harry Quinn.

"How about you, Gene?"

"I dunno," answered Salvio. "Listen to me, Reata.

Nobody's got a brain like yours. But remember that Jeff Miner is in there, and maybe the smooth-faced gent is even slicker than Jeff. They're LaFarge men."

"They'll kill Bob Clare, the first move we make from the outside," said Reata. "That means that one of us has to be on the inside. That means I've got to get into that house. Well, that ought to be easy . . . there's an attic story over the kitchen where they're all sitting around. You two get close and wait. When you hear my yell, smash in that kitchen door and start shooting." That was all he said.

He stood up and left them without another word, and, as they watched his form dissolve in the thick of the night, Harry Quinn muttered: "It's better to be on the right side of the fence, and the right side is always Reata's side. But tell me, Gene. How's he goin' to do anything to the gang in there? How's he goin' to handle 'em and save Bob Clare, even if he gets inside?"

Salvio answered: "Why, you know how it is. Where the rest of us leave off thinking, Reata just begins."

XIII

"The Trap Door"

Reata went around the house as fast as he could go, while still scanning with care the means of egress. He found what he wanted at the back of the old building—a beam that projected out from the edge of the roof, perhaps used as a hoist when the place was being built.

Over that beam, at the very first cast, Reata lodged the noose of his lariat, and a moment later he was handing himself up the slender line, walking the logs of the side wall at the same time with the tips of his boots. Once on the roof, it was easy for him to slip through a dormer window and into a room where the air was laden with a faint odor of rats.

Beneath him, he could hear the sounding of the voices of the people in the kitchen, and now he pushed ahead with his eyes closed and his hands extended before him. That is far the best way of moving through darkness, instead of straining the eyes where nothing can be seen. He found the door, in that manner, and out of it he stepped into a hall. Still progressing toward the voices underneath, he found another door, and beyond this were the rough, sharply angled timbers of the roof rafters.

The voices were directly beneath him now, and, through the darkness, rays and long slashes of brightness struck upward, touching the rafters and the crosspieces with staring eyes of light. One thing above all else struck the eye of Reata. And that was a square, irregularly sketched in broken streaks and points of light upon the under surface of the roof. Reata located the source of that square and found that it was what he had hoped—a trap door that gave down upon the middle of the kitchen floor, and very useful, of course, insofar as kitchen supplies could be cached up here in the attic and immediately reached at any time by means of a ladder.

The door was there, but it was closed, the light soaking only through the chinks and crevices around the edge of it. The great question was whether or not Reata could lift that door and give himself free access to the kitchen without making a sound to attract the attention of the people beneath him. There was still another danger. Unless the door had been opened recently, dust was likely to have accumulated around the edges of it, and a fall of dust through the lantern light beneath was sure to bring attention.

So, with his fingers prying around the sides of the door, Reata gained a handhold and at once started to lift. He put on that pressure very slowly, for by infinite slowness he hoped that not a creak would come from the strained wood and that not a groan could be wrung from even the rustiest hinges. One thing gave him some hope, and that was the tense tone of the conversation beneath him. For he heard the voices of the tall man, Jeff Miner, saying grimly: "Now we gotta have the showdown, and we gotta settle things. We been waitin' too long already . . . I'm sick of it. Listen here to me, Tony. Are you goin' to talk sense, or ain't you?"

"I'll talk turkey," said Tony.

If they were talking turkey—it must mean life or death to Bob Clare—in that case a few little outside disturbances would not easily be noticed. Therefore, Reata increased his pressure on the edge of the door. Yet he still used such caution that the long and painful strain made his arms ache to the shoulders. He had to set his teeth and then smile as he had been smiling a great deal during the last day and a half. But what could any pain of the muscles be compared with the long-drawn, grinding agony of nerves that clamored for rest? As he had endured that torment, so he endured this.

If the brain of Reata had spoken audibly, just then, it would have been heard repeating, over and over again: "Bob Clare . . . Bob Clare . . . Bob Clare!" For the name of the man was haunting him, beating in his ears. Death, which had reached for him in Clare's cabin, was now extending its hand toward his rescuer. Could he in turn avert the touch of it?

Still drawing the trap door upward, he soothed himself by repeating silently, over and over, that fate would not let him fail, but that it was preordained that he must succeed. For he had paid the price; he had made his effort; he had rallied strong helpers to work at his side, and, furthermore, he had bought the brain of Pop Dickerman to aid him. Aye, and at what a price!

Now he had the door raised almost straight up. There was no longer that agonizing strain on his shoulders. A wide square of light shot upward through the gap that had been made in the ceiling. It seemed to Reata that light was almost as strong as the sun. He had to steady his excited nerves a little before he could realize that the up-striking light was, as a matter of fact, very dim—only such as extended through the porous top of the lantern that stood on the top of the central table in the kitchen, almost directly beneath him.

The heat of the cookery, the rich odors of it, kept stealing up to his nostrils. Then came a sudden exclamation, Tony crying out: "What the devil dropped that dust on me?"

He was there by the table. His wide sombrero jerked back, and he stared straight upward into the face of Reata.

A frightful tenseness, a frightful realization that he had failed at this last moment when the door of success was literally opening under his hand—that was what froze Reata. Then he understood that what was so very clear to him, looking into the light, was all obscured to Tony Clare, looking away from it. Holding his breath, Reata waited.

But the head of Tony remained strained back only for an instant. Then the sombrero flopped forward again as Tony continued to rub his eyes and swear softly.

"There's a wind comin' up," said Tommy Alton, "and that's pretty sure to knock loose a lot of dust in an old shack like this here."

"Damn such a place!" said Tony. "It always looked to me like what it is . . . murder!"

"You got that word on the brain," said the sneering voice

of his mother, from the stove where she was busy with her cooking.

"Wait a minute, Tony," said Jeff Miner, who was standing farther to the side, "you gotta remember that there's justice, ain't there? And justice kills, pretty damned often?"

Tony stretched out his long arm and pointed toward the chair in which his half-brother sat, thoroughly tied, hand and foot. "I been talked to so long that I'm pretty nigh talked out and talked down," he declared. "You all keep tellin' me that Bob is a sneak and a man-killer. But I dunno . . . somehow there's something that comes up in me all the time. Ain't he my father's son?"

"Hi!" screamed Inez Clare, suddenly alert with mischief and anger. "Your father's son! And ain't you got a precious lot of reason to love that there father of yours?"

"Aw, quit it, will you?" answered Tony. His voice fairly ached and groaned with weariness.

"Ain't you able to see sense?" demanded big Jeff Miner. "Ain't there any sense in you, Tony? This gent has to go down. You dunno what he's done. Make him answer up about the men he's killed. You tell him, Bob Clare. Talk up like a man and admit how many men you've killed."

Bob Clare was perfectly steady. The long strain of the day had told on him, and those fluctuations of despair and of hope as he saw the instinctive affection of his half-brother wax and wane through the hours.

"Damn me if I wouldn't pretty nigh rather die myself than to keep on talkin' about him so much," said Tony Clare. "Look it here, Bob. How many gents you bumped off?"

Bob Clare merely smiled and, sardonic as it was, that smile made him seem younger again.

"He won't talk!" exclaimed Jeff Miner, who seemed to be taking charge and dominating the scene. "There's a good reason why he won't talk. There's a list of twenty dead men behind him, and that's why he shuts up!"

"Twenty?" exclaimed Tony, in both awe and horror.

"It's a lie!" answered Bob Clare. "Five men . . . that's all."

"Yeah, he'll admit he's knocked over five," said Jeff Miner. "But there's plenty more. He's a killer . . . is what he is. He kills for the sake of killin'."

"I've never killed a man tied into a chair," answered Bob Clare. "But I'm through with the talking. It's no use. I know that I'm a dead man, and I'm dead because I was a fool!"

"Because we turned out smarter than you!" said Inez, jeering.

"Because I was a fool . . . because I didn't follow good orders and stay at home. But I've got an idea, somehow, that this night is a thing you people are going to remember. I've a mighty bright idea that you'll remember it for a long time."

"Your friends are goin' to trail us down, are they?" Jeff Miner sneered.

A strange smile crossed the face of Bob Clare. "*One* friend will," he said.

Reata, by this time, had laid the trap door flat open and now crouched at the edge of the opening, searching his brain for the thing that he could do, and finding no answer.

"One friend? Hell, you got no friends!" said Jeff Miner. "All you got is a lot of hangers-on that foller around after you because like a fool you chuck your money away to 'em. There ain't a man of the lot that'll lift a hand for you, and there ain't a one that don't laugh behind your back."

The queer smile remained on the lips of Bob Clare.

"If you'd said that a couple of days ago," he answered, "I might have been able to believe you. But things are different now."

"Found a partner, have you?" snarled Miner.

"Aye," said Bob Clare gently. "A partner!" His glance, as he spoke, flashed upward right toward Reata, as though an instinct had told him where to find the thing of which he had spoken. The glance went down again instantly. In the gloom, he had been unable to see the open trap and the man above it, but the words and the look lodged in the very heart of Reata.

He would do something, of course. With the deadly coil of the lariat in his hand, he could noose one of the men around the throat and then hurl himself at one of the others. And after that? Well, after that some miracle might happen. But still he waited, since the ultimate moment had not come.

"We'll take a chance on what any of your friends can do," said Miner.

"Wait a minute," said Tony Clare. "Ma, go out of the room, will you?"

The woman jerked her head around toward Tony. He threw off his sombrero. There was a sudden and a cold passion in him that Reata could guess as soon as the screening hat was removed.

Inez, after a moment, without a question, stepped in front of her son and examined his face.

But Tony seemed unaware of her; his gaze went over her, past her to the bound figure of Bob. And now with a shudder of joy Inez Clare stepped away from her son and walked swiftly out of the room.

When the door slammed heavily behind her, Tony Clare said: "You been handy with guns. You've been and fought your way through a lot of bad scrapes. Now I'm goin' to give you a chance to cut your way through this here one." He turned to Miner. "Cut them ropes and turn him loose, Jeff," he ordered.

"What's the idea?" asked Jeff Miner.

"Him and me," said Tony, "we ain't goin' to do no murder. We're goin' to fight it out fair and square. Cut him loose, and then give him back his gun."

XIV

"The Fight"

There was more than the treacherous blood of his mother in the heart of Tony—that was clear. Something leaped in Reata as he heard the speech. Something could be done now, perhaps. If Tony were occupied even for a moment with the prisoner, then Reata could strike a double blow with great advantage, from his height. And with his call, he could bring in Dickerman's two wildcats who crouched somewhere outside, near the door of the kitchen, ready to respond. They would not fail Reata in this pinch. By all the dread that the great Pop Dickerman inspired, he could be certain of that.

Jeff Miner was saying: "Tom, whatcha think of it?"

Alton sat on the edge of the center table, not far from the lantern. He now shrugged his shoulders, and his calm, good-natured face turned from one brother to the other.

"Sure," he said. "Why not?"

"All right, then. I guess it's as good a way as any," remarked Jeff. He went deliberately to the chair, cut the ropes, and gave Bob Clare's gun back into his hand. "I'd take and chuck you into the river, if I had the doin' of it," he said, staring unflinchingly into Clare's eyes. "But the kid's gotta have his way, and he's gonna have his party."

Bob Clare fingered the gun thoughtfully.

241

"Stand up!" shouted Tony, with a sudden fury.

"Tony," said Bob Clare, "you're remembering that we have the same father?"

"Yes!" yelled Tony, the rage loosening and rushing through him. "We got the same father, and a mean one. He hounded Ma. He raised hell with her life. But it's because we got some of the same blood in us that I'm givin' you a chance to fight for your life, instead of bashin' in your head like the others wanna do. Stand up!"

Bob Clare sighed. He looked at the sourly grinning faces of Jeff Miner and Tommy Alton.

In a flash the thing was clear to Reata. Of course . . . the ropes that had bound the arms of Bob Clare all the day and shut off at least a part of the normal circulation had left him numbed, half helpless in leg and arm. And for him to attempt to use the revolver now would be suicidal.

Yet, he would not ask for any mercy. Reata could guess that beforehand. To point out to Tony that the fight was a murder and not a real battle would have tasted, to the fine honor of Bob Clare, like a cowardly appeal for life. No, he would not make his appeal. Instead, he rose slowly to his feet. Would he even lift a hand against this man who was half his own blood? Reata doubted it.

They made a magnificent picture as they faced one another, almost of a height and of bigness, with something more noble and powerful in Bob and something more handsome and dangerous in Tony.

The noose formed under the fingers of Reata. He made it ready for the cast. The idea had come to him at last. It was not at one of the men that he would make his throw.

Tony was saying savagely: "Ma was double-crossed. You know that she was double-crossed. It ain't me that I care about. I don't want none of the dirty money of a man that hated me. I don't want it, and I wouldn't have it . . . but Ma was treated crooked . . . and now you're goin' to pay for it!"

Reata saw the lips of Bob Clare part, but the argument that was about to come forth was never uttered. Bob Clare set his teeth and endured the rank injustice of this speech. After all, it would be hard to root out of the mind of Tony a belief in which he had been schooled all the days of his life.

"Tom, stand back there ag'in' the wall with a handkerchief in your hand," said Tony. "When you drop it, we'll shoot."

Of course, there was a portion of this plan that Tony could not comprehend, but which was clear enough to Reata. No doubt Jeff Miner and Tommy Alton would take no chance that Tony might be killed. The first bullets would fly from their own guns into the heart of Bob Clare.

As Jeff stepped back to take up his appointed station, Reata made his cast. Fair and true the lithe shadow of the thin rope dropped. It whipped over the lantern, gripped it with a slight jangling sound, and then, with a strong jerk, Reata snatched the light out of the room. The violence of that upward motion put out the lantern's flame.

Below him, in the darkness, there was a moment of frozen silence. Then, before he heard a stir, he yelled at the top of his lungs and dropped through the trap door to the kitchen beneath. He had forgotten the table. It crashed under his feet, and rolled him headlong over the floor.

Pandemonium filled that room with shoutings and stampings. A gun flashed and roared. Instead of pitch darkness, from the cracks of the old stove, red spots and thin slices of firelight stared through the black. Then something smashed heavily against the outside door, but without beating it down. That would be Salvio and Harry Quinn trying to get in. Who would have dreamed that in the door there was strength enough to resist the onset of two such men? Reata saw and knew these things while he rolled dizzily across the floor. Then he struck a body and toppled its weight on himself.

"Get Bob Clare! Get Bob Clare!" the wild voice of Jeff Miner was yelping from a different part of the room.

Then the rest of the scene went blank for Reata, to some degree, because his hands were totally filled in struggling with the man he had crashed against. The fellow was big, weighty, and fast; the grip of his hands bruised the flesh right through the clothes.

A hammer stroke whirred past the head of Reata as he struggled to get the lariat's supple coils untwisted from underneath him. He heard the clank and iron crashing of some tool that had broken as it missed him and shattered on the flooring. A revolver, perhaps? He put his left hand under his chin and swung the elbow back and forth. It struck heavily into flesh and bone. The weight that pressed him down relaxed a little, groaning with shock of the blow.

At the same time the outer door of the room went down with a mighty crash, and he heard the singular, high-pitched yell of Gene Salvio going into action—like the cry of a mountain lion beset by a pack of dogs.

Then guns filled the room with booming and with electric, red flashings. By those flashings, the lightning hands of Reata were guided. It was the split part of a second that he needed to bring the loop of the lariat over the shoulders and the arms of the man who had been pinning him down. A moment later, in spite of the desperate struggles of the other, he was tied, and rolled in the rope—a package of cursing humanity.

Someone had yelled out in a stricken voice; a heavy body suddenly struck the floor. And then swift footfalls were fleeing.

From the throat of the man Reata had just tied issued the ringing voice of young Tony, shouting: "They've got me! Save yourselves, boys! There's too many of 'em!"

"Get after 'em!" yelled Reata. "Gene . . . Harry . . . after 'em! One of them may be LaFarge himself! Move fast!"

Move fast? Aye, but never so fast as galloping horses—the noise of hoofbeats was rapidly drawing away from the cabin now.

"The woman! The woman!" cried Reata. "She's back in the house."

The voice of Salvio panted at the open doorway, his head and shoulders dim against the horizon stars: "They're gone . . . the woman and one man. Who's left in here? Harry, who's that groaning on the floor? Get a light."

The jangling of metal on metal, then, as a lantern was lighted.

As the light spread, Reata first saw the set face of Tony on the floor at his feet, and then, near the fallen table, the body of Jeff Miner lying in his own blood.

Smooth-faced Tommy Alton was gone, and he had had forethought enough to take with him Inez Clare.

But the victory was with Reata. The fullness of it made tinglings of pleasure run through his blood, for now he was gripping the hands of big Bob Clare. Clare, totally unhurt, although the coat had been torn from his back during the struggling in the darkness, Bob Clare was now laughing joyously and wringing the hands of Reata.

XV

"End of a Gunman"

The miracle had been performed. There was a great red welt along the face of Harry Quinn, beneath the bandage that encircled his head. Otherwise, not one of the attacking party had been scratched. Guns could not find their mark in that hurly-burly. Chance had favored the bullet from Salvio's gun that laid out big Jeff Miner. The victory was complete, and as a token of its completeness here was Tony Clare in their hands!

His half-brother was leaning over him, saying: "Nothing is going to happen to you, Tony. You stood up for me all day, and I'll stand by you."

But Tony only stared at him, with excessive poison and malice in his eyes.

Reata and Salvio and Harry Quinn solemnly shook hands with one another. There was a lasting wonder in the eyes of the last two as they stared at Reata. But Salvio smiled a little.

"I dunno that it knocks the breath out of me so much, Reata. I been and seen you before doin' things that couldn't be done."

"Never mind that," urged Reata. "Here's a poor devil bleeding to death. Let's give him a hand."

"Leave me be," said Jeff Miner. "I'd rather die in a gutter than have your hands on me."

"Let the rat die that way, then!" snarled Gene Salvio.

But the rapid hands of Reata already were cutting away the blood-soaked coat of Jeff Miner like the rind from an orange.

Only when he saw the purple mouth of the wound on the breast of Miner did Reata desist. He laid back the fragments of the coat across the naked body. His own coat he rolled and pushed under the head of Miner.

"It's finished, eh?" said Miner, his mouth pulling out to one side in a sneer.

Reata said: "I'm sorry, old son."

"Sorry, are you? Then you're a fool," said Jeff Miner. "You got me this time . . . you gents. But it had to be that way. Nobody walked on two legs that woulda been able to lay me out in fair fight with the sun to see by." He glared at them, silently cursing each face with his eyes.

"Give me your flask, Gene," said Reata.

A pint metal flask was instantly passed to him by Salvio, and Reata put it carefully to the lips of the wounded man. Jeff Miner took a long drink. Afterward he lay back with his eyes closed, his lips parted, breathing rapidly, audibly. His color was altering now. Through the deep stubble of unshaven hair, his face looked gray-green. When he opened his eyes, he stared across at Tony Clare, who was sitting up against the wall.

"All because I pampered a young brat," said Jeff Miner. "I coulda bumped off Bob and done the job clean and neat. But I made a fool of myself. That's why I deserve what I got." He centered his gaze on Reata. "You're him that done it," he said.

"I didn't even carry a gun," said Reata gently.

"You're him that done it," said Jeff Miner. "The gun didn't matter. That was a tool. You're him that done it." He nodded his head. "If ever I'd seen you this close before," he continued, "if ever I'd had a chance to see the yaller come into the gray of your eyes, I sure woulda know how to look out for you, Reata." He kept on staring. "Bill Champion?" he said suddenly.

"Well?" asked Reata.

"You're him that done in Bill Champion. You killed Champion, Reata! You're the man."

"Yes," said Reata.

Jeff Miner sighed. "It kind of makes me feel better," he said. "Damn my heart but I had to feel bad when I thought of bein' done in by a nameless brat of a kid, like you looked. But the gent that done in Champion . . . he done in me, too. You're goin' to have a name for yourself, one of these here days. If only you used a gun . . . that bit of a lariat, that ain't a man's tool for a fight."

Reata said nothing for a moment, then he suggested: "Take it easy, Jeff. You're going out, old-timer, and maybe there's something on your mind. If there is, say it to me, and I'll see that it's done."

"Will you do something for me?"

"I will."

"Then take hold of your damned rope and go and hang yourself, will you?"

Reata shrugged his shoulders. "I want to serve you, Jeff," he said. "Any messages?"

"Yeah, if you ever see Tom Alton, tell him he's a coward and a cur."

"I'll tell him that," said Reata.

"That's all."

"No word for any woman, Jeff?"

"I been a man. I ain't been a mollycoddled fool," said Miner. "There ain't no woman for me."

"You're going to have a proper burial," said Reata. "Tell me what you want on the stone."

"On the stone?" said Miner, his voice growing huskier, with a distinct rattle in it. "Why, put on the stone. . . ." But here he coughed, and the cough brought up fast-breaking bubbles of blood to his lips. He choked, and, vainly gaping his wide red mouth for air that he could not draw into his lungs, he caught up a stick with a charred end that lay near him and scrawled rapidly across the floor, a sweeping, flowing signature: **Gaston LaFarge.**

It was the same signature, to a flourish, that had appeared on the greenback. And Jeff Miner dropped from the elbow on which he had raised himself and lay without a struggle or a tremor, dead.

Gene Salvio, on one knee, staring at the name, gasped out: "It's LaFarge himself! That's his signature. Reata, we've caught the king of them! We've wiped out LaFarge!"

Reata, staring at the same signature, slowly straightened to his feet, and drew a long breath. He remembered what Dickerman had said of LaFarge. It seemed impossible that in the very beginning of the feud the great LaFarge had gone down. And yet there remained on the floor the great sprawling signature.

Afterward, they turned their attention from the covered form of the dead gunman to Tony Clare, and Reata asked him: "Could you recognize this man, Tony? Is this LaFarge himself?"

"I never seen him," answered Tony sullenly. "I don't know nothin' about him, and I don't want to know."

"His mother must have done the bargaining with LaFarge," said Reata. "Now, Bob, what's to become of Tony?"

"I'd like to turn him loose," answered Bob. "I would have been a dead man long before the end of this day, except for Tony. But if I turn him loose, he'll be back with his mother in no time, and then she'll start some more of her murder tricks. I've got to keep Tony with me for a safeguard, for a while."

He turned to his half-brother and said: "I'm sorry, Tony."

"Sorry? You lie!" Tony sneered. "You're glad. Just the way I'd be glad if I'd managed to get the best of you in the fight. You'd've been sorry, though, if this here Reata hadn't come on me like a cat that can see in the dark!"

Bob Clare stared at the speaker with a strange mixture of sadness and disgust. Then he turned back to Reata. "It's over and ended," he said. "Inez won't dare lift a hand while I have Tony with me. We've won, Reata. A few days ago I was a dead man . . . a walking dead man. Now I can take a breath and a drink again. I can stop being a fool!"

"It's a good thing to stop being," said Reata, with a smile. "But Rafferty Hill is going to be pretty down on me, old fellow."

"Why?" asked Clare.

"Because you were a light that shone pretty bright for the town," said Reata. "And now you're out!"

About the Author

Max Brand is the best-known pen name of Frederick Faust, creator of Dr. Kildare, Destry, and many other fictional characters popular with readers and viewers worldwide. Faust wrote for a variety of audiences in many genres. His enormous output, totaling approximately thirty million words or the equivalent of 530 ordinary books, covered nearly every field: crime, fantasy, historical romance, espionage, Westerns, science fiction, adventure, animal stories, love, war, and fashionable society, big business and big medicine. Eighty motion pictures have been based on his work along with many radio and television programs. For good measure he also published four volumes of poetry. Perhaps no other author has reached more people in more different ways.

Born in Seattle in 1892, orphaned early, Faust grew up in the rural San Joaquin Valley of California. At Berkeley he became a student rebel and one-man literary movement, contributing prodigiously to all campus publications. Denied a degree because of unconventional conduct, he embarked on a series of adventures culminating in New York City where, after a period of near starvation, he received simultaneous recognition as a serious poet and successful author of fiction. Later, he traveled widely, making his home in New York, then in Florence, and finally in Los Angeles.

Once the United States entered the Second World War, Faust abandoned his lucrative writing career and his work as a screenwriter to serve as a war correspondent with the infantry in Italy, despite his fifty-one years and a bad heart. He was killed during a night attack on a hilltop village held by the German army. New books based on magazine serials or unpublished manuscripts or restored versions continue to appear so that, alive or dead, he has averaged a new book every four months for seventy-five years. Beyond this, some work by him is newly reprinted every week of every year in one or another format somewhere in the world. A great deal more about this author and his work can be found in THE MAX BRAND COMPANION (Greenwood Press, 1997) edited by Jon Tuska and Vicki Piekarski. His next **Five Star Western** will be THE BRIGHT FACE OF DANGER, a James Geraldi trio.